Seeking Safe Harbor

SEEKING SAFE HARBOR

Suddenly Everything Changed

Albert A. Correia

Kamel Press

Please visit
www.KamelPress.com / Correia
to see more from this author!

Visit us at
www.KamelPress.com
to see more great books!

ISBN-13:   978-1-62487-045-3 - Paperback

                978-1-62487-046-0 - eBook

Library of Congress Control Number: 2015944164

Published in the USA.

*This book is dedicated
to
my children,
to my step children,
and to my grandchildren,
those now alive and all those to come.*

They are the reason the future is so important.

Chapter 1

ZACH had felt uneasy for over a week, even before they left the island, and the large blip on the radar that was bearing down on them did nothing to ease his concern. Why would a big ship change course to go after a forty-one foot sailboat at two-thirty in the morning? Was it a pirate? Pirates were better known to work the South China Sea and the Indian Ocean, but there were some here in the Pacific, too.

Whatever was on their tail, though, looked too big to be a pirate. The radar blip was huge. He looked back again but still saw nothing. The weather was calm and the water's surface almost flat, which was why they were motoring instead of sailing, but a heavy layer of clouds prevented light from the moon or stars to sneak through to lighten the sky around them.

Whoever was behind them wasn't using running lights, which concerned him even more. Anybody not using running lights out here in the middle of the ocean had to be up to no good. His own lights were on, so whoever was navigating the big ship could see them, and a ship that big had to have radar; they had to see the small boat's little blip. In fact, whoever it was had changed from a course that was parallel, but several hundred yards to their port, to a course that put them directly behind the sailboat. That had to be intentional.

Watching the radar, he estimated the big ship's speed at sixteen or seventeen knots, more than double the rate the sailboat was motoring. The monster ship was catching up quickly. He wished he had the night vision goggles he kept by the charts in a drawer in the salon, but he couldn't take the time to get them now.

Zach's next look at the radar brought a worried, "geez" from his lips. The blip was almost on them, and he saw no evidence it was veering off its collision course. He could now hear the rumble of engines, and when he looked back, he could see a massive object looming near that was even darker than the black night.

He didn't have time to warn Stacey and the kids; he had to act now. Because the huge thing behind them was slightly off to his port side, he cranked the wheel hard to starboard, gunning his single sixty horsepower diesel to full speed. The forty-one foot ketch lurched sharply to the right, moving as fast as a small diesel can move a full keel, seventeen-ton craft through salt water.

Within moments, he could feel the boat rising and their speed increasing as a massive wall of water shoved them out of the way. Holding the wheel as tight as he could, to try to keep control of the vessel, he chanced a look back and saw the side of a massive ship charge by, its thick steel hull not missing them by more than ten yards. He'd never seen anything that big at sea. It was like a skyscraper, and it displaced vast volumes of water.

The initial phase of the wake from its bow cutting through the water caused a wave thirty feet high. The sailboat, which was no more than a toy by comparison to the huge ship, was atop it. The action of thousands of gallons of water was twisting the small boat at will, turning the bow even further to starboard.

He knew that if he let it, the wave would roll them and capsize the boat. Still holding the wheel as tightly as he could, he strained to turn it to port. He used every bit of his strength, but it wouldn't turn. He moved off to the side and pushed hard against the wheel, using every ounce of his weight and every muscle in his legs, his back, and his arms to leverage it ahead. It seemed like an eternity, although it was just seconds, and the wheel finally began to turn.

He got back in position behind the wheel and continued turning to port. The bow slowly turned left as the boat slipped down the front side of the wave. It was diving, but almost back on course when the bow hit the ocean's more normal, flatter, surface. The bowsprit dug into the sea and, for a moment, it seemed like they were going to dive deep into the water. As the wave passed, the stern dropped and the bow came up, water gushing in all directions from the freed bowsprit. The boat bobbed like a top dropped from above into a bathtub, but the now relatively calm waters let it settle a little. A secondary wave of the big ship's wake hit them, but this time it only rocked the boat a little.

Zach reset to his original course. He would be following the big ship now, but he had no choice. The GPS wasn't working, and he didn't know celestial navigation. He'd set his course for the big island of Hawaii when they left the little island they'd been staying on, and he didn't dare change course. Any slight deviation and they could miss the Hawaiian Island chain entirely.

Stacey rushed up from the aft cabin, and their fifteen-year-old son, Glen, came up from the salon at the same time. Their thirteen-year-old daughter, Denise, was a step behind him.

"What's going on?" Stacey asked breathlessly.

"We were almost run down," Zach told her. He pointed forward. Algae, disturbed by the big ships props, glowed in its wake. That was all they could see ahead. Their boat was still rocking from the huge ship's wake, even though the cause of the disturbance was now hundreds of yards ahead of them.

"It felt like we were being knocked down," Glen said.

"We almost were," his father said. "There's a big ship up there, and it came through like it was trying to run us down. In truth, a knock down would have been a lot better than what they seemed to have in mind."

"Why would someone do that?" asked Denise.

"I have no idea," Zach admitted.

"What's going on, Zach?" his wife asked again, this time with the sound of distant worry in her voice. "Everything seems out of kilter lately, like nothing is going right and there's nothing we can do about it."

"I told you what it is," Glen said. "It's war."

"We can't jump to conclusions," Stacey said. "And how would that explain a ship trying to run us down?"

"I don't know," Glen said, "but the last thing we heard on the radio before it went on the blink was the news that North Korea was planning to attack South Korea and would nuke the U.S. if we interfered."

"They've been saying that for fifty years," Zach said, "and nothing has ever happened, except that we let up a little on our sanctions each time. That's what they're after again."

"Yeah," Glen said, "but did the radios all go out before? Did the GPS system go out before?"

"No," Zach replied calmly, "but we were never on an uninhabited island when we heard it before. Anything could go out of whack out here, and we'd never know what caused it."

"Was the ship that tried to hit us from North Korea?" Denise asked. "Or China?"

"No, I don't think so," Zach replied. "But it was too dark to see much."

Stacey studied him. "You say that like maybe you did see something."

"Not really. As I said, it was too dark to make out much."

"There's a big difference between 'not much' and 'nothing.' What did you see?"

"Well, it looked like there was a flight deck up above the hull, but that can't be."

"A flight deck," Denise said. "Isn't that what

aircraft carriers have, like the one we saw in San Diego before we left?"

"Yes, honey," Stacey said.

"Which is why it can't be," he reasoned. "There's no aircraft carrier around this part of the Pacific, and if there were, it would almost have to be American. And no American Navy ship, especially a gigantic aircraft carrier, would try to run some strange boat down. Look, it was dark, and my eye just caught a glimpse of something, and, you know, it was like a quick impression. I've seen a ship like that before, the last time was just a week ago, so when I saw something that reminded me of it, my mind interpreted. There's no substantiation for what is obviously a wild, and wrong, conclusion. Happens all the time."

They fell silent. That was probably it, but they knew Zach was as level-headed as they come. It wasn't like him to see something that wasn't there.

They all looked forward, each in deep contemplation. The only thing they could see ahead was a slight trace of glowing algae, and that, too, soon disappeared.

Chapter 2

STACEY was at the wheel at a little after seven the same morning when the radar showed a blip ahead of them. She kept her eye on it to see if it was coming or going, and asked Glen, who had joined her in the cockpit twenty minutes earlier, to keep his eyes on the horizon in case something came into view.

She soon determined that the object wasn't moving. They were on a heading of twenty-nine degrees, the course from the island in the Marshalls they'd left three days earlier, to the big island of Hawaii.

The July sun was still far enough to the north to make seeing things in the water difficult at that time of the morning. It was off to the right and not directly in their vision, but the glare forced them to shade their eyes on that side. Neither could see anything yet, so they weren't sure if whatever was out there was a ship at rest or an island. They had seen the chart for this area and didn't remember any islands, but Glen went below to retrieve the chart to be sure. He brought it up, shaking his head.

Stacey had no doubt that Glen was right, but had him take the wheel so she could check it out. They'd learned long ago that there was usually plenty of time to double and triple check everything. When on a more than four-month family cruise that covered many thousands of miles, being thorough, and careful, was a must. She first made sure it was the right chart, and then examined it closely. She nodded. "Okay, we can be fairly certain there's nothing permanent out there," she said to her son, "so it has to be a boat of some kind. The question is, why is it stopped?"

"A fisherman?" Glen asked.

"Maybe, but I wonder what they could be looking for in waters this deep?"

"We'll soon find out," he opined. "It's dead ahead." He reached below the seat and unlatched the door to the storage bin under his seat, looking for binoculars. The first case he pulled out was for the night vision goggles. "A new spot for these?"

"Yes," Stacey replied. "We thought they were convenient, as well as safe, being with the charts below, but we learned last night they have to be even more convenient."

He nodded. They were always learning something. He replaced the goggles and pulled out the 10x35mm binoculars, the ones they used for long distances. Things kind of bounced with them, but whatever was out there was a long way off. When closer, they'd use the 8x35mm binoculars, which weren't as powerful but were easier to keep focused.

Stacey folded the chart and set it on the cockpit seat next to her. Glen locked in the autopilot and took a seat across from her. Both turned to face the bow, their eyes glued to the water in front of them, He used the binoculars, and she looked with bare eyes. Up until a few days ago, coming across another boat out here in the middle of the Pacific Ocean had been a pleasure, but now that the radios and GPS had lost their signals, and after what had happened just hours before, they were leery of what lay ahead.

He saw it first and pointed to the spot.

She saw it, too, but it looked like no more than a little dark spot on the water to her. He steadied the binoculars and focused in, then whistled.

"What?" Stacey asked.

"It's really big."

She stood and looked at the radar for the first time in several minutes. "You're right. This blip is a pretty good size already, and we're still miles away."

They continued on for several minutes more, with Glen's binoculars constantly pointed at what was up ahead. Finally, he said, "Mom, that's an aircraft carrier."

"An aircraft carrier? You must be mistaken. What would an aircraft carrier be doing here, just sitting around doing nothing?"

"Look for yourself." He handed her the strong binoculars.

She looked, adjusted the focus, and studied

the ship ahead. She held the big glasses as steady as she could so she could get as good an idea as possible of what was out there. When she was sure of what she was looking at, she handed the binoculars back to her son. "You're right, as usual." She started back toward the hatchway and ladder leading down to the aft cabin, where Zach had been sleeping for the past two hours.

"Mom, are you going to bed?"

She stopped, turned to look at Glen, checked her watch, and then came back to sit where she'd been before. "No, I don't think anyone is going to be sleeping much today. Unfortunately, that includes your father, who's only slept two hours in the last thirty-six. I'll let him sleep a little longer, but something's very wrong and we're going to need him up here very soon."

Chapter 3

STACEY let Zach sleep another half hour, and by the time he got to the sailboat's cockpit, he was able to get a good look at the aircraft carrier with the 8x35mm binoculars. He went over the whole ship and after a couple of minutes, his binoculars followed something down from the flight deck to the water. He focused in on a spot at the waterline.

"What is it?" asked Stacey.

"They've lowered a boat." He swept the area for miles on either side of the aircraft carrier with the binoculars. "There's nothing else out there."

"What does that mean?" asked Denise. By now, all four of them were on the deck, three looking at the big ship from the cockpit and Glen forward on the bowsprit, watching the carrier with the more powerful glasses.

"No way of knowing at this point, but they could be coming here."

"What for?"

"That, honey, is another of the questions I have no answer for at the moment," he told his daughter.

Glen, who had been engrossed in what he saw in the distance, hadn't heard their conversation. He called back, "Hey, dad, they're sending a launch our way."

"Can you get a good look at it with those powerful binocs?"

"It's still pretty far away, but it looks like it's more than a small shore boat. Maybe forty or fifty feet. I think they've got a gun."

"What?"

"I can't be sure, but it looks like a bazooka, or rocket launcher or some other kind of weapon attached to the deck on the bow."

Zach and Stacey stared at one another. What had been the family cruise of a lifetime was turning into a nightmare. "What do we do?" she asked.

He shrugged. "We get out our two little weapons and wait."

"What can we do with a .30 caliber rifle and a pistol against a rocket launcher and God knows what else they have?" she asked. "We should have brought more weapons."

"I didn't expect to be confronted by pirates out here, let alone the U.S. Navy."

Zach went below and came back with a lever action carbine and a 9-millimeter automatic handgun. He handed the pistol to Stacey.

"I can take that, Mom," Denise said. "I'm a better shot than you."

Stacey smiled at her daughter. "You are that,

but a thirteen-year-old girl shouldn't have to be defending her life like this."

"Maybe not, but it looks like that's the way it is."

Stacey pulled her daughter close and hugged her, squeezing tightly for a moment.

"Look, we're not sure yet that there's any danger," Zach told the women. "Let's put the weapons down but keep them close, just in case. We'll know soon enough if we're going to need them."

He looked at the other boat again, sweeping the whole of it. When he got to one spot, he stopped and studied it for a few moments.

"What is it?" asked Stacey.

"The writing on the side. It looks like it's in Chinese or some other Asian language."

"What does that mean?"

"No idea. The carrier is U.S. for sure, but that small boat is... I have no idea what it is."

They all watched for several minutes as the boat from the carrier moved toward them. There was no longer any question. It was heading directly at their boat. Then, Glen jumped up and began running back to the cockpit, yelling, "Two guys went to that little cannon or whatever it is up front. They're loading it."

Zach leveled his binoculars on the boat's bow. "Geez, he's right, and they're aiming at us. Get down, everyone."

Before they could move toward cover, they heard the frightening sound of a shell being launched. It blazed right at them.

Chapter 4

ZACH pushed Stacey and Denise down while Glen leaped toward the cockpit. They weren't yet under cover when they heard the frightening sound of something whizzing by overhead. They looked at one another in amazement as they heard an explosion.

Looking back, they saw a fifty-foot powerboat less than a mile behind them, its bow on fire. They'd been so focused on the aircraft carrier and its launch, they hadn't bothered to look at the area behind them or check their radar for over half an hour. In the past, that might not have made a difference, but things had suddenly changed.

As they started to get up, they heard another boom and were rocked a moment later by the wake of the boat that had come from the carrier as it rushed past, heading for the burning boat. As it passed, they could clearly see that the lettering on its side was Asian. Everyone aboard, though, looked American. The second shell destroyed the wheelhouse of the crippled vessel, and as the armed boat approached, five armed men opened fire with assault weapons. For a few seconds, there was return fire, but that ended quickly. When they were alongside, four men jumped aboard where there was another short volley of small arms fire, and then silence.

The family watched as the navy crew brought two men out from below. Even though they were wounded, the prisoner's hands were bound behind their backs. The crew took the prisoners aboard the navy boat, and then returned to the burning craft, transferring things from the burning boat to their own. Zach and his family couldn't see what they were loading. The men worked quickly, obviously in a hurry to get away. When they had what they wanted, they motored thirty yards out, then turned back and launched one more shell at the boat's hull. The final shot hit right at the waterline, ripping the bottom to shreds. No longer having anything to hold it up, the boat was gone in minutes, leaving only a small oil slick and a little flotsam to mark the spot.

The vessel from the carrier headed back toward the sailboat. When they saw it coming, Glen grabbed the carbine and Denise started for the automatic.

"Keep them ready," Zach told the youngsters, who were growing up quickly. "But don't shoot unless you have to."

As he walked over to the rail to watch the boat approach, a loudspeaker came on. "Ahoy, there, you aboard the ketch, *La Sirena*," came a booming voice. "I am Commander Joseph A. Kotchel of the United States Navy. With your permission, we would like to come alongside your vessel. We have things to discuss."

By that time, the other boat was thirty yards away. Zach leaned out and yelled, "What things?"

"What just transpired this morning, for one."

"We saw what happened."

"But, you don't know why it happened."

"We don't care why."

"Oh, but you will when you hear the story. What's more, it is essential that we discuss what the immediate future holds for you."

"Our future is none of your business!"

By now, the other boat was within twenty feet and the two men were talking directly to one another.

"Perhaps not," said the commander, "but it is a conversation we must have." The naval officer was a man of average height, not more than thirty-five. His manner was polite, but firm. "I can understand that you are wary of having us board your vessel after what you witnessed here, but I assure you that you and your family are safe. If it will make you feel more at ease, I will come alone, and will leave my weapons aboard the vessel here. I see you have weapons. I will not object if you want to keep me covered while we talk. My men will not fire upon you."

"Very well," Zach said. "Come alone and unarmed. Once you are aboard, though, have your men move your vessel at least fifty yards away." He had seen what they could do; they were trained, well armed and outnumbered his family, but it was not in his nature to give in easily. The mariners were willing to talk, so they might do it his way.

"Agreed," the commander said. He removed his holster and laid down his assault rifle. As soon as the boats were adjacent, only rubber fenders keeping them from rubbing against one another, he stepped easily aboard the ketch. Zach took his arm to be sure he was steady and then cautiously shook the officer's hand. Zach was slightly taller than the navy man. Both were muscular and obviously athletic.

"My name is Zach Arthur, and this is my wife, Stacey," the civilian boat captain told the navy officer. "The two people holding guns on you are my son, Glen, and my daughter, Denise. They are both excellent shots."

The naval officer took them in at a glance, seeing four trim, well-proportioned people. Stacey was a runner, and at age thirty-eight still had the waist of a fit twenty-year-old. Glen was already over five-foot-ten and Denise was tall for thirteen. He shook hands with each of them.

"Now," Zach said, "since you feel it is so important that we know; tell us what the devil is going on here."

"We got word yesterday that a terrorist group, the most vicious kind imaginable, had captured a boat and was pirating boats in this area, killing everyone aboard." The commander nodded toward the spot where the boat had gone down. "We were looking for them."

"Looking for them? Are you aware that it was us you almost ran over this morning?"

"Yes, of course. My captain and I offer our

apologies. We thought you were them," and he, again, nodded toward the spot in the ocean. "When we saw you were flying an American flag, we altered our course to miss you."

"Altered your course?" Zach seethed. "You kept coming straight at us. The only reason we're alive is because I was able to get out of your way at the last second."

"It takes a little distance for an aircraft carrier to change directions, "and it happens slowly. Again, my apologies, but even if it didn't appear to you that way, we were trying to avoid hitting your boat in those final seconds. And, we did miss you."

"Okay, I'll grant that what you're saying is plausible. But, why did you stop here?"

"We thought the terrorists might be after your boat, but wouldn't try if we were visible."

Zach was aghast. "Are you telling me you used us as bait?"

"I wouldn't put it quite that way. But, we did think that if they thought they were alone with you, they would try to kill you. As it turned out, we were right. Fortunately, they didn't have radar and we were far enough away that they didn't see us until it was too late."

"I've never been in the navy," Zach said through clinched teeth, "but I was an Army Ranger for five years. Never would we have even considered using civilians to lure the enemy. I'm sorry, Commander, but none of what you've said makes any sense to me. What you've done in the last five or six hours is unconscionable. All of that aside, why would I believe that a multi-billion dollar United States Navy Aircraft

Carrier is out hunting for a few penny ante terrorists instead of doing something, you know, a bit more important?"

Kotchel didn't respond immediately. When he did, he asked, "Do you mind telling me where you've been for the last week?"

"We were on one of the Marshall Islands for five days. A little atoll, actually. The last three days, we've been at sea."

"Have you read a newspaper, or listened to the news at any time in that period?"

"There aren't any newsstands in the middle of the Pacific. And we lost any kind of radio signal while we were on the island. But, what could happen that is so earth shattering that it causes these kinds of things?"

"Earth shattering," Kotchel said thoughtfully. "That's a more apt description of what has taken place this past week than you could possibly realize, being as you haven't heard the news. Come, Mr. Arthur, I think you and your family had better take seats in the cockpit. You don't want to be standing when I tell you what has gone on this past week."

Chapter 5

Z ACH and Stacey sat on one side of the cockpit, Glen, and Denise on the other. The
weapons had been set aside, but were handy,
just in case. Commander Kotchel took a seat in
the middle, behind the wheel.

"Before I start, I want to make something
clear. What I'm about to tell you is going to
be a shock, so prepare yourselves for the worst.
The very worst you can possibly imagine."

"We're at war, aren't we?" Glen asked.

Kotchel glanced sympathetically at the boy,
then turned to the parents. "You could say that,
but it goes beyond being 'at war.' Far beyond."

"What could go beyond being at war?" Stacey
wanted to know.

"It's North Korea, isn't it?" Glen added.

"Again, it's more than that. The easiest
explanation is simply to say that the world, as
you know it, is gone. It's been obliterated!"

"What?" Zach and Stacey cried in unison.

Glen and Denise leaned forward and stared in disbelief at the navy officer.

"You'd all better sit back and listen while I give you an overview," the commander said, his voice becoming stern. "Hold your questions until you have a picture of what has happened." He looked at each until they nodded their assent. He took a breath, and his eyes revealed the pain he felt as he began to tell them what happened.

"Yes, to the best of our knowledge, North Korea was the first to fire at its major adversary, South Korea. The first missile was conventional. South Korea responded in full force and, without warning, North Korea sent a nuclear missile into the heart of Seoul, destroying much of the city. China warned the United States to stay out of it, and for the first few hours, we did. But when North Korea used a nuclear weapon, we took action against them. When we did, China attacked our naval forces in the region with such ferocity it shocked everyone. That by itself might have led to what followed, but there was more. Much more."

Kotchel sat back and shook his head. "At the same time that was going on, Israel and Iran attacked one another. No one knows what the final straw was that caused it, or who fired first. It all happened so fast. Within twenty-four hours, both gave up on conventional weapons. Again, it's muddled who did it first, but they both began firing off missiles with nuclear warheads, ending any debate about whether either of them had them. It was clear that they both did, and they had enough to destroy whole countries. However, Israel has

– had – the most efficient anti-missile system ever invented, and blasted Iran's weapons out of the sky. Their own hit with such devastating force, they completely destroyed Iran. That brought Russia in. They immediately fired nuclear missiles at Israel, overwhelming their anti-missile system, and the ones that made it through wiped the country off the map. That action brought a nuclear response from NATO.

"In the meantime, the United States retaliated against China. We'd been strengthening our forces in the area, so the response was not only fast, it was devastating. It had only been two days since North Korea attacked South Korea, and the U.S. and China were still using conventional weapons. Then, I suppose because others were already using them, and they had little hope of defeating the United States in a conventional war, China decided to take us by surprise and attacked with nuclear weapons. And it wasn't our forces in Asia they went after. They attempted to destroy our mainland, sending nuclear missiles to every major city in the United States. The U.S. was indeed taken by surprise, but as soon as we saw what was happening, we retaliated in kind."

"The Northern Lights," Denise whispered.

"What was that?" Kotchel was caught off guard by the remark.

"We thought we saw lights in the sky to the north a few nights ago," Stacey said. "We wondered if it was the Aurora Borealis."

"If only it were," said the navy man. "But, it's too late for the spring showing, and too early for the autumn."

"I told yo..." Glen started to say, but his voice trailed off when he realized how unimportant his being right was now that they knew what it must have been.

Kotchel continued, but thought it best to veer away from the main subject for a minute. "By the way, if you're wondering why our carrier isn't on the bottom of the sea, we were on our way from San Diego to Hawaii at that time. We were ordered to change course for the South China Sea. By the time we got there, it was pretty much over. Most of our navy was already on the bottom of the ocean, as were almost all the North Korean and Chinese ships. We were involved in a few skirmishes with smaller ships and won them all. We've had some damage, but nothing major. He looked out at the boat he'd just come from. You probably noticed that the craft we're using isn't U.S. A carrier isn't equipped to do some of the things we've had to do this past week, so we captured that vessel from the North Koreans three days ago. As you saw, it's been really handy.

"But, back to what has happened in the world. While all I've told you so far was going on, Pakistan decided to take advantage of the confusion and nuked India, their archenemy. India retaliated with their own nukes. By then, it was as if everyone in the world had gone mad. No one dared wait to be attacked. It seemed that attacking first was the only way they could survive. Countries were emptying their arsenals. When NATO forces responded to Russia, Russia launched missiles at every NATO country and all their allies, which pretty much includes every democracy in the world. China followed suit. All the major economic centers in the United States, Canada, and Europe were being annihilated, but everyone got off just about every one of their own nukes before the sites were wiped out. At any given moment, there were hundreds of nuclear missiles flying in every direction imaginable. Some anti-missile missiles were up there, and they knocked many enemy missiles out, but there weren't enough of them to ward off the deluge."

He stopped to draw a breath. As he'd known would happen, the Arthur family was sitting in total shock. Their eyes were wide and their minds were racing. Zach and Stacey were holding hands; she was gripping him so hard, Kotchel could see the muscles bulging in her hand.

He went on. "While we still had some form of mass communications, we learned that an estimate of at least four billion people were killed in the first..."

"Four billion?" gasped Stacey. "Did you say four *billion*?"

"Yes. Well over half the population of the world was annihilated in the first four days. It's been the most devastating time in human history, worse than even the most pessimistic dooms-dayers predicted. Every major city was wiped out. New York, Tokyo, Beijing, Shanghai, Hong Kong, Mexico City, Sao Paulo, Rio de Janeiro, Paris, Rome, Moscow, Berlin, Toronto, Los Angeles, Manila, Mumbai, and any other metropolitan area you can think of, no longer exists, except for some suburbs. Even those are mostly uninhabited. What the bombs didn't kill, the radioactivity did or soon will. Europe and the Middle East are gone. So, too are Russia and China, although some people are still alive in small parts of eastern Russia and western China. Every military base in the world of any consequence, big or small, was destroyed. Our carrier is only one of maybe a hundred military ships still in existence. Except for our carrier, and I think two cruisers, the rest are all small. One of the cruisers is ours, the other Chinese. You see, I'm not talking about a hundred American ships. That's all that's left in the whole world.

"You already know about Pakistan and India, but it didn't stop there. Country after country, most of whom no longer have the core of their elected leadership, began attacking whoever they perceived to be their enemies. Venezuela attacked Colombia, Guatemala attacked Mexico, and Cambodia attacked Vietnam. Heck, even Argentina attacked Brazil, and they had been friends the week before. Nicaragua attacked Costa Rica, who didn't have an army, only their police to defend them, but then Honduras attacked Nicaragua. And on, and on, and on. The nuclear holocaust is over, but only because about every nuclear weapon that had ever been made was either used or destroyed. The country squabbles continue, however, and they are vicious. Violent fighting continues, even within countries, including some of those that in the past resolved their differences peacefully at the ballot box.

"The parties that have been out of power

for years, if not forever, are attacking what is left of the existing power structure. The only places in the world that have any semblance of order are the bottom two-thirds of Africa and the Australian Outback – well, all of Australia, except for the coastal areas. Not that Africa is all that peaceful, but all they have going on is their usual in-house conflicts. Terrorists, or gangs, or whatever you want to call them, are openly killing anyone in their way. That's happening everywhere."

He involuntarily looked back at the spot where the boat had been sunk and paused to let all that he had told them sink in.

"Now," he said, inhaling deeply, "I suspect you have some questions you'll be wanting to ask me."

Chapter 6

WHAT the Arthur family heard was so appalling that none of them felt the will to speak for well over a minute. Zach was the first to break the silence, attempting to keep a quavering voice calm.

"The United States? Is there still a United States?"

"Yes," Kotchel answered, trying to sound positive. "It's not what it was, but its better off than most of what used to be the other major nations."

"Do we have a Congress?" Stacey asked. "A President? A Supreme Court?"

"Yes, but from the bits and pieces of information we've received, it's all changed. It's not clear what all those changes are. Congress was out of session, so many of our representatives were at home and survived. The President and Vice President were killed when Washington was hit, as were all members of the U.S. Supreme Court.

As you have no doubt surmised, Washington was destroyed, along with almost all of the Atlantic Coast. The Speaker of the House of Representatives was visiting relatives in Iowa and is alive. He was sworn in as President by the nearest federal judge. No one knows for sure if the judge had the power to do it, but the Constitution designates the Speaker as next in line and there was no one else around to do it. The members of Congress that could be found are meeting in an undisclosed location in Kansas."

"Undisclosed? Why undisclosed?" Glen asked. He'd been taking it all in like a horrible history lesson. Now his mind was full of questions.

"I'll answer as best I can, but the simplest explanation... there are gangs and terrorists throughout the United States as well as the rest of the world. There are numerous factions and they're vicious. People, and groups that were prepared, have been able to fight them off and are surviving. Others are barely able to find food and water and can't protect themselves. Until whatever military people that are still alive can be found and a new structure established, and until police forces can regroup, people, especially those in leadership positions, are in serious danger. If any are found by the terrorist elements, they will be killed. They must operate in secret."

"Are you getting orders?" Zach asked.

"It's spotty. Originally, we were told to stay in these waters and keep our eye out for troublemakers and people we can help. This morning, we were able to do both. We haven't received any new orders, so we will continue doing what we've been doing."

"But, you're an aircraft carrier," Glen said. "How can you stoop to this kind of thing?"

"Son," Kotchel said, not showing any anger at the youngster's comment, "in emergencies, we do what is needed. Nothing is too petty." He looked toward the big ship. "Actually, we are still a carrier, and we still have sixteen planes aboard. Not much fuel, but we could get them up, if necessary. It's just that at this moment, there isn't the need for us to act in the capacity of an aircraft carrier."

"Sir, is it the new President and what's left of Congress telling you to do that?" Glen asked, trying to get a handle on the chain of command.

"No, my boy, it doesn't work that way, even in as dire a situation as this. What's left of the joint chiefs has managed to get together and they're trying to reorganize our military. It won't be easy. It will have to be a volunteer force for some time to come, so they have their work cut out for them. I think they're in Oklahoma, but I don't know, and don't want to know. There's no point in talking about things out of our reach. Look, for the purposes of this talk, we'll accomplish more if we restrict our discussion to those things that are pertinent to yourselves and your situation at the moment. What do you want to know that pertains to your own lives?"

Stacey had a question that had been in her mind from the start, but she could barely get it out. "San Diego?" she murmured.

Kotchel asked, quietly, "Your home?"

She nodded, biting her lip.

"I'm sorry."

"Are you sure?" Zach inquired, trying to keep his voice steady.

"I'm afraid so.   Everything around there, from Camp Pendleton in the north, to the naval facilities in the southern part of San Diego, was obliterated in the first wave of nuclear strikes."

Stacey covered her face and Denise began crying.

"What about the inland coastal area of Central California? Santa Maria?" Zach asked.

"I don't know for sure. It may be okay, if okay is the correct word. The problem would be getting there. Ports and even small marinas were targeted. Oxnard had a naval base, so it was hit hard."

"My parents live in Santa Maria. We'd planned on laying over in Oxnard when we went to visit them. That's where we were going after Hawaii," Zach said. "Her parents live – lived – in San Diego. Us, too, and we were planning on getting Glen and Denise back in time for school. My business is – was – there."

"So, our assumption was right, Hawaii was to be your next stop."

"Yes."

"I'm sorry to be so blunt after giving you such terrible news, but you need to rethink that decision."

"We have to get supplies. We have enough for three weeks, but that's cutting it close and anything can happen out on the water. We need more. It's as simple as that."

"We thought that might be the case when we saw what your heading was, but I have to tell you, the island of Hawaii is very dangerous. We don't think anything major hit them, but the other islands were decimated and the survivors swarmed to the big island. There's widespread looting for what is left to eat and drink. Fortunately, our Commanding Officer gave some thought to the problems you would be having. Kind of an apology for almost running you over, I think. We took everything we could off the boat we sank. There are at least a hundred large cans of beans and all sorts of vegetables, six tons of coffee, quite a few medical supplies, and some boat equipment that may come in handy. Oh, and some dynamite."

"Dynamite?" said Stacey. "What were they doing with dynamite?"

"They were a gang of terrorists. There's a lot they could do with dynamite, none of it good. It might useful to you in some good ways, though."

Denise frowned with unbelieving curiosity at that. "What could we do with dynamite?"

"Oh, I don't know," admitted Kotchel. "Maybe you'll come to a place where you need to blow away some rocks away to get into shelter.

"We'll take it," said Zach. "I have no idea what's in store for us, so anything has potential at this point."

"That's the mindset you'll need. There's also a sextant if you need an extra one."

"I wish I had a use for it," Zach said, "but I don't know celestial navigation."

Kotchel whistled. "With the GPS system in shambles, you're going to need it."

"We could use some lessons."

"I'll give you a quick lesson, but there's no

time to teach you everything. I think I may have a book I can give you, though."

"That would be great! We're fast learners. The kids are, anyway. They took their exams two months early so we could come on this trip."

"Be glad they did and you made the trip," Kotchel said, then quickly went on before they began to think about what had been lost while they were gone. "I see you have some small weapons here." He pointed at the carbine and pistol still lying on the cockpit seat beside Glen and Denise. "Is this all you have?"

"Yes," Zach replied, worry lines beginning to crease his forehead. "We never anticipated anything like this."

"Who could?" the commander wondered aloud. He eyed the weapons. "I see the guns are by your children. You said they can use them. Is that true?"

"Everyone here is trained, and they're all excellent marksmen."

"Assault weapons?"

"We've never had any and my family has never been trained to use them."

"But, you're an ex-Army Ranger, so you know them well."

"I do, but we have none, and I doubt we can buy any now."

"There were six fairly modern AK-47s aboard that boat and enough ammo to hold off an army for months. We have all we need, so they're yours if you want them."

"Absolutely!" Zach exclaimed.

"Six?" Stacey said. "But we saw only two prisoners."

"Four were killed by the missile hits or by our gunfire when we boarded. They went down with the ship."

"We saw that the two men you captured are wounded," Zach said. "Stacey is a nurse. Maybe she can be of some help?"

"Thanks for the offer but we have a medic attending them, and we've got doctors on the carrier. They'll be well taken care of before joining eighteen others in our brig."

"You have eighteen prisoners already?"

"I imagine we'll have a hundred before this is over. Although we'll find an island as soon as we can that may be able to sustain them and let them go. We have stores for a couple of months, but after that, we'll be foraging for food for our own personnel." He straightened, realizing he was off topic again, and said, "Okay, back to you people. Is there anything else we can do for you?"

"We have a little diesel and enough water for about three weeks. We could use a lot more of both. Is that possible?"

"We can't spare any diesel. Thank goodness you have a sailboat and your only real need for the motor is in dead calm waters. As far as the water goes, we can give you a three-month supply if you want. We have two desalinization plants on board the carrier, so fortunately we have plenty of that."

"I don't know what to say," Zach said. "This is a bit overwhelming."

"The world is going to need strong people, good people. You appear to be good people, and you've got to be tough to be out here cruising like this, so you're exactly what the world will need. If we have been of help, we're glad. Let me call my crew over and we'll unload what we have, and then we can go over to the carrier to get the water and give you some celestial navigation lessons with your new sextant."

"If you don't mind, I'll give the family some lessons on the AKs while you're still around."

"Fine, and we have some experts who can bring you up to speed if you're a little rusty."

"A little practice never hurts," Zach agreed.

Commander Kotchel stood and motioned to his crew to come over, then turned back to Zach. "Okay. Please understand that the reason we can only give you a short lesson is because we have to get down to Samoa. We got word just before we went after the terrorists that there's some massive gang activity there. And, you need to be heading for California."

"We'll be on our way by nightfall," Zach concurred.

"Zach, the package," Stacey said.

"Package?" asked Kotchel.

"There's a package of medical supplies in Hilo that we were planning on taking to my mother," Zach explained. "She is into holistic medicine and there are some herbs that apparently only grow in this area."

"Forget them," the naval officer recommended. "I'm sympathetic and use as many natural cures as I can myself, but it's not worth the risk."

"I'm sure you're right," Zach said.

The commander's boat came alongside and he went to the bow to tie a line to a cleat that a crewman tossed aboard the sailboat. Glen went aft to tie another line there.

Once the supplies were unloaded onto the sailboat, the naval officer walked over to get aboard his boat.

Zach called to him. "Commander Kotchel, how can we thank you for all of this?"

"By surviving!"

Chapter 7

WHEN the sun came up the next morning, it shone on a family that had spent the night in sad reflection. Stacey's parents, most of their friends, cousins, uncles and aunts, schools the children attended, their home, their business, everything they were used to had been in San Diego.

San Diego was gone. Gone! The people dead, the buildings reduced to rubble. They could only hope that Zach's parents and a brother who lived in the Santa Maria area were still alive. Even if the area hadn't been bombed, had gangs taken over?

Over the the years, they'd seen people who were supposed to be taking part in peaceful protests against some relatively minor thing turn into violent mobs. If simple differences of opinions and the hope for something better did that to people, what would such massive devastation – the loss of homes, food, water, friends, loved ones, just about everything they'd ever had – do to them?

Zach finally went to bed at two o'clock in the morning. Stacey, still mourning the loss of her parents and friends, opted to stay at the wheel, using the time to gather her thoughts. When he came back on deck at eight, she was still at the wheel. They'd been taking two hour shifts at the helm, but now she insisted they all sleep while she kept the boat on course – and allowed her mourning to steer its own course. She finally come to grips with the reality. Her parents were gone, and her family needed her.

"Did you sleep okay?" she asked.

"Better than I expected. I guess having had only two hours in the last couple of days took a lot out of me."

She took a seat next to the wheel when he took over.

"I've been thinking about your parents," she said.

"Mine?"

"Yes. For now, I have to put my own out of my mind. Yours have to be our goal. They're the strongest people I've ever met."

"They are tough," he agreed.

"They're survivors. I think they're still alive," she said.

"I hope you're right. I believe you are. They always stay prepared for an extended time of self- sufficiency, so they should be able to hold out until we can get to them."

"So," she made eye contact with him, "you think that's where we should go, too?"

"Yes. Besides being my parents, they are, as

you said, really strong. Commander Kotchel was right, but it's not just the world that will need those kinds of people. So do we."

"We're strong, too, Zach. Including Glen and Denise."

"I wasn't saying we aren't. I know we are. What I'm saying is, strong people will need to band together. The old saying, 'there's strength in numbers,' is true. Never more so than now."

"I agree. You know something, though?"

"What?"

"Strong as your mom is, she'll still need those medical herbs."

Zach didn't reply right away. He looked off in the distance, then turned back to Stacey. "Would you get me the chart for the Hilo area?"

"We're going after the herbs?"

"For diesel. Commander Kotchel was right about everything else, but he was wrong about our need for fuel. We need more. In the months to come, there could be many boats after us, and in calm weather, we will be sitting ducks if we depend only on sails. Besides, we may have to go from port to port, and we need to be able to get in and out in a hurry, directly, not having to tack as the wind demands. And, yes, I want to take my mother what she feels she needs. Being as Oxnard was hit hard, we can head for Santa Barbara after Hilo, dock the boat, and go to Santa Maria from there."

Stacey returned with the chart, and Glen and Denise were with her. "They're all for it," she said.

"I want you to know it could be dangerous," Zach told the children.

"Oh, we know that," Denise said brightly, "and we've already talked about it. We think we need to establish right away that we're going to live as we need to, not like some cowering fools, living the way fear dictates."

Zach looked at Stacey. "Remind me again... exactly how old is she?"

"According to the birth certificate, thirteen, but sometimes I think it's off by at least ten years."

"Actually, those were Glen's words," Denise giggled, "but I would have said the exact same thing if he hadn't."

Glen raised his eyebrows and looked askance at his sister. "Anyway," he said, turning his focus back to his parents, "we're with it a hundred percent. Besides, we all know how to handle AK-47s now, right?"

"You learned fast, but you still have a lot more to learn," Zach advised his son. "The main thing, though, is that you're on board with the plan. We're gonna be in for some difficult times and need to pull together all the way."

He locked in the mechanical autopilot and sat with Stacey on the seat behind the wheel. The children sat on the seats at either side of them. Zach rolled out the chart and studied it carefully.

"When we sailed into Hilo on our way from California, we approached Hilo Harbor directly from the east. I'm sure you remember that even though the town is on the eastern part of Hawaii, it's located on an indentation, and the town and bay face north." He traced a finger along a line that ran north from the eastern part of the bay. The line, which was the breakwater, turned and went west, eventually stopping, leaving an opening at the western part of the bay. "This breakwater protects the bay, and the entrance isn't very wide. For us, that's good; but it's also bad."

"Why's that, Dad?" Glen asked.

"What we need to get for my mother is supposed to be with that fellow George that we met at Aunt Millie's Hilo Hotel. That's where we need to go."

"Hey, that was a really neat place," Denise chimed in.

"And George is a neat guy, assuming he's still around. He's the hotel's concierge, although I doubt that's what they call him there. He does a little of everything and is the kind of guy who knows how to get things. We need to find a supply of diesel fuel, and if anyone can get it for us, it's him."

"You haven't answered Glen's question, honey," Stacey reminded him. "I think I know both the good and the bad, but we need to all be on the same page."

"Absolutely," Zach agreed. "The configuration of the breakwater is good, because the water will be calm. We can sail in quietly and anchor in that little niche between little Coconut Island and the mainland, which is near the hotel. I'll take Denise with me and row the dinghy over to the mainland. You and Glen will need to watch the boat. There's no telling who. . . or what. . . will be waiting there in hopes of capturing a boat."

"That's the bad?" Glen asked. "There may not be any bad guys there at all, you know."

"True, but that's only part of it. The worst part is, we have to go back out through that little opening between the breakwater and the mainland across from it. That's a great place for an ambush. We'll be an easy target for anyone on land, and if they have boats, we'll be in real trouble."

"We're armed," Glen said, "and we're all darned good shots".

"Yes, but I sure hope it doesn't come down to that," Zach said, "There's a good chance it will, though." He turned his attention back to the chart. "Okay, here's where we are." He tapped the chart with his index finger. "We're southwest of the island. We're going to have to stay quite a distance south so we won't be seen. We'll sail far enough past that we still won't be seen when we turn north. Then, we'll turn west and follow the same course we followed when we went there last time."

Looking at each of them, in turn, he continued, "The difference is, we went in by daylight before and used the motor once we were inside the harbor. This time, we have to remain unseen. We're going to sail the whole way at night, never using the motor. Any questions?"

"Will there be lights on the breakwater, or the town, to help guide us?" Glen asked.

"No telling," Probably a few, although I have no idea if they still have electricity. For all I know, there may be fires. But, that doesn't matter. The radar will show the landmasses, the breakwater, and the larger boats. We'll just have to hope there are no little rowboats out there for us to run over."

"We can't let our guard down. It isn't going to be easy," Stacey said, looking at the children to be sure they understood.

"From now on," Zach added, his voice low, "nothing is going to be easy."

Chapter 8

WHEN they got near enough, they could see there were a few lights scattered around the town, but the multitude of fires gave off the most useable light. The glow of those fires framed mainland Hilo enough that the Arthurs could make out buildings off in the distance as they approached land.

They set their course to run parallel to the long westward leg of the breakwater, about fifty yards north of it. The radar gave them a view of what was on or near the water, away from the fires.

As near as they could tell, there were seven ships at anchor – they weren't moving, anyway. None was in the path of their destination. There might be a canoe or dinghy in the way that didn't show up on the radar, but they'd have to chance that.

When they were slightly past the eastern edge of the Hilo Bay entrance, they turned due south. Zach went aft, dropped the mizzen sail, and tied it down. With Denise up front on the jib, Glen on the mainsail, and Stacey at the wheel, they turned again when they passed the breakwater, this time southeast. That should take them to where Hilo Bay and Reed's Bay mingled. Specifically, it was a spot a little east of Coconut Island and north of the point where Aunt Millie's Hotel sat.

With the mizzen sail out of the way, Zach went forward and lifted the anchor from the compartment at the *La Sirena*'s bow. He stepped onto the bowsprit with it and prepared to drop it when they reached the spot they were seeking. There were no lights on the little island they were planning to anchor next to, but there were some on the mainland where they calculated Aunt Millie's Hotel was located. The fires and lights that were interspersed throughout Hilo provided sufficient light for them to see where they were going. It was just enough for them to see that nothing appeared to be in their way.

Unfortunately, they knew it might also be enough that they could be spotted by anyone looking in their direction.

When they reached the area that looked best for anchoring near their objective, Zach raised his arm. Stacey spun the wheel to port, turning the boat into the lightly blowing wind. Denise and Glen immediately dropped the jib and main sails, and the boat slowed, then halted. Zach dropped the anchor. It hit bottom with twenty of the fifty-foot chain still above water. He slowly let the chain drop foot by foot until all of it was beneath the water, then let the line out a few more feet and tied it off on a forward cleat.

In normal circumstances, he would let more line out so the boat could swing freely. But in normal circumstances, they wouldn't be this close to shore. If he could get the diesel as he wanted, it would require his rowing their little dinghy back and forth several times, and a longer distance meant more time rowing. They didn't want to spend a minute longer in this place than was absolutely necessary.

The boat settled, with Coconut Island to the left, the mainland behind, and Reeds Bay on the right. Four boats were anchored in Reed's Bay and they had seen three more on the other side of Coconut Island when they came in. There was no movement on any of the boats or on Coconut Island. Two of the boats looked like they were burned out. From time to time, they could see a shadowy figure running on the mainland, and they heard voices off in the distance. They were yells, not conversations.

They thought they saw a guarded light that might have been coming from behind closed blinds in the structure they remembered as being Aunt Millie's Hotel. It gave rise to an optimism that was as guarded as the light.

They walked softly to the stern, their rubber-soled shoes making no sound. Zach and Denise picked up AK-47s from the cockpit on their way. Zach and Glen untied the lines holding their eight-foot dinghy to the two davits extending back from the stern, and the little boat sank quietly into the water.

"We should be back within the hour," Zach whispered to Stacey. "I'll call as soon as I find

George and get a handle on the situation." He showed her the battery operated two-way radio he had in his pocket. "If we run into trouble, we'll call... if we can. Be prepared to make a quick exit if you have to."

"We're not leaving without you and Denise," Stacey whispered back. But her voice was sharper than his was.

"I appreciate that!" He took a breath and attempted to whisper with a softer tone, realizing she must be scared. "And that's the last thing I want, but we have no idea how bad things are here. We're in survival mode now, and we need to do what we need to do."

"I'm not an Army Ranger," she reminded him, "and my family is all that matters to me."

He didn't argue. He turned to Glen and pointed to the left side of the boat. "Keep your eyes peeled for anything that doesn't belong on the port side. Your mother will be doing the same on the starboard side."

With that, he and Denise slung their AK-47s onto their backs, the strong canvas slings securing them there, and Zach stepped quickly down an aft ladder onto the dinghy. Denise followed, with Zach helping steady her when she was in the boat. When she was seated and the dinghy steady, Glen handed Zach one oar and Stacey gave him another. He slipped them into the oarlocks and shoved off toward shore, rowing the short distance quickly while Glen and Stacey grabbed two more AK-47s and took up their guard duties.

When the bow of the dinghy pushed up onto a small sandy spot on land, Zach jumped off the forward end and pulled it five feet onto the beach. He tied the small line at its bow to a bush as Denise stepped off, and they both looked around to get the lay of the land. They could make out a pathway through the shrubbery to their left that appeared to lead up a gentle incline to a level where they could see buildings.

Zach motioned for Denise to follow him as he started up the path. Their eyes constantly scanned the dark area as they approached the level of the buildings. There was no movement around them, but anything or anyone could be out there, hidden by the dark bushes. The path led to a swimming pool that overlooked the bay.

"That looks like the Aunt Millie's pool," Denise whispered.

Zach nodded his agreement and started around the pool. As he rounded the corner of the pool near a clump of shrubs and tall palms, a figure ran out from behind a dark shrub and charged at him.

Chapter 9

ZACH felt... more than saw... the attack coming. The shrub was ten feet away, and the distance gave him time to swing into action. He immediately realized that for someone to attack this way, he must be unarmed.

Zach wasn't ready to kill, so he dropped his weapon and went into a crouch with his arms outspread. Meeting the attacker with a shoulder into his stomach, he wrapped his arms around his unexpected foe's upper body and threw him hard to the ground. When the man tried to get up, Zach caught him on the side of his face with a powerful punch. The single blow knocked the man unconscious.

Denise, who'd un-slung her AK-47 when she saw her father in a fight, came up beside him. "Wow," she whispered, "that was quick."

"Quicker than it should have been. There's something wrong with this guy. I got a look at his eyes for an instant. They looked crazed. He may be on drugs, or maybe he's just starved. Whatever it is, he wasn't up to what he tried to do."

"What are we going to do about him, Dad?"

"I suspect he's out for a while, and our time is limited, so we'll have to forget about him and get on with what we came for. There might be others like him, though, so keep an eye out." He motioned for her to follow, picked up his weapon, and started for the hotel once again. There were three paths leading from the pool to the hotel, and Zach chose the one in the middle. It led to the lobby. The glass door was locked, and the lights were out, but he was sure he saw movement there moments earlier.

He made no attempt to break in but, instead, stood silently watching the interior, his assault weapon at his side. Denise followed his lead, standing beside him. As his eyes adjusted, a shape began to materialize behind the check in counter. The shape wasn't moving, but Zach thought he recognized the contours of a somewhat familiar bald head.

He kept his voice as soft as he could while trying to get the words heard on the other side of the lobby. "George, it's me, Zach Arthur, and my daughter, Denise."

The shape didn't move for several seconds. Neither did Zach or Denise. The shape finally disappeared, and a moment later Zach could see a crouched shadow creep to the side of the lobby and move slowly along the wall. He made no move to raise his weapon, and continued to stand silently while the person inside was apparently sizing him up.

When the shadow disappeared again, he guessed what was happening. He would have done the same. The person – he was convinced it was George, the man he was looking for – went out to the pool via one of the other doors and approached him from the rear. He didn't turn, even when he felt a presence come up behind him.

"Drop your weapons!" Zach recognized the voice.

"I will keep it down at my side, George, but there are bad guys out there. I need to keep it ready for immediate action, just in case I need it. You do remember us, don't you?"

"Yes, but I don't know what you're doing here. You have a sailboat. You were free of this place. Why would you come back to an island that's fallen victim to anarchy?"

Zach turned to face the man. George was around forty-five years old, in good shape and alert. He had a small pistol aimed at them, which Zach ignored. "We need fuel, and from what I recall, there's no one better at locating things than you. We only learned about what has happened less than two days ago. Apparently this island is better off than most places."

George dropped the arm with the pistol and looked at Zach in stark shock. "Better off than most? My God, we've been overrun by gangs. People are killing others over a pint of water. I've been holding them off as best I can with this little .38, but that's only because no large group has converged on us yet. It's just a matter of time."

Zach thought for a moment. He had an idea,

but held it back for the time being, hoping he wouldn't have to use it. "George, we can be of great help to one another. We need diesel fuel. We have money."

"Money?" George laughed. "Money is worthless! If you gave me a million dollars in small bills, the only way they could be of any value is using them to start a fire to roast food."

"I was afraid of that, but I have something better than money, anyway. How would you like an AK-47 and ammunition?" Even in the dark, Zach could see George's eyes light up. He looked at the weapon in Zach's hand. "Like that one you have?"

"Yes, if you can get us diesel. We need as much as you can get."

"There are six fifty-gallon barrels on the dock over on Reeds Bay."

Zach whistled. "Three hundred gallons would be fantastic. I think I know that dock, and if we came up next to it, my deck would be a little below the dock, so we could roll the barrels onto the boat. But that's around the bend, and tough to sail into."

"It's the only diesel around here that I know of and, at the moment, it doesn't belong to anyone. The boat that it was meant for sank. For two AK-47s, it's yours."

"Two? You have help?"

"All the help left, but Millie is still here."

"Aunt Millie, the owner? I thought she was old and no longer involved."

"Old, yes, but she can do more than any two people I know. She isn't involved on a daily basis, but she's here now and ready for a fight.

I wouldn't want to come up against her if she had an AK-47. I'm going to be glad she's on my side when that crowd of thugs decides to try to take over the hotel."

Zach had two more weapons than there were people aboard but he had hoped to keep the extras in reserve for more trades later on. Of course, the fuel would be useful for bartering, as well, and there wasn't time to haggle. "Okay, George, two AK-47s and six magazines."

"Ten!"

"Eight!"

"Deal!" George exclaimed. "These two guns?" He pointed at the weapons Zach and Denise held.

"One, but I need to keep one handy. I'll give you the second one and the other seven mags after we've loaded the fuel."

"Fair enough. I'll take the one to Millie – she's keeping watch on a second story balcony. She has a .357 magnum, but will love this baby. I'll join you in a minute, and we can sail over to Reeds Bay."

"Will there be anyone there?" Denise asked worriedly.

"It's unlikely anyone is there now. There's no food anywhere around the dock, and people are starving, so all the looting is being done in the commercial areas. Right now, anyway. If anybody sees your boat, though, or hears something going on, we're likely to have some unwanted company."

Chapter 10

GEORGE was back in less than five minutes. The three of them made for the boat, skirting the pool and stepping around the man who was still lying unconscious at its side.

George looked curiously at the fallen man, and Zach said, simply, "He jumped me," as they walked around him.

When they got to the water, Zach held the dinghy steady as Denise and George climbed aboard. He gave it a good shove and jumped in himself. He took the oars and rowed them quickly to the sailboat, pulling up to the stern where the boarding ladder hung.

"I'm going to keep the dinghy in the water," Zach said. "No telling what we're going to run into." He looked around the dark land surrounding the hotel, knowing there could be a dozen people hiding there like the man he'd knocked out. All the lights and fires were farther away, near the center of Hilo, but the people were desperate and were liable to do just about anything.

Denise grabbed a rung of the ladder and began climbed up, her rifle hanging loosely by the canvas sling over her shoulder. George followed, and Zach was right behind him. Once aboard, Zach explained the situation to Stacey and Glen. "We need to sail her around the bend over there, nodding toward the point that separated Hilo Bay from Reeds Bay, and then back toward the dock. We'll only use the mainsail."

Stacey and Glen sprang into action, knowing what was expected of them. They'd been in emergency situations before, although those were storms and somewhat different from what they faced now. The sailing would be easier in these calm waters, but in those other situations, there wasn't the possibility that someone might open fire on them at any minute. Glen pulled up the anchor as Stacey started removing the bungee cords that were holding the mainsail to the boom. Zach was already at the mast winch, pulling the sail up. Denise was at the wheel.

"What can I do?" George asked.

Stacey didn't hesitate. "Go aft and watch for bad guys. Stay away from the center of the ship, or the mainsail boom is likely to cold-cock you. Wouldn't want that to happen!"

A light wind was blowing toward land, so the bow was pointing away from shore, within thirty degrees of what their initial course would be. As soon as the sail started going up, the boom swung to the starboard side, and the *La Sirena* began moving. Glen hauled the anchor up and left it on the deck in case they needed it later. Denise turned the wheel to starboard. The boat was soon moving at a few knots, the wind coming in over the port side as they headed almost due east. Within ten minutes, they were abreast of the opening between the two bays.

Stacey nodded at Denise, and the girl again turned the wheel, this time ninety degrees to starboard. Stacey had moved to the pulley that controlled the mainsail boom. She let it out so that the boom swung all the way around until it was almost at a ninety-degree angle to the hull of the ship. The wind, which was now coming directly over the stern, hit the sail full on and they moved at a rapid pace.

It only took a couple of minutes for them to pass the rocky point that extended out to separate the two bays. Zach went over and grabbed the line that controlled the boom. "I'll guide it over, Denise. When I say 'now,' make the turn... but not too fast."

She nodded, and when Zach gave the word, she began making the turn. As Stacey winched in the line, Zach walked the boom across the boat. They were soon sailing west, headed straight for the dock, the wind coming in over the starboard rail.

George, himself no stranger to boats, had never seen things done more smoothly. He moved to the center cockpit to avoid having to yell. "The barrels are in front of the third building from the right."

"Good," Zach replied. "That means we can make a wide turn, and it'll give us plenty of room to ease up to the dock."

With the moonlight, and the fires blazing in the town behind them, the boaters could see the buildings easily. It also made them more visible than they would like.

Stacey relieved Denise at the wheel.

George looked inquisitively at Zach.

"I know what you're thinking," Zach said, "and you're right, Denise is a great helmsman. But, Stacey was at the wheel in three Transpac races. She can put a forty-one foot boat within an inch of any line you draw for her."

As they approached the dock, Zach began lowering the sail, and Stacey turned slowly to port so they could let the slight wind push them gently up to the dock. When they were twenty feet away, Zach dropped the sail all the way, and wrapped a single bungee around it. He then went to the stern and grabbed a shoreline. Glen was on another line at the bow. With the sail down, the wind pushed the boat toward the dock slowly. When they were three feet away, and Zach and Glen were ready to jump up to the dock to secure the lines. A powerful gust of wind hit the boat broadside. Stacey reacted quickly, turning the wheel hard to port. She'd done everything possible to save the situation, but it wasn't enough.

They slammed into the dock. She kept it from hitting hard enough to damage the boat, but it still caused the one thing they'd been trying to avoid.

It made a loud banging noise.

Chapter 11

E VEN before the boat stopped rocking, Zach and Glen had the lines at its bow and its stern wrapped around cleats on the dock. The boat settled against the heavy posts that held the dock up.

"I'm sorry I couldn't stop it from hitting," Stacey apologized.

"Nobody could have," Zach reassured her. "Unfortunately, Mother Nature decided to have a little fun at our expense, and we're all at her mercy when she does that. It does limit our time here, though. No telling who heard it."

He spotted six barrels. "Are those the ones, George?"

"Yep."

"We need to get them over here, fast. Rolling them will be the quickest way. Stacey and Denise, you'd better keep your weapons off safety and ready. Watch for bad guys. They could come from either side."

The three males rushed over to the barrels. Each knocked one over and rolled it toward the boat. Glen lost control of his, and it rolled right onto the aft deck, banging hard on the teak deck and rolling over to the far side, where it came to rest against the railing.

"Sorry, Dad!"

"That's okay, Glen, that's where we would have..." Zach started to say, but cut off his comment when the sound of gunfire interrupted him.   Stacey had stepped up on the dock and opened fire at a spot near the corner of one building over from where the barrels were.   He could see a few men ducking for cover, but several others were heading their way, undaunted by the risk.

Zach rolled his barrel onto the sailboat, making no attempt to avoid chipping the teak deck or the rails. "No time to be neat," he stated flatly, and George did the same.   The barrels came to a stop near the one Glen had rolled onto the boat.

They ran back for the other three barrels, knocking them over as Denise, still aboard, joined her mother in shooting in the direction of the advancing men.

Both were intentionally missing, but Stacey yelled, "Stop where you are or I will aim the next rounds directly at you."

Most of the men slowed down, then stopped. When two didn't, Stacey shot them in their legs.

The other men gathered to confer.   Zach, George, and Glen took advantage of the lull to roll the other three barrels onto the boat. The large barrels cluttered the aft deck, leaving little room for the crew to maneuver, but that was of no concern to them at that moment.

"Untie the aft line," Zach yelled at Glen as he started the engine. "Quick, Stacey, undo the bow line and get aboard." He pushed the throttle full ahead as Stacey, her weapon still in hand, jumped up and undid the line, which was already beginning to tighten. Zach was turning the boat away from the dock when she tossed her weapon aboard and jumped, grasping a rail as the boat picked up speed.

* * * * *

Six of the men had regrouped. They ran to try to catch the boat, but stopped abruptly at the edge of the dock when George shot at their feet. They jumped back as the wood chips flew. By the time they regained enough courage to move ahead, the boat was out of reach.

One of the men was armed with a rifle but saw the futility of trying to go up against five people armed with assault weapons. "Is that skiff still down by the old cannery?" he asked.

"Well, yeah, Cody," another said, "but there ain't much fuel in it."

"All we need is enough to cut them off before they get out of the bay," said the armed man. "I want that sailboat."

They all ran north, heading in the direction the sailboat would take as it sailed toward the bay's entrance. By the time the La Sirena reached the point, the men had run over the little hill at the base of the narrow land mass that separated the two bays.

They were sliding down the levee leading to the old cannery as the sailboat, instead of heading out of the bay, turned to head toward the anchorage near Aunt Millie's Hotel. Though they had the fuel they wanted, there was still business they had to complete.

The hotel was less than a half mile from the old cannery.

Chapter 12

WHEN he was sure there were no obstacles in the way on the course to the hotel, Zach turned and watched George help Glen stand up the barrels of diesel fuel. Stacey had gone below for some line and just returned to the aft deck to tie the barrels securely against the rail.

"The future looks pretty bleak here, George," Zach said after a minute. "What are your... long term plans?"

"I'll stay and help Millie with the hotel," George replied without hesitation.

Stacey looked up from the barrel she was tying down. "I think I know what Zach has in mind. You handled that weapon very well back there, George." She looked at Zach and nodded her approval.

"It will be months, probably years, before anyone needs a hotel around here," Zach said. "George, you're welcome to come with us."

"I appreciate the offer, but I can't leave Millie.

We've been working together for so long, she's like my own mother."

"How are you going to live?" Stacey asked. "There can't be any mode of transportation set up to bring goods in, and those marauders must be taking everything of any use out of the stores."

"Millie and I have been survivalists for years. We've stocked enough water, canned goods, batteries, medical equipment, and everything else we'll need for at least six months. Now, with these weapons and ammunition to ward off thieves, we'll be fine."

"As far as supplies are concerned, it sounds like you're better off than us," Zach admitted. "Even with what we got from the U.S. Navy added to what we had before, we'll have to stretch it to last more than a couple of months. I'm not the best fisherman in the world, but I catch one now and then, and..."

The sound of an explosion interrupted him. He stopped talking and looked toward a place on land where fire had broken out. "George, is that the hotel?"

Pain was etched into the hotel man's face. He nodded, but didn't say anything for a few moments. Then, "Zach, I've got to get there, fast. Millie's alone."

Zach nodded. They'd been moving at half-throttle, but he now pushed the lever forward all the way. When he was as close to shore as he felt safe with a full keel that extended at least eight feet below the water line – more with as much weight as they had aboard – he turned the boat full around so that it's bow was pointing toward the eastern portion of the breakwater. He shifted to neutral and let the engine idle.

Glen went forward to drop the anchor, but Zach called to him. "No. Glen, we don't have time to anchor. With all the noise we've made in the last fifteen minutes, we're likely to draw a crowd. We have to be prepared to get out of here without delay."

George was starting to climb over the port rail, but Zach grabbed his arm. "We'll take the dinghy."

"You're going with me? You don't have to."

"In whatever this world is turning into, good people have to stick together," Zach replied. "Stacey, can you keep the boat steady?"

"Yes," she agreed, and jumped up to the wheel. "I'll tie down the last two barrels later."

"Denise, stay with your mother." Zach said to his daughter. "But keep your eye out for unwanted company. Glen, you come with us."

Denise still had her automatic weapon in hand, and indicated so to her father.

"Good! George, Glen, follow me." He slung his automatic weapon over his shoulder and rushed aft, scooting around a barrel and climbing down the ladder they'd used earlier. He grabbed the line holding the dinghy and pulled the small boat in. When it was close enough, he stepped aboard, holding onto the ladder to steady himself. George and Glen followed him aboard, both with automatic weapons slung over their shoulders.

George removed his rifle and looked around as Zach untied the line and shoved off from the sailboat. Clouds had begun to cover the moon every now and then, but at that moment, the moon gave them ample light to see where they were going. The dinghy headed toward shore and picked up speed as Zach took the oars and started rowing.

Glen stepped to the bow and picked up the line that was used to tie the dingy to the sailboat, then waited in anticipation. The second they touched shore, he jumped off and pulled the dinghy onto dry land. Before he moved it three feet, Zach and George were there to help. When they had it completely out of the water, they all ran toward the hotel.

Fire was blazing out of half the hotel's windows on one side of the building. As they rushed toward the back door, another explosion rocked the building. That one was at the front of the hotel, but it was powerful enough to shake the ground under them, almost knocking them down.

They regained their balance and continued toward the hotel. As they approached the door, they heard gunshots over the noise of the crackling blaze. The shots came from the second floor, where George had left Aunt Millie. There were only two shots, not the rapid-fire bursts that would indicate it was Millie using the automatic weapon George had given her.

Chapter 13

THE six men found the worn skiff tied to a ramshackle dock next to a cannery that had been abandoned several years earlier. They climbed aboard, and the fellow who'd known it was there flipped the outboard motor's gas lever on and pulled on the starter cord. The motor coughed, turned over once, but didn't start.

"C'mon, Harley," the one with the rifle said, "get this thing going."

"If you're so smart, Cody, you do it," Harley snapped back.

"Will one of you do it for crissake?" another pleaded. "Look, they're headed toward shore. If you guys quit messing around, we can get that boat while it's right over there."

With two more pulls, Harley got the engine going. It sputtered, but they began moving jerkily toward a spot near Coconut Island – the spot where they were almost sure the *La Sirena* was headed. They watched as the sailboat made a turn and stopped with its stern toward shore. In the moonlight, they could see three men get in a dinghy and row to shore.

"Did you see that, Cody?" asked one of the men. "Weren't there just three guys on that boat?"

"That's all I saw. So that means all that's left aboard is two gals."

"Gals with guns," Harley reminded them.

"Yeah, but they're still just gals," Cody scoffed. "What can they do?"

"Didn't you just see what they can do?" Harley shook his head "Man, they shot Gus and Arnold while we was standin' right there."

"That had ta be the woman," Cody reasoned. "The other was just a kid."

Harley cut the engine. "We'd better sneak up on 'em," he explained when the others looked at him inquisitively. "Let's paddle."

"Ain't no oars," the fellow who'd seen the *La Sirena* headed toward shore said.

"Paddle with your hands, Marty! But keep it quiet."

"You be quiet," the other snapped.

"You all be quiet," whispered Cody. "We can't sneak up on 'em if you're all beatin' your gums at one another."

When they got a little closer, Harley whispered to Cody, "Hey, the boat's kinda moving back and forth. I think someone's at the controls."

"That's gotta be the woman," Cody whispered back. "That means all we gotta deal with first is the kid. Let's move real slow and easy like to the back a' the boat. I think they got a ladder there that the three guys used. Slick, you and Marty go up first. Grab the girl and keep her quiet. I'll be right behind. If the woman is at the controls, I should be able to get hold a' her before she can grab that automatic rifle of hers."

He smiled crookedly. "Capturing two gals along with a boat is like getting a big bonus. We can make good use of both of 'em, if you know what I mean."

"I don't know, Cody," Harley said in mild protest." She looked pretty tough. What if she's got that assault rifle right on her?"

"Then I guess I'll just have ta kill her and we'll settle for just the kid."

* * * * *

Stacey controlled the *La Sirena*, moving the sailboat forward every time the wind and current shoved it toward land. Denise kept watch. She walked slowly along the deck on the sides of the boat, stopping every few feet to scan the area. A full swing around the boat took between three and five minutes. She started her last round aft on the starboard side, and walked forward to the bow.

It was while she was heading in the other direction that the skiff with the six men aboard snuck in toward the boat's stern. By the time she walked back on the port side, they were hidden by the boat itself and the barrels that now blocked her view of what lay behind the boat.

As she passed the cockpit where Stacey was at the helm, she thought she heard a noise. It sounded like something bumping into the boat's stern. She brought her AK-47 down to waist level and hurried back.

She was maneuvering around the barrels when an ugly, dirty man jumped up from the boarding ladder and grabbed her shoulders. There was another right behind him.

"Ya might's well put that gun down little girlie," the man who held her shoulders smirked, "Cause yer mine now."

Chapter 14

GEORGE didn't bother searching for keys. Pulling his AK-47 off his shoulder, he blasted out the glass back door. The three rushed into the building through the shattered opening without stopping. Fire was already spreading to the stairs at the right of the lobby.

"I left Millie up there!" George cried out as he rushed to the stairs, taking them two at a time on his way to the second floor.

"Millie!" he shouted when he reached the second floor hallway.

"Don't come any closer or I'll shoot," came a strong female voice from a room two doors down the hallway.

"Millie, it's George. Thank God you're safe. Come on... we have to get out of here!"

A slender, white-haired woman of about eighty years appeared in the doorway. She carried a .357 magnum in her hand. "George, some men tried to break in."

"Where are they?"

"I got two of them. The others got away before I could get a shot at them. Maybe I should have used that repeater you gave me."

"They must have thrown some powerful Molotov cocktails into the place. It's an inferno."

"That's why I shot them."

"Unfortunately, the damage has already been done. Now we have to get out of here." He took her hand and started to lead her to the stairs.

"Wait," she told him, breaking away from his hold. She ran back into the room and came back carrying the assault rifle in one hand and the .357 magnum in the other. "There are still some very bad people out there. We need all the defense we can muster."

"I agree. Let's go."

When they got to the lobby, they saw that Zach and Glen had found fire extinguishers and were trying to put out the raging fire.

"Aren't those the people you were saving the herbs for?" Millie asked.

"Yes, it's the Arthurs."

Zach turned when he heard them coming. "We tried to control the fire, but it's no use," he called to George. "It's spread too far. We have to get out of here. George, you'd better change your mind and come with us."

"I can't leave Millie."

Zach looked at the old woman. She looked back defiantly. It wasn't lost on him that she had weapons in both hands. He made a decision. "Bring her."

"Where are you going?" she wanted to know.

"California," Zach replied.

"I can't leave my hotel!"

"Millie, in half an hour there won't be a hotel," George told her. "With the island in the hands of the kind of people who did this, it will be years before it can be rebuilt."

She looked around and sighed. "Okay, but we're coming back."

No one doubted her resolve, but it wasn't the time to discuss the future. "Fine," Zach said, "but right now we have to go!"

"We have food, water, ammunition, radios, and first aid equipment in that section over there," George said, pointing to the left side of the building. "The fire hasn't reached there yet."

The second Molotov cocktail had been thrown onto the second floor at the front of the left section of the building. The first one had hit the right side and that side was now completely engulfed in flames. Fire was working its way back on the left side. The rear hadn't been destroyed yet, but it soon would be.

"We can use all we can get," Zach agreed, "but we're running out of time. Let's all get what we can carry on one trip to the dinghy. Then we're on our way."

George led the group across the lobby and down a hall to a room with no number on the door. They could feel the fire scorching the floor above. It was threatening to break through to that area and was likely to do so at any moment. "Here's where we store our survival supplies," he told the others. He didn't consider keys; he just shot the lock and kicked the door open. The room was filled with boxes, jugs, and bags.

Millie stepped in first and pointed to one

area. "Canned foods are there," she said. "How are you fixed for water?"

"We were okay," Zach replied, "but with two more bodies, I think we should take some extra."

"In the jugs," she told him. "We've got medical supplies over there." She pointed to some white boxes. "They seem to be getting more important by the minute."

"I'll take a jug of water and some canned goods," Zach said. "Glen, you grab the medical supplies."

"Millie and I will bring what we need," George announced.

They all loaded supplies in their arms and started to walk out, but George stopped. "Hey," he called to Zach, "Those herbs you ordered are right here. Still want them?"

"Yes," Zach replied without hesitation.

"Okay, I've got them."

They hurried down the hallway and out the door to the pool. The clouds had covered most of the moon, but there was still enough light that they could see that the man Zach had knocked out was still lying by the pool.

As they stepped around him, gunshots erupted ahead of them. Zach dropped what he was carrying and darted for the dinghy. There was no doubt where the shots were coming from. Someone had opened fire on the *La Sirena*.

Chapter 15

DENISE tried to pull away from the man, but he tightened his grip on her shoulders, his calloused fingers digging into her flesh. He came straight at her from the front, so the automatic weapon she was carrying just above waist level was not only pointed at his stomach, it pushed into a gut that hung over his belt.

"My... my gun is pointed right at you," she warned him in a tremulous voice

"C'mon, kid," you ain't gonna do nothin' with that thing an' you know it."

She'd never been so frightened, but tried to look stern. "If you don't let go, I... I'll shoot."

He tightened the grip on her shoulders even more and leaned an intimidating, unshaven, and grimy face close to hers. His breath caused her to gag. Then she saw a third man climb aboard behind the one that was holding her and another one behind him. As he edged around the first two men, she could see that this one was carrying a rifle. He looked past her toward her mother at the wheel.

Pushing at the man in front of him to clear space, he began to level his rifle at Stacey. The man behind her main antagonist was shoved ahead, moving her foe even closer to her. That made the ugly assailant even bolder. He let go of one shoulder and reached for her weapon. At the same time, the frightened teenager saw a fourth man's head peek over the deck from the boarding ladder.

It all happened so fast; she didn't have time to think. The one thing that was evident despite the fear that possessed her was that she was out of time. She closed her eyes and did the only thing that might get her and her mother out of this. She pulled the trigger.

The rat-tat-tat of the bullets firing was deafening to her. The impact of the slugs driving into the man's stomach knocked him backward with such force he took the man behind him over the aft rail with him. They landed in the skiff, where the last two men were starting to follow Harley up the ladder. Seeing what had happened to their compatriots, they changed their minds and instead jumped into the water and started swimming back the way they'd come.

Cody, who was sliding around the side of the men who'd boarded ahead of him, managed to duck away as they went overboard. He leaned against a barrel, using it for leverage to straighten up. The girl was shooting, so he changed targets, swinging his gun around to shoot her.

Stacey saw Denise start back to investigate

the noise. She continued to keep the *La Sirena* steady at first, but when she realized there were men sneaking aboard, she abandoned the controls and un-slung her weapon. She watched in horror as Denise shot a man, but an even greater travesty was in the making. As Cody brought his weapon around to shoot her daughter, she fired.

The weapon was on single shot, but one was enough. The bullet caught the would-be assassin in the chest. He staggered backward, caroming off the barrel he'd used a moment before to straighten himself up. He, too, plunged over the rail into the skiff.

Harley was about to climb aboard, but he saw enough to discard any further dreams of commanding that sailboat. He dove into the water and swam after his two buddies.

* * * * *

Zach didn't see the first part of the saga, but he got to the water in time to see one man fall over the aft rail and another dive in, swimming in the direction two others were headed.

As he pushed the dinghy into the water, he called out, "Stacey, Denise, are you okay?"

Stacey came to the rail. "We're fine, but hurry. I don't know if there are any more thugs around here."

Glen came up next to him, still carrying the supplies he brought from the hotel. He started to say something, but stopped when he heard a motor start off at a distance.

"What's that?" he wanted to know.

"It sounds like a boat's motor," Zach replied worriedly. "And not a small one. It's out there in the bay somewhere. With all this noise, we're beginning to draw the kinds of crowds that spell danger. I don't know who or what that is out there, and don't want to know... but we may find out soon enough. We need to load the supplies, quick, and get out of here. We're better off at sea."

They met George and Millie halfway up the hill. The two hotel people were overloaded with bags, jugs, and boxes. "We got about all you dropped," George said breathlessly. "We left just a few canned goods back at the pool."

"We have to forget them," Zach said, "Let's load what we have into the dinghy and get it to the boat."

When it was all loaded, there was only room for two on the dinghy. Zach helped Millie aboard and then turned to George. "Do you swim?"

"Like a fish."

Zach put his weapon in the dinghy and nodded for George to do the same. "Glen," he said to his son, "row the supplies and Millie out to the boat. George and I will swim."

Both men were in the water and swimming before Glen had a chance to get settled at the oars. George was on the side where the skiff bobbed quietly in the water. He grabbed the side and lifted himself up. He saw three bodies at the bottom. He had no way of knowing that one was alive, but the guy was unconscious so he wasn't aware that there were two bodies on top of him. George gave the skiff a shove toward shore. He heard splashing off to the right, but whoever was out there was moving in the opposite direction, so he discounted it as being an immediate threat.

Zach got to the boarding ladder first and climbed it in seconds. He found that Stacey had abandoned the controls. She was sitting at the side of the cockpit, trying to soothe her sobbing daughter.

When Denise saw her father, she jumped up and hugged him, her body shaking. Stacey looked pityingly at her, then at Zach. She shook her head slowly, a signal that he should use caution.

"Dad, I shot a man! He was grabbing me, and I... I... I shot him."

His heart went out to her. What had the world come to that she had to do such a horrible thing? He patted her hair softly. "Sweetie... you had no choice. We're living in an awful time, and there are terrible things happening all around us. We have to do what we can to survive."

"I... I think I killed him."

"We have no time to find out. We're in real danger as long as we stay here."

The dinghy arrived and Glen, George, and Millie began hauling the supplies up to the sailboat. Leaving her daughter in the hands of her husband, Stacey went over to help.

"We'll just have to drop them in the salon until we have time to organize," she said. She went down the ladder to the salon with a load, set the items down on a table, and reached up to take what George was passing down to her. In less than a minute, everything was stashed in

the salon. She went back up. "We're set here, |
she told Zach.

"Good!" He dropped his arms from around
Denise. "We have to go, Sweetie."

"I know." Her voice was weak, but steady. She
stood straight. "I'm ready."

Zach stepped into the cockpit and took the
controls. The boat was drifting toward shore and
its bow swung to starboard but as soon as he
pushed the lever forward and turned the wheel,
the vessel straightened out and moved forward.

The others were looking for places to settle
in, but Zach warned them, "Everyone, we heard
a motor start somewhere in the outer bay. There
may be someone out there waiting for us, so it's
too early to relax. Keep your eyes open and your
weapons ready."

They could hear the sound of another running
motor in the distance as they rounded Coconut
Island and motored toward the bay's entrance.
There was sufficient light on the water in the
direction they were headed for them to see a
dark shadow with the shape of a motorized boat
leaving the bay.

The shadow disappeared behind the dark
breakwater.

At the same time, the sound of a motor
pushing a big boat also went away.

Chapter 16

"I F THEY'RE waiting for us, it will be behind the breakwater to our right, so I'll keep as far left as I can," Zach told the others. "Keep an eye out on that side as well. That's the mainland, and there's no telling who might be lurking in the dark over there."

The *La Sirena*, which had left this bay little more than a month before in daylight, sailing proudly with the wind, was doing it much differently this night. The sails were tied down, the motor was running at near full throttle, and the dinghy, which normally hung from davits off the stern, was trailing behind.

The normally clear deck now had six heavy barrels of fuel lashed to the rails on the aft deck. Boxes, bags, and tubs were strewn around the salon they now used for eating and conversing. Before, a relaxed crew had viewed the local scenery in awe of its beauty as they passed. This night, they were tense and armed, all eyes on the lookout for gangs and terrorists – or whatever the people who turned to killing and looting for survival could now be called.

As they passed through the bay's entrance, George said, "I think I saw movement on the mainland."

"Everyone keep down," Zach ordered as he turned the boat, which had been headed due north, to a northeast heading. It didn't put them directly on their course to California, but it did take them away from a mainland where danger now lurked around every corner.

Nothing happened, except that the boat began to rise and fall more noticeably when the *La Sirena* left the calmer bay waters and entered the more active ocean currents. The swells weren't large, but the wind was picking up and they could see an occasional whitecap in places where the moon shone upon the water.

When there was no move against them from the mainland, Stacey reasoned, "Either those over there aren't armed, or they have no boat and saw no point in shooting at something they couldn't catch." She moved over to the port side. "I think we'd all better come over here," she told everyone. "If we're going to be attacked, it will be by that boat we saw slip in behind the breakwater. If they do come after us, it will be from the starboard side, so we can keep under cover here behind the upper hull of the cabins and the cockpit."

"Do you think they're still there?" Denise wanted to know. There was still a tremor in her voice. "I don't see anything."

"Their lights are off, and in the dark, anything around the breakwater rocks would be almost impossible to see," her mother said. "They must still be there, though. They haven't had time to go anywhere, and we haven't heard their engine for some time now. That means they're just sitting there."

"What do you think they're doing?" Glen asked.

"Waiting," said Millie. It was the first time she spoke since being introduced.

"Waiting for what?" Denise asked.

Millie shook her head. "I don't know for sure but I don't like what I'm thinking." She checked to make sure there was a round in the chamber of her automatic weapon.

They heard a motor start.

"Where is that coming from?" cried Denise.

"It sounds like it's coming from over there by the breakwater," George answered.

"Everyone... do as Stacey suggested," Zach said. "Get over on the port side and stay under cover until we find out what's happening."

The sound of the motor was getting louder. There could be no question about its destination. It was headed right at the La Sirena. Zach began to slow the sailboat down.

"Shouldn't we try to get away?" Millie asked.

"This is a sailboat," Stacey told her. "It's built to be propelled by sails. Our engine is only big enough to get us in and out of small places and move us a little in dead calms. Any powerboat in the world is at least four times faster. Trying to outrun whoever is back there is fruitless."

Zach didn't add that he decided that if there was going to be a confrontation, there was no point in getting farther out to sea. If they were somehow forced to swim, it might as well be from a point closer to the breakwater. "Let's wait to see what their intention is," he said. "Everyone stay down, and make sure your weapons are off safety."

When the powerboat was thirty yards away, it slowed and a light came on, shining on the *La Sirena*.

"Ahoy, there, sailboat *La Sirena*, this is the Hilo Coast Guard." The voice came from the powerboat. Even though the moon wasn't covered by clouds at that moment, the people on the sailboat could see nothing on the other boat except the light that was shining in their faces. They couldn't tell what the man looked like or what he was wearing. "We need to board your boat to check for contraband," the voice went on.

In a whisper loud enough to be heard by those aboard, but not thirty yards away, Zach asked, "George, is there such a thing as the Hilo Coast Guard?"

"Never heard of it," George answered.

"Me neither," Millie said. "And I've been here for eighty years."

The point of origin of the light moved.

"Zach," Stacey observed, "that's not a mounted light. It's only a powerful flashlight, and whoever is holding it just changed hands."

"Good observation," he said. "They're bad guys, so we're going to have to fight. I'm going to put it on autopilot, gun it, and then I'm ducking down in the cockpit. Be ready."

It took only a few seconds for whoever was at the controls of the powerboat to react when

Zach increased speed. The sailboat had opened up more distance between the boats in that short time, but the powerful engine roared, and the powerboat was closing in on the *La Sirena* quickly.

When it was again thirty yards away, the light was still shining on the sailboat, and those aboard the supposed Coast Guard boat opened fire.

A hail of bullets tore into the sailboat.

Chapter 17

"EVERYONE stay down!" Zach yelled the second the bullets started flying.

"We're sitting ducks with that light on us," George said over the noise of the fusillade.

Zach was well aware that the real problems were that they couldn't outrun the powerboat and that the light made them too visible, but he hadn't worked out a solution yet.

As if reading his mind, Denise called out, "I could knock it out, Dad."

"I know you could, Sweetie, but it's too dangerous for you to get up to do it right now. Stay down while I try to come up with something."

From his location at the bottom of the cockpit, Zach couldn't see what was happening on the narrow deck between the cabin and the rail. All the other members of the crew and their two guests were lying low there. Bullets were either flying over their heads or hitting the hull or the masts and sails. Several bullets punctured holes in two of the barrels of diesel. He knew that... unlike gasoline... diesel wasn't highly flammable, so there was no explosion or fire, but he also knew that they were losing valuable fuel.

Glen and Denise were lying near the front of the cabin. He put a finger to his lips, then crooked a finger and urged her to follow him as he crawled forward. She crawled after him, and when he was in front of the cabin, she crawled up next to him.

Having seen that everyone was in the center or toward the back of the powerboat where they were still standing and visible, the people were concentrating their fire. So far, nothing was hitting where the two youngsters were now. Glen whispered in his sister's ear, "As long as we're careful, they won't know we're up here, so we can do things."

"If I slide around to the other side of the cabin, I can get a shot at that light from the corner," she whispered back.

"That's what I was thinking. Be careful, though. Move real slow. And wait until I'm below."

He pointed to the hatch that was in the center of the boat, a few feet forward of the cabin. The cabin top was two feet higher than the deck at that point, so their actions were hidden from the others on the boat and, more importantly, from the people who were shooting at them.

"What are you going to do below?"

"I have an idea," was all he said before he lifted the hatch, slid through the opening, and lowered himself onto the large V-berth bunk bed in the cabin at the front of the boat.

Denise didn't waste time asking any more questions. She edged over to the starboard front corner of the cabin and peeked around. All she could see was the light, and it was getting nearer. Fortunately, it was still pointed at the cockpit, so only a little peripheral light hit where she was hidden. As long as she didn't make any quick moves, they shouldn't notice her.

She was right-handed, and if she shot the way she usually did, she would have to go all the way out from her cover or raise her head, shoulders, and part of her upper body over the cabin. Either would be more dangerous than leaning around the corner and shooting left handed.

Ever so slowly, she brought her rifle around and positioned the butt against her left shoulder. It would be a little awkward shooting that way, but her father was a thorough man and he had them all practice from both sides. Besides, she reasoned, it was the same person aiming.

She was an excellent shot and one bullet would normally do the trick. However, with the light shining so brightly, she couldn't be sure of the exact spot it was coming from. What was more, the wind driven waves were rocking the boat enough to make a single shot chancy. She left the weapon on automatic. She knew it tended to kick up and to the right when fired, so she aimed at the lower left of where she thought the light was emanating. She squeezed the trigger gently.

Her shots couldn't be heard over the sound

of all those coming from the powerboat, but the bullets ripping into the boat all around them told the shooters that someone was firing back. She didn't hit the powerful flashlight, but her shots caused the holder to shift, giving her a better idea of where the light was coming from. She re-aimed and squeezed the trigger again.

She shattered the light with her second volley, but that gave the men aboard the boat a fix on where the return fire was coming from. Two of them shifted their target area to the front of the sailboat and blasted it. Bullets flew around her, and she ducked frantically back behind the cabin. In the excitement of the moment, she didn't feel anything hit her, but noticed blood on her arm. She looked to see a three-inch long slit on her lower arm. It wasn't deep and only a quarter of an inch wide. She looked at it in wonder. She had never been wounded before but instinctively knew that a bullet nicked her.

She was a thirteen-year-old girl. Two days before, her most serious considerations were coping with the changes in becoming a teenager and going from elementary to high school. In the last half hour, she provided cover fire against a pack of thieves, killed a man, and was wounded in a battle for their lives. There were bullets hitting all around her, and she could hear a boat full of men bearing down on them, intent on killing her and her family.

Life had changed.

Chapter 18

"WHAT'S happening up there?" Zach yelled from the cockpit. "Who knocked out their light?"

"It was Denise, Dad!" Glen answered from below in the main cabin.

"Denise?" cried Stacey from the side of the cabin. "Are you all right?"

"I'm okay, Mom," Denise called out. "I shot out their light!"

"Good job! Stay down," her mother said, not knowing what else to advise a girl who had the courage to shoot a man who was attacking her and then shoot out the light that was making them easy targets.

Zach crawled over to look down into the cabin. "What are you doing down there, son?" It was unlikely anyone from the other boat could hear them over the noise of the gunfire, but Zach was a careful man and had lowered his voice to an audible whisper.

"Looking for the dynamite," Glen responded in the same tone.

"Great thinking! *Wow... keeping a cool head and coming up with this good an idea under stress are a couple of abilities few people have,* he thought. "Glen, this idea could give us the edge we need. The dynamite is up here in the cockpit storage bin. Come on up, but keep your head down."

He slid back toward the rear of the cockpit so his son could climb up into the space between the cabin doorway and the wheel. While Glen was getting settled, his father lifted the lid of the storage bin, keeping his head below the top of the cockpit where bullets were flying. He reached in and felt around for the dynamite. His hand felt what he was looking for, and he brought up a stick.

After checking the fuse, he again reached into the bin. "This fuse is six inches long," he told Glen. It'll take too long to burn down to the dynamite." He pulled up a knife. "I'll cut it to just over two inches."

Glen whistled. "That'll burn down fast,"

"It has to be fast. I figure eight seconds." Zach raised his voice slightly. "Stacey, George, can you hear me?"

"Yes," both replied in loud whispers.

"Me too," said Aunt Millie.

"Sorry, Millie, of course you too. Denise, can you hear me up there?"

"Barely, but I can."

"Good, because I can't chance speaking louder. I can hear them getting closer. They don't know our capabilities, so they will be cautious, but

they have to try to board us. We need to let
them get close. When they're ten feet away, I'll
yell 'now' and everyone start shooting. Which of
you three are closest to the bow?"

"Me," said Millie.

"Okay, Millie, crawl to the forward part of the
cabin. You and Denise will be shooting from that
area. Stacey and George, go toward the stern as
far as you can and still have protection from
the aft cabin. We can't have anyone shooting
from here, because Glen will be here with the
dynamite, and I'll be at the wheel."

"When I give the word, and they start giving
cover fire, light the fuse, Glen. Wait five seconds.
I will count out loud to five so you don't have
to. I've listened to the gunfire from their boat.
I know they have an automatic weapon, but it
sounds like they only have one. It doesn't sound
like they have many men, or weapons. You
four use your automatic weapons to keep them
pinned down during those five seconds. Glen,
when you hear me say five, throw the dynamite
into their cockpit. It has to hit the cockpit,
because if it hits the deck, it may roll off. As you
throw the dynamite, I'm going to hit the throttle
hard and turn away from the powerboat. I figure
we will have three seconds to get away from the
blast. Is everyone set?"

When all had responded, Zach added, "Okay,
now I'll slow down to let them get closer."

"That's the most precise and optimistic plan
I've ever heard in such a short span of time,"
George commented doubtfully.

"Yes, it is. But I made plans like this before
when I was in the army."

"Did they work?"

"Yes, for the same reason this one will."

"Which is?"

"Because it has to."

* * * * *

The clouds had again partially covered the moon, cutting visibility. With their powerful flashlight no longer functioning and natural light suddenly limited, the men on the powerboat could no longer get a good bead on their targets. They stopped firing, and their leader, a gruff looking man with sunken eyes, told the man at the helm to keep moving, but don't go alongside yet.

He looked skeptically at the sailboat when it slowed down and ordered his man to slow down, too. He wasn't about to let them call the shots. He saw guns aboard the sailboat before everyone hid, but he didn't know how many or what kinds. One, he knew from the bursts that knocked out their light, was an automatic weapon. That was near the front of the boat. If they had one, they might have others.

As long as its crew stayed hidden, the sailboat looked like a ghost ship, and he didn't know what to expect. However, he'd seen their boat clearly in the light, knew where everything was, and knew they had weapons. He wouldn't blunder in not expecting resistance. That worked yesterday, but these people seemed more alert.

However, they knew nothing about his boat or about how many men or weapons they had.

He hadn't fired his own automatic, so they wouldn't know they'd be up against two. He and his men were aggressive, which was a big advantage, and their boat was faster. And, they had an even bigger advantage. They'd lost everything and had nothing more to lose.

He stationed one man with an automatic weapon, along with one with a single shot rifle, at the front of the boat. He instructed them where their target was at the front of the sailboat and where to board it when they moved in close. He had a third man, this one with a single shot rifle, take cover in the stern. He joined him with his own automatic weapon. Their target was the cockpit and aft cabin, and they would board the sailboat ahead of where they saw the barrels. The man at the wheel of the powerboat was unarmed.

A sixth man was below, nursing two gunshot wounds he received when he was holding the flashlight. Denise's shots hit the arm holding the light in two places. Neither wound was life threatening, but there wasn't a fifth weapon, so he saw no point in remaining on deck and in harm's way.

"Okay," the leader said when they were all in place, "It's time. Let's move in. When we're close, I'll yell 'now' as the signal to open fire. Pin them down, and be ready to board when we're alongside."

The powerboat moved relentlessly in on the slow moving sailboat that seemingly had no one in control.

Chapter 19

THE moon slid out from behind a cloud as the powerboat neared the *La Sirena*. A whitecap broke between them, but the frothing wave didn't alter either boat's course as the space between them narrowed to twenty feet, then to fifteen. As they drew closer, everyone in both boats became more nervous.

Those on the sailboat felt great fear. Bullets had careened around them for several minutes and they knew what it felt like to be sitting targets.

Those on the powerboat felt the confidence of men in control... yet they couldn't help but wonder what still lay ahead when they reached that sailboat. They hadn't anticipated such resistance from the small group. They had no doubt that they would get what they were after, but they also knew that they were going to have to fight for it.

When the shooting had stopped, Zach peeked

over the top of the cockpit to see where the powerboat was. No one shot at him, so he continued his vigil. At first, he saw little more than a dark shape. But when the clouds moved away from the moon, he was able to pick out general characteristics of the boat.

It appeared a little longer than their own, maybe forty-five feet. As with most of those boats, the front three-quarters was for cabins and storage, and the back section was the cockpit, with controls at the forward part of that section, attached to the rear of the cabin section. The fuel tanks would be below. A stick of dynamite going off on the deck back there would blow the tanks.

His eyes swept back and forth, trying to pick up signs of life. There was one man in the open, sitting on a port side seat at the controls of the vessel. It seemed strange to Zach that one man would be so open and vulnerable while everyone else was obviously hiding, but he quickly decided the reason had no bearing on what was about to occur.

It was time to act.

"Now," he commanded. He didn't think he was overly loud, but it sounded like the word echoed across the water. Undeterred, he began counting.

Stacey and George rose up above the aft cabin and began firing at the stern area of the powerboat, and Millie rose up above the forward cabin and started shooting. Denise, when she saw the bow of the powerboat move up even with their own bow, slid on her stomach along the front of the cabin, edging toward where Millie was. When Zach gave the order, she opened fire, too, shooting as she inched backward.

To their dismay, four men on the powerboat, two behind their own forward cabin, and two in the aft cockpit, also lifted up and began firing at the sailboat. Those on the sailboat had assumed that by opening fire with automatic weapons, the shooters on the other boat would stay under cover. That might have been the case, but it happened that the powerboat's leader yelled "now" at the same time Zach did, so both sides opened fire simultaneously.

In less than a second, it had become a fierce firefight. Bullets ripped into the fiberglass around Denise; she stopped edging and started scrambling to get behind the cover of the port side of the forward cabin. The others stayed as low as they could, but never stopped firing.

Glen lit the fuse when Zach gave his command. At the count of one, he raised up to get a bead on his target. He saw the powerboat's cockpit a little behind where he was. That would be an easy throw. He raised up and cocked his arm, ready to throw. At that instant, a bullet hit the shoulder of his throwing arm.

He spun around, but knew he had to get rid of the dynamite. The count had not yet reached three when, with what strength he had left, he threw the dynamite at the powerboat.

It landed on the other boat, but on the deck ahead of and above the cockpit.

The man nearest it, the one at the wheel, saw the boy throw something at his boat. When it landed a little ahead of him and to his left, he saw what it was and immediately recognized that he and the boat were in serious danger. He jumped up to grab the dynamite.

Zach was at the wheel, in front of Glen, and didn't see his son get hit. He looked off to his right from where the opposing gunfire was coming. He was shocked to see the dynamite land at the wrong place... and much too soon. His count had barely hit three.

My God, he thought... *that guy is going to throw it back at us!*

Chapter 20

THERE wasn't enough time to get out of throwing distance, but Zach knew he had to try. He pushed the throttle full ahead and cranked the wheel hard to port, away from the powerboat. "Grab handholds, everyone," he yelled. He had no time to determine if anyone aboard heard him.

The boat didn't react as fast as he liked – it seemed like minutes to him – but it was actually a quick movement in the water and that created a three-foot wave at the starboard stern. The wave moved toward the front of the boat, where another wave approached from the opposite direction. The two crashed into one another between the two boats, creating a huge comber that shot upward.

It raised the *La Sirena*'s stern ten feet in the air and almost capsized the powerboat. The powerboat rode it out, but the port side rose so high that the round stick of dynamite started rolling around the deck at a rapid pace. It rolled right under the grasping hand of the diving helmsman and off the higher level into the cockpit. It continued rolling until it hit the foot of the group's leader, who was trying to keep upright by holding onto a fishing chair attached to the deck toward the back of the cockpit. He was occupied with trying to stay on his feet and neither saw the dynamite, nor felt it hit his foot.

The helmsman turned frantically and saw the dynamite was more than fifteen feet away. Its blazing fuse was burning with unrelenting progress toward the packed explosive. He didn't know much about sticks of dynamite but knew enough to realize that that this one was about to blow. He also didn't know what the fates might hold for him in the roiling waters below, but it couldn't be worse than what awaited him if he stayed where he was for another second. He dove into the churning sea between the boats and disappeared under the swirling waters.

There were two explosions. Not one second after the helmsman hit the water, the fuse burned to the end and the dynamite went off. That first explosion blasted the powerboat's aft section apart. That sent the fishing chair, the helmsman's chair, all the equipment that had been there, and the two gunmen high into the air. It also ripped open the top of the fuel tanks.

Sparks hit the highly flammable fuel, and since it was an older, gasoline-powered boat, they ignited a second explosion. That one was massive. It lifted the broken, shredded boat skyward and shot pieces of it in all directions. The two men who had been shooting from the front of the boat were killed instantly as shrapnel ripped through their bodies.

The eruption caused a voluminous hole where the powerboat had been, the escaping water rolling out in giant waves in a full three-hundred-and-sixty degree circle. It hit the *La Sirena* almost instantly.

The sailboat's stern had returned to the ocean's general level moments before, but it was lifted again, this time more than twenty feet. That caused the bow to plunge downward. Everyone had heard Zach's warning and grabbed handholds, so no one was thrown overboard. Everyone was holding onto rails, wheels, or lockers. Their hands stayed where they had handholds, but when the bow began to nose-dive, their bodies swung downward.

Instead of moving through the wave, the sailboat, its prop now out of the water and screeching in the open air, was carried on top of the huge swell for a few moments before moving with the water downward. The crew could do nothing but hang on, their feet dangling toward the bow, which was pointed toward the bottom of the sea.

Everyone except Denise had secured their weapons by slipping their arms through the straps. Denise had still been rushing backward toward the port side of the boat to be next to Millie when she heard her father yell out. She used the extra second to get to where she was heading instead of slinging her rifle before she grabbed onto the handrail on top of the cabin. To secure the weapon, she rolled on top of it. When the sudden movement caused her body to fall away from the deck, it freed the weapon from under her weight. The boat was still in the pull of the swell, but the wave began to flatten out a little. The angle of the deck went from forty-five degrees to less than thirty degrees.

At that angle, the gun didn't rush away from her, but instead slid at a tantalizing speed toward the bow – and the ocean below it. She was holding on to a handrail on top of the cabin with both hands, but removed one so she could grab for the weapon. In the last half hour, she grew attached to it – it saved her life, after all – and she didn't want to lose it. It slipped under her hand and continued on its way toward the bow. She let go with her other hand and again grabbed for the rifle. It was still out of reach.

A wave hit the port side of the boat, which was still riding the swell, and shoved the bow several feet to starboard.   The rifle changed directions, and began to slide toward the side of the boat. Denise went after it. She slid on the wet deck, heading for the teak rail on that side of the boat. It was a sturdy, solid teak rail, but there was ample room between the stanchions for a rifle – or a scrambling, sliding girl – to fall right through.

Chapter 21

THERE was just enough light for Millie to see Denise let go with her first hand. She began scooting after the girl, moving her hands along the handrail she was holding onto instead of removing them as they moved.

When Denise let go with her other hand, Millie quit scooting and rushed to catch up. When Denise lost control and began to slide toward the ocean, Millie was close enough to shoot out a hand to grab the teenager's wrist.

Denise looked gratefully at the old woman, but pleaded, "My rifle. I've got to get my rifle."

Millie spoke with compassion, but firmly. "Honey, you're worth a heck of a lot more than a rifle. Let it go. I'll pull you up."

The sailboat was carried by the wave for several seconds, the stern high, the bow down and moving to starboard. Then the wave that hit the boat from the side dissipated and the swell that had been carrying the sailboat finally passed through. The water was leveling off, the hole left by the explosion quickly filling again with water. The *La Sirena* rocked as the water sloshed around it, but it began to settle as the ocean resumed a gentle roll in the aftermath of the disturbance.

"Well," Millie said as she helped Denise scramble back to where she was previously, "it looks like we made it through that all right." She let go of the girl's wrist.

"Yes, thank you! You saved my life!"

"That's a nice thought" the old woman said, "but I think providence had more to do with it. The boat straightened up at the right moment."

The boat was now moving smoothly, powered by its small diesel engine, the propeller back underwater. They no longer needed to hold onto the rails, but most did, anyway. Denise let go with one hand and rubbed the wrist of the other. "Say, you're strong."

Millie laughed. "I wouldn't say strong, but I'm not weak." She saw the blood on Denise's arm and lowered her head to look at it. "What is that? Did you scratch yourself when you started sliding?"

"I'm not sure what it is. It happened around the time I was shooting at the light."

Millie took Denise's arm and lifted it so she could get a closer look at the wound. "It's too dark to see much, but I swear it has signs of a burn. I think a bullet zipped right through there."

"I was thinking the same thing, but I really don't know. I didn't feel it when it happened."

"Things ought to get a lot calmer now," Millie

surmised. "We should be able to get some lights on so I can take a better look at it. I'm sure you people already had medicine and bandages, but we brought some, too, and they're in the main salon. I imagine they're strewn all over the place after what we went through, but they should be easy to find. I'll collect them up and have that little bullet wound taken care of in a jiffy."

They started back toward the cockpit, but before they were halfway there, their mission was interrupted.

* * * * *

When the giant swell hit the boat, Zach jumped up to resume his place at the wheel. He knew he would be powerless to control their course... among other things, the rudder and propeller were out of the water... as long as the stern was sticking so far in the air, but he wanted to be ready when the time came.

As it was, the boat went straight ahead until a wave hit the bow on the port side, causing it to yaw to starboard. Immediately after, the boat settled in the water, and the rudder and prop moved back down below the water line. That put him in control of the boat's movements, so he eased the throttle forward and turned the wheel slightly to port to get them back on course.

The prevailing winds from Hawaii to California blow directly into the face of a boat, so sailboats under sail have to tack most of the way. The *La Sirena* was temporarily powered by its engine, which allowed it to follow a direct course.

The ocean still hadn't settled completely, but Zach decided the boat's slight rocking wouldn't stop them from doing some checking into their situation.   Many bullets had hit the boat, and they'd been tossed around violently by the explosion-born waves. Things could be broken.

"Glen, go below and get the twelve-volt flashlight. I want to check our perimeter before I turn the lights on."

"Dad, I'm wounded," Glen said from behind.

Stunned, Zach turned to look at his son.

"What did you say?" cried Stacey from the side of the aft cabin.

"I was hit in the shoulder," Glen replied. "That's why I had to throw the dynamite early."

Both parents were at his side in a second, and Denise, already halfway back, ran the last ten feet to get to him. Millie quietly headed down to the salon.

When he saw the blood, Zach tore off the youngster's shirt so they could get a look at the wound. Both he and Stacey got close to inspect it, but it was hard to see in the dark just how much damage was done to the shoulder. "We need light, Denise," he said.

"I'm on my way," she replied as she hurried down the ladder into the salon.

A few seconds later, she returned with a large flashlight. Millie was right behind her with bandages, anti-bacterial medicine, a bottle of painkillers, and a bottle of water. George was on his way down the ladder into the salon.

Stacey took the light and backed up a little. The flashlight was almost as powerful as the one that had been shining on them, so she told Glen to close his eyes and look away before she shined it on his shoulder.

Zach looked at the wound. It was on the outside top of his right shoulder. Despite all that had happened, it had only been a minute or two since it happened and the blood was still flowing heavily. He saw that Millie had come up next to him with the medical supplies and water. "Great, Millie. Thanks!"

"I used to be a nurse," she told him. "It was a long time ago, but I remember quite a bit."

"Take a look," he said, moving aside so she could get in close.

Millie poured water on a cotton swab and cleaned around the wound. She looked closely at it, and then told Glen to move his arm back and forth. He did, wincing as he did so.

"Okay," she said, "now up and down."

He again followed her orders, and again winced in pain

"Was the pain you felt in the muscle or the bone?" she asked.

"I don't know. Kinda in my skin, it seemed like."

"Yeah, that's what I figured. It missed the bone, or you wouldn't have been able to move your arm that way."

"Mind if I take a look?" Zach asked. "I'm no doctor, but I had to do some first aid on a couple of wounded guys in the Middle East."

It was Millie's turn to move over so he could get a better look.

He wiped more blood from the wound and examined it. "I agree. No bone damage. Go ahead and treat the wound."

"I will," she said, preparing the bandages. "Then I'll fix Denise's wound."

"Denise?" cried Stacey, almost dropping the light at the same time.

"It's nothing," Denise protested. "Not anything like Glen's."

Zach checked on Denise while Millie was treating Glen's wound. She had to grab Stacey's arm more than once to keep the light on it. Stacey kept looking over Zach's shoulder to see her daughter's wounded arm.

"It's only this," the girl said, showing them where the bullet creased her arm. "Like I said, it's nothing like what happened to Glen."

"It's not so much what it is," Stacey said, a note of forlornness in her voice that was not in keeping with her usual upbeat attitude. "It's what it could have been." Her children were injured. "What have we gotten ourselves into?"

Zach put his arm around his wife. "It's not what we got ourselves into," he reminded her. "It's what has happened to the world. We had nothing to do with it, but I'm not sure there's any way we can stay away from it. Once we've checked on my mother and father, though, we're going to try."

Millie finished dressing Glen's wound and turned to work on Denise. "I've given your son the strongest anti-pain medicine I have – strong aspirin," she told the Arthurs. "It's not on par with what you get at a hospital, but it will help. I recommend he get some rest now."

"He's been sleeping on a berth we made out of the dining table area," Stacey said. She quickly shunted her feelings of despair aside and was

ready to get on with what needed to be done.
"That's not an issue, but we need to clean up
down there first.'

"I've got almost everything picked up," George
called out from below.

"Great... thanks, George!" Stacey said. "You
and Millie have already been a great help. Glen,
I'll set up your bunk."

"And your daughter's arm is bandaged," Millie said. "She ought to rest, too. In a few days,
she'll be as good as new. It'll take a little longer
for your son, though."

"Thanks, Millie," Stacey said. "You can sleep
with Denise in the V-berth. There's a couch that
makes into a bed for George on the side opposite
where Glen sleeps."

"Before we settle in," Zach advised, "I need
to do what I started out to do before we heard
about Glen's wound. We need to know we're
finally alone out here. Stacey, after you get Glen
set up, check the radar for larger craft. I'll use
the flashlight to look for small boats nearby."

He took the flashlight from Stacey and started
around the boat, shining the light out over the
ocean as he went. Stacey set up Glen's bunk
quickly – it was just a matter of turning the
table over on a swivel and adjusting the seats.
Denise got the sheets out and put them on the
bunk as Stacey went back up to the cockpit and
turned on the radar.

Once they got Glen settled in, Denise and
Millie went to the forward cabin. Both climbed
onto the V-berth bunk without bothering to pull
the blankets back or disrobe. In seconds, they
were asleep.

George went up to the deck and joined Zach walking around the vessel. After adjusting the radar to study different distances for over two minutes, Stacey turned it off and went to join Zach and George, who were just then nearing the bowsprit.

"There's nothing as far as the radar reaches," she told the men, "except for the island behind us, and there's nothing moving around it."

The men looked relieved to hear that. They had already looked over the starboard side of the ocean and it was clear. Zach shined the light dead ahead now, and all three looked out for anything that wasn't part of the ocean. There was nothing but water. They continued around, all scanning the ocean as far as the light shined.

Zach even shinned the light directly below them to be sure there was nothing near or attached to the boat. They were determined to inspect every inch of the ocean around them.

It never occurred to them to check what was on the boat itself.

Chapter 22

N O ONE saw the automatic rifle behind them. It slid back toward the center of the forward deck when the boat rocked and the port side raised up for a moment, and it stopped at the center when it hit the hatch that Glen had used to go below deck.

They were looking the other way and it was dark, so they wouldn't have seen it, anyway. It was the next day before they saw the weapon again, and it wasn't any of them who found it.

The three continued looking out over the port side until they reached the stern. They maneuvered around the barrels of fuel. Zach shined the light on the barrels and discovered that three of them were hit, and fuel leaked out onto the deck.

Fortunately, the boat was watertight and the fuel had washed overboard. It would require some cleaning up the next day. Probably a sixth of the fuel was lost, but it didn't pose a problem.

Zach next passed the light over the dinghy, which was trailing along behind the boat, tied to it by a twenty-foot line.

"We won't need the dinghy any more tonight, Zach," Stacey said. "Should we bring it in and hang it on the davits?"

Zach flashed the light on the little boat, shaking his head. "No, we'll need to clean it up before we hang it, and none of us is up to that right now. We all need to get some rest tonight. Tomorrow, we'll do a thorough inventory, check the damages, and clean up whatever got broken in our skirmishes. You and George should head below and get some sleep. I'll take the first watch. George, how much experience do you have on boats?"

"I've done some fishing and a bit of sailing," George responded. "And if we're under power, I can handle a watch with no problem."

"That's good, because we'll keep the motor going until we get things in order tomorrow," Zach told him. "However, I'm not turning any lights on, including the running lights, for the time being. We'll rethink that once we're clear of the islands. Right now, we need to get as far away from here as possible, and I want everyone else to sleep all night. We'll do three-hour watches. George, I'll call you in three; you'll wake Stacey for the watch after your turn."

"Sounds good."

"I'll show you your bunk and get some linen out for you," Stacey told him, leading him down into the salon.

When the two were gone, Zach took one last look behind the boat. They were leaving Hilo and the big island of Hawaii behind them. He could see a faint light in the sky where the city was, probably the result of the fires that were growing in size. He glanced again at the dinghy, which was skipping through the waves behind them. All looked in good shape, so he moved into the cockpit where he could keep an eye on things.

All was quiet. The *La Sirena* motored smoothly away from Hawaii and everyone except Zach was asleep. He was comfortable, looking out into the dark night and periodically checking the radar.

Even when the light shined on the dinghy, no one had noticed the fingers that grasped its transom. As time passed, and all but the man on watch slept, and the sloshing waters hid the sound as a man's arm reached over the transom.

He slowly climbed into the little boat.

Chapter 23

STACEY was on watch when the sun rose the next morning. Whatever the skies might be like in other places in a world ravaged by a nuclear holocaust, there was no unpleasantness in the skies over the Pacific Ocean east of Hawaii this day.

It was the kind of day that made the Arthur family fall in love with cruising. The sky was a clear and pristine blue, artistically enhanced with a few cotton-like clouds. The sun threw light out upon an ocean that rippled with small waves pushed by light breezes, and there was just enough nip in the air to tell Stacey it would not be an overly hot, nor cool, day. There was enough wind to tell her that they would still make good time when they hoisted the sails and turned off the engine.

It was a beautiful sunrise, and she decided to walk to the front of the boat to see it better. The autopilot was on, so she needed do nothing before she climbed over the side of the cockpit onto the port side deck. A quick glance back over the diesel barrels told her there were no boats in the waters behind them for miles Satisfied with that, she looked left and right, with the same result, and then started toward the bowsprit to get an unobstructed view of the of the rising sun.

Like her husband, she was a thorough person. It occurred to her that looking over the barrels had given her a look at the ocean several hundred yards distant, but nothing closer. There was space between two of the barrels, so if she craned her neck a little she could get a better look. She stopped, turned, leaned to her right, and looked between the two barrels. In that way, she could see the ocean that was nearer, and the corner of the dinghy they were towing.

She saw nothing there except the ocean and the corner of the dinghy. She wasn't interested in the dinghy, and paid it little heed at first. But something seemed... strange. Was that a part of a shoe she saw?

She reached back into the cockpit and grabbed the weapon that she kept on the seat beside her during her watch. Bending over and keeping behind the barrels, she stepped quietly toward the stern. Peering over the last barrel, she was able to see the entire dingy – and the man who was sprawled across it, apparently asleep, or unconscious or...

"Hey!" she yelled. The prone man did not move. She called again. Then again, louder.

"What?" Zach called from the cabin below.

"You better come up here, Zach. We have a... situation."

A second later, the hatch leading down to the aft cabin slid open and Zach climbed up on the deck. He had on shorts and a t-shirt, and an AK-47 was in his hand. The deck above the cabin was over a foot higher than the deck Stacey was on, so he could see the dinghy as he walked over to join his wife. He stepped down and walked over to the aft rail.

He shook his head. "He couldn't have been there the whole time," he opined.

"No," she agreed. "It was dark last night, but you shined the light on the dinghy, and I certainly would have seen a body if there'd been one there."

"He must have come from the boat that was after us... but how?"

"Are you going to kill him?" asked Millie, who heard the commotion and came up behind them to look over their shoulders at the man lying on the dinghy.

"No," Zach stated emphatically. "Maybe the rest of the people in this world have come to that, but we haven't."

"Besides," Stacey added, "for all we know, he's already dead."

"Don't think so," Millie advised them. "I can see a slight movement of his back."

The two Arthurs turned to stare at the white-haired woman.

"What? You think I'm blind just because I'm getting a little older? Look for yourself. It's faint, but he's breathing. Not sure how good of shape he's in, but he's clearly alive."

"I see it," said Denise, who had come out on deck and was atop the aft cabin. Glen and

George came up behind Millie.

"It's too bad, then," Zach sighed. "That means we have a prisoner on our hands." He turned to his son. "How's the shoulder?"

"It hurts when I move my arm, but it's not as bad as I thought it would be."

"Denise, how's your arm?" Stacey asked.

"It's just a scratch," the girl replied. "It's nothing."

"Good," Zach said, half in jest. "Because I need you to go below and bring me the .38. The AK-47 will be too cumbersome to carry down there."

"What are you going to do?" There was a hint of concern in Stacey's voice.

"You saw what happened when you tried to wake that fellow up by yelling, so I need to get on that dinghy and shake him into consciousness. Otherwise, we'll lose valuable time dragging him behind us half the day."

"Be careful, Zach. We've seen what that kind of man is capable of."

When Denise returned with the pistol, Zach stuck it under his belt at his back. He told his daughter to go to the wheel and keep an eye out for any other vessels while they checked out the man in the dinghy. "If you see anything, let us know and take it out of autopilot. We'll decide what to do from there."

"What about me?" Glen was eager to help.

"You need to rest that shoulder," his father told him. "You might just as well stay above decks, though."

"How about I redo the dressing on that wound?" Millie asked.

"Good, and thanks, Millie. Stacey, you and George stay here." He handed George his weapon. "I'll have the guy covered on the dinghy, but you keep your eye on him, especially when he first gets aboard and I'm still climbing the ladder."

He climbed over the rail and down the ladder. When he was on the bottom rung, he pulled the line in until the dinghy was right below him. He tied it off and watched the man for several seconds before risking getting into the small boat.

The dinghy had two seats that extended from one side to the other, and the man was draped over both. One leg was bent and totally inside the dinghy, but the other was straight out, the foot slightly outside the boat. He appeared to be slender and about as tall as Zach. His clothes were still soaking wet. Zach concluded the man must have crawled up from the water and passed out as soon as he was safely in the small boat.

He stood over the man and nudged him with a foot. The fellow stirred, but didn't wake up, so Zach nudged him harder. This time, the man opened his eyes and raised his head slowly. The first thing he saw was a gun pointed at him. He looked higher, and saw Zach staring down at him.

"Who are you? And what are you doing here?"

"You blew up my boat," the man mumbled weakly. His head dropped down again.

"You were trying to kill us."

The man didn't raise his head, but turned it

a little and looked up at Zach. "No. They were, not me."

"They?" Zach felt no sympathy for the man but decided to listen to what he had to say.

"The pirates."

Zach shook his head. He could see this was going to take some time, and the dinghy was no place to hold an inquiry. "I'm going to move to the back of the dinghy, and you are going to go up that ladder there. Keep in mind, you're our prisoner. There are two automatic weapons trained on you up there, and I'm behind you with this pistol. One false move and you're history."

"I'll do whatever you say. Being your prisoner will be a lot better than it was being theirs." The man started to get up, but quickly fell back down. "Give me a second." It was a quiet plea. "I'm pretty weak."

Zach said nothing. He waited but his eyes never left the man.

Breathing heavily, the prisoner got to his knees slowly. He moved over close to the ladder and grabbed one side with one hand and then brought his other hand around to grab the opposite side. Using the ladder for stability, he stood. Then, still moving slowly, he climbed the ladder. When he got to the top, it appeared he didn't have the strength to climb over the rail. George set his weapon aside and took an arm to help him over. As soon as the man was on deck, George released his arm and retrieved his weapon.

Zach was over the rail a second after the prisoner. "Sit here on top of the cabin," he told the man. "We have a lot of questions."

"Do you mind if I stretch my legs a bit?" man asked. "They had me at the wheel of my boat for three days straight, and my muscles are really tight."

"I suppose a few minutes won't make a difference."

"Do you think you can trust him to not try to make a break for it?" George objected.

Zach looked around at the ocean that seemed to go on forever in all directions. "Where could he go?"

"Good point," George agreed. "But..." He set his weapon aside and patted the man down thoroughly. He nodded at Zach. "Nothing."

"Okay, walking around the deck is good exercise when you're at sea..." Zach started to explain to the man.

"I know. I am – was – a boat owner."

The man walked unsteadily toward the bow. Millie was over to one side with Glen, redressing his wound. Denise was at the wheel. Zach, Stacey, and George watched the man go, and then lapsed into a discussion about what Zach and their new prisoner talked about while on the dinghy.

When he got to the front of the main cabin, the man's legs appeared to give out, and he squatted and sat on the cabin top. He looked back and shrugged his shoulders at his captors, his hands out, palms up, letting them know he had no ready explanation for why he wasn't able to go any further. He turned to look out over the bowsprit at the vast ocean in front of them. Something on the deck, to his right, caught his attention. He looked down and saw the AK-47 lying next to the hatch. He studied it for a moment and then looked back at his captors. They were in deep conversation.

He reached down and picked up the weapon.

Chapter 24

THEY could see the man bring the weapon up to waist level. He looked it over before turning toward the stern where the three were standing. The rifle swung around with him, and it ending up pointing where he was looking, directly at them.

"Drop it!" Zach ordered in a loud, firm voice.

"What?" the man said. He looked up to see three automatic weapons pointed at him.

Zach fired a warning volley to the man's side, the bullets zooming past and out into the Pacific. "The next ones won't miss."

The man dropped the weapon. In seconds, Zach, Stacey, and George had him surrounded.

"How did you get that weapon?" Zach demanded.

"I found it laying right here," the man said. "Just now."

Stacey picked it up. "It's an AK-47, the same as what we have."

Denise locked in the autopilot and joined the group at the front of the cabin. "That could be mine," she told her mother. "I thought it fell overboard last night, but maybe it didn't."

"You didn't say anything," her mother said.

By that time, Millie and Glen had come up from the salon to investigate the ruckus.

"We were all busy fixing wounds," Millie pointed out. "Besides, she almost went overboard herself."

"What?"

"She was trying to stop the gun from going over."

"Millie stopped me as I was sliding," Denise added.

"Oh, Sweetie," the girl's mother said, hugging her, "I'm so sorry. Last night was such a horror."

Zach joined them in the hug. After a few seconds, he broke away and sat down on the cabin top. "Unfortunately, last night may be the kind of thing we will be having a lot of in the future. With any luck, we'll have enough free time to get better prepared on our trip to California. We all have a lot to learn."

He turned to the man who was ostensibly their prisoner. "To start with, though, we need to learn something about you. What's your name?"

"If it's all right, I think I'd better sit, too," the man said. Without waiting for approval, he sat. "My name is Ron Tillman."

"Why were you and your people trying to kill us last night?"

"As I told you before, I wasn't." He put up a hand when Zach started to protest. "Let me tell you the story. "That was my boat. I lived aboard and used it mainly for fishing. When the world went crazy, I was almost out of fuel so I anchored in the harbor. The four pirates – there's no other word for them except pirates – boarded my boat and took me captive three days ago."

He paused and looked around, his eyes coming back to rest squarely on Zach's. "I've had nothing to say about what happened aboard since. None of them knew much about boats, so they kept me alive and forced me to do all the piloting. In those three days, they attacked four small boats looking for food and fuel. None of the boats had much of either, so they killed the people aboard and scuttled the boats."

He sighed and looked down. They couldn't read what was in his eyes when he looked up. There might have been sorrow in them for a moment, but that changed quickly. When he looked back at them, they saw neutrality.

"Oh, I tried to be heroic," he went on, his voice low. "For a while. After they killed the people on the first boat and sunk it, I refused to do any more piloting. They tied me up and beat me. Several times. When that didn't work, they threatened to kill me. That did. I saw that they had no compunction about doing that, so I relented and continued driving the boat, biding my time until I could find a way to escape. I'm a good fisherman, so they were living mainly on the fish I caught. By the way, if you have food, I'd very much appreciate some. They ate almost everything I caught and allowed me barely enough to survive on."

"Their plan," he took turns looking them in the eye, "was to get to the U.S. mainland. But they knew they could never get there on my boat because they would never find enough fuel. When they saw your beautiful sailboat and saw those barrels you have back there, they thought they hit the jackpot. They decided to take it over, keeping a couple of you around to run it."

"A couple of us?" said Stacey. "And the rest?"

"Everyone else would have met the same fate as the people on the other boats they attacked. Me, too, I'm sure... being as they would have had no more use for me. Dead people don't pose a threat, and they don't eat, either."

"You tried to sink us," Zach stated firmly. "You, personally."

Tillman looked at him questioningly.

"The dynamite," Zach prompted. "You tried to pick it up and throw it at us."

"That? Look, all I knew was that someone threw a stick of dynamite at us. If I didn't get rid of it, it would destroy my boat – which, by the way, it did. What would you have done? I had no idea where I was going to throw it, but I sure as heck intended to throw it away from my boat. As it turned out, it was my chance to escape. When it rolled away from me, I dived overboard to get away from the explosion. When I came up, I saw your dinghy trailing along behind you. It took every ounce of strength that I had left, but I somehow got to it. I held on until it looked like most of you had settled in for the night, and then I managed to climb up into it. I guess I passed out right away. The next thing I knew, you had a gun pointed at me."

"What's that bruise on the back of your arm?" Millie asked.

"Where they hit me, I suppose," Tillman said, twisting his arm around so he could look at it, "although they mostly hit me on the back."

"Zach, do you mind if I take him down to check out his bruises?" the former nurse asked.

"No, go ahead. It's time for us to get some breakfast, anyway. Then we need to start cleaning up."

Millie helped Tillman walk to the cockpit and helped him climb over and down the ladder to the salon.

"What do you think?" George asked when they were gone.

"I don't know," Zach admitted. "He could be telling the truth."

"I think he is," Stacey said. "He seems to be in bad shape."

"Diving into a rampaging ocean and struggling to stay afloat would do that all by itself," George pointed out.

"Either way – whether he's our guest or our prisoner – he's here and will be until we reach California," Zach said. "We'll treat him with respect, but we can't treat him as one of us."

"How do we do that?" Glen asked.

"First," his father said, "we keep all our weapons away from him. We'll have to watch them closely from now on." He looked at Denise, who nodded. "Second, we'll have to have two people awake at all times when he is. I'll let him stand watch, but one of us will be watching him throughout."

"Do you think he can really fish?" Glen asked.

"He'd better be able to," Stacey replied. "With the extra mouths to feed, we'll need the extra rations."

"I'm glad you didn't add what I thought you would." Zach said, a small smile playing on the corner of his lips.

"Which is?" she asked, attempting to maintain a look of innocence.

"Because I certainly can't," Zach answered.

"I believe," Denise cut in, "that message was implied by how the statement was formulated."

All eyes turned to the girl who was trying, with little success, to look intellectual. For the first time in days, the family had a good laugh.

Chapter 25

BREAKFAST was a different experience than any meal they ever had, either on this trip or at any time. The food was the same as what they had been having and the preparation didn't involve anything new, but that was where the similarity ended. In addition to the three new people, the conversations were what might be heard on the battlefield, with talk centered on the fighting they in which they had just engaged and what battles might lay ahead.

Once breakfast was over, they went to work, sobered by the retelling of what they were forced to do the night before. Simply giving voice to those horrid memories engendered even more alarming visions of what awaited them in the new, unknown world that lay ahead. It was seemingly unspoken knowledge that keeping busy would help them concentrate on more mundane – and calming – issues, those having to do with everyday life.

The Arthurs always kept good track of what they had on hand, so it didn't take long to tally up an inventory that included the meager new supplies they got from the hotel. There was not enough to sustain the three new people on board, but having them was better than not.

They found locations for the new things. Because they had a "prisoner" aboard, they locked the AK-47s away. Zach, George, and Millie kept their handguns on their persons. The dinghy was lifted to the deck and cleaned. Barnacles had attached themselves to the bottom in the short period it had been in the water. It was soon hanging on the davits that extended out over the water at the rear of the boat. The sailboat's deck was scrubbed, getting rid of the fuel and blood that had stained it, and the barrels at the stern were rearranged to even out the weight.

All told, they counted twenty-one bullet holes in the boat's structure but none of the bullets had hit anything vital and did not inhibit their ability to sail the boat. As they had originally thought, there were holes in three of the barrels, all in the top one-third portions of the containers, so they still had most of their fuel left.

Millie found that Ron Tillman had multiple bruises on his back, but only a few resulted in cuts. She dressed and bandaged them in short order. Because of their injuries, both he and Glen were told they didn't have to participate in the cleanup, but both elected to lend a hand. They, possibly even more than the others, saw the value of keeping their minds on small chores.

By ten a.m., all was ready for the hoisting of the sails. When Zach gave the word, Denise cut the engine, and he raised the mainsail. At the same time, Stacey was raising the mizzen sail on the aft mast, and within seconds, Glen had the jib up at the front of the boat. Denise disengaged the autopilot and was at the wheel. There was a ten-knot wind coming from the northeast, and that was enough to move them along comfortably. The boat leaned only a little to starboard with the wind hitting the sails over the port side.

"Dad, with the wind coming from where it is, we can stay right on course for a while," Denise advised her father.

"Good. Keep that course as long as you can."

George and Millie watched in awe as each member of the family did their job with coordinated proficiency. "You people are really good," George said. "I've been wanting to learn how to sail, and now seems to be the perfect time."

"A person is never too old to learn," Millie added. "Teach me, too."

Zach readily agreed. "It will be my pleasure. We'll need all the knowledgeable hands we can get on this trip. Okay, let's start with what we're doing right now. A boat can sail in any direction except directly into the wind. The wind is coming in from the northeast. The course we're on is almost due east, so the northeast wind is coming in on the port side, over the front quarter of the boat. It's at about thirty degrees off our bow. As long as it keeps coming from there or moves in a northerly direction, we're okay to stay on this course. Sailing this way, into the wind, is called reaching, or beating. If the wind moves even a little south, however, and I'm afraid it probably will, we will have to fall off and head in a southeasterly direction."

"Won't that take us off course?" asked Millie.

"Yes. We'll be tacking from that point on. That is, we'll head southeast for awhile, and then come about." He laughed and took a moment to explain the second sailing term. "All 'coming about' means is that we'll change directions. In this case, we'll change to a northeasterly course. At that point, the wind will be coming in over the starboard front quarter of the boat. We'll keep doing that, changing course, for most of the trip. First southeast and then northeast. The idea is... we will end up going to a point in the middle, almost directly east."

Millie thought that over and had a question. "If you keep changing, and we're out here in the middle of the ocean, how will you know you're really heading toward the right spot?"

"Good question. Wait here." He went below and came back with the sextant Commander Kotchel had given him, along with the book of directions. "At noon," he said, holding the book up to be seen, "I'll get a reading, and then I'll be able to determine exactly where we are." He thumbed through the book, looking for the chapter on noon sightings.

Millie watched dubiously as he searched. "If you don't mind my saying so, I get nervous when someone has to look at a book when he's about to do something he's supposed to know how to do. We're a long way from land."

"I understand your concern," Zach admitted.

"This is not the way we usually do things. In the past, we had a GPS – that means global positioning system – but the system was knocked out of service, so we have to revert to this method. It got people around the globe for hundreds of years, so I'm sure it will get us to where we want to go in California."

"But," Millie persisted, "you really don't know how to use that thing, do you?"

"Millie, it's not that hard," he replied, hoping to calm her. "Besides, we have a compass and charts, and the sun always comes up in the east. Even without the sextant, we'd hit California."

"But where? California is a very long state, so we might end up a hundred miles from where we intend to go."

"No, not that far off. Look, I..."

Ron Tillman had been watching all that had taken place and now stepped in. "Zach, if you don't mind, I'd like to help."

"Help? How?"

"I never did get around to buying a GPS. I've been using a sextant since I was a kid, and it's taken me many places. I can keep us on course and teach you at the same time. In exchange, I'm like George and Millie. I would love to learn to sail, and what better time than now. It seems like the perfect quid pro quo."

Zach didn't respond right away. He still wasn't sure about Tillman and wasn't keen on giving him the ability to sail the boat away if the opportunity presented itself. On the other hand, there would be nothing else to do for weeks in a confined atmosphere so he was going to learn just by watching, anyway.

Besides, everyone, including himself, would be more comfortable knowing that someone who knew how to do it was taking the sextant readings.

He reluctantly nodded his acceptance of the offer.

Chapter 26

SEVEN days at sea went by more quickly than any of them ever expected. The weather was warm and there was enough wind to move the boat along at an average of about five knots. During most of the daylight hours, Millie, George, and Ron were learning the intricacies of sailing.

The winds, as Zach predicted, started coming from almost due east, and so they began the tacking procedures he outlined – first southeast and then northeast. That gave everyone a chance to participate in the "coming about" exercise many times each day. Every time that happened, the wind changed to the opposite side of the boat from moments before. The booms swung around to the other side, and the sails were trimmed so that they caught the winds in the optimum manner, maintaining the maximum speed. The new members of the crew were learning fast.

Ron proved himself an excellent fisherman. He, Glen, and Denise tossed their lines over the side every morning. The teenagers watched and mimicked everything he did. They were convinced they did exactly the same things, but he caught three times more fish and his tended to be larger. They caught plenty of fish between them, which saved the canned goods they had in storage.

"Dad, what's wrong with me?" Glen asked. "Why can't I catch fish like that?"

His father commiserated. "Son, there's nothing wrong with you or Denise. Or me, for that matter. You've seen me fish. I can't catch as many as the two of you, no matter how hard I try. Some people just have the knack, and he is one of them. That is really handy in the situation we're in at the moment. We're eating really well and not depleting our supplies in the process. If you really want to learn, though, keep watching. Maybe you'll pick up enough that someday you'll be a great angler, as well. I suspect that a large part of the "knack" is a combination of experience and patience."

Because he was so useful, Ron was growing on the family, but that did not mean they didn't still keep an eye on him. There were always two armed people awake when he was, and one was always far enough away so that if he overpowered one, the other would be able to call for help and, if necessary, shoot him.

Because all three of the new people had come aboard on short notice and hadn't had time to pack, Zach and Glen shared what few clothes they had with Ron and George. Stacey and Denise shared with Millie. It wasn't a perfect arrangement, especially being as they were limited in how much they could wash and dry things on a forty-one foot boat in the middle of the Pacific Ocean. Fortunately, not one of them had the slightest interest in making a fashion statement – at least not in the situation they were in at the moment.

It wasn't easy with seven people aboard instead of four, but they maintained a habit that they determined was important for people living in close quarters. At some point every day, each person went to the forward deck to be alone for at least half an hour. No one was allowed to bother them in any way during that time. Most didn't feel they really needed that, yet they all felt a little more serene after their time alone.

As all the bunks were taken, Ron moved around to sleep. He used one of the Arthur family's sleeping bags and sometimes slept on George's bunk. When George and he slept at the same time, he either slept on the bunk Glen used or they inflated a mattress for him and he slept on the salon floor, back away from the galley area, which was close to the ladder leading up to the cockpit. Every day, Ron did a noon reading with the sextant and then spent the next hour or two going over the results with the other members of the crew.

They spent their evenings playing card games, studying, or sitting around talking. Their conversation often consisted of telling tall tales from the past. Other times found them drifting toward what they might find when they reached their destination.

"Say, if we've been averaging five knots, that's almost six miles per hour, right?" George asked shortly after they had dinner on the seventh night. They were all sitting around the cockpit enjoying a starlit night, and his question was not directed at anyone in particular. Not waiting for a response, he continued. "According to what I've learned, a knot is about one point fifteen statute miles, which means we've been traveling at about one hundred and forty miles per day. So we've come around nine hundred and eighty miles." He stopped to do a little calculating.

Those who spent time at sea on a sailboat immediately picked up on his error, and even Ron and Millie seemed to figure it out. None chose to tell him what it was yet. They just smiled and waited for him to give them the conclusion he was working out.

"Based on that, we'll be in California in about ten or eleven days," George said, "not the month or more you guys guessed it would be that first day. That's great!" No one joined him in celebrating the likelihood of a quick trip. He looked around. Everyone was either looking pityingly at him, or smiling smugly. "What?" he asked, his brow furrowed.

"I'll go get the chart," Zach said. He went down the steps into the salon, returning a minute later with a large chart. He spread it out over the seat where was sitting, and shined a flashlight with red lens in place to preserve their night vision and prevent them from being seen. "Ron," he said, "what did today's noon sighting show our coordinates to be?"

Ron took a pad from the back pocket of his

shorts and thumbed through it for a few seconds. When he came to the page he wanted, he read it, then put an index finger down on a spot about one fourth of the way from the Hawaiian Islands to California. "Here's the coordinates for where we were at noon today."

George looked over their shoulders. "Hey, that spot can't be more than five hundred miles from Hilo, not almost a thousand."

"That's about right, George," Zach told him. Remember, we're not sailing straight at California. Half the time we are heading toward Mexico, and the other half the time toward Canada. Actually, we have been lucky so far. We have been able to sail at close angles to what a direct course would be, so we gained some good distance. Sometimes we must sail further off target, and that means we gain less distance with each tack."

"This," George sighed deeply, the wind gone from own his sails, "is going to be a long trip."

"Nobody in a hurry chooses a sailboat as a means of getting from place to place," Stacey said. "On the other hand, no other kind of transportation is as enjoyable, and we go to places that people who limit themselves to cars, trains, and planes can only dream about."

"Maybe so, but I can see this becoming pretty boring."

"Not likely," Ron said, looking ahead. "Not in the near future, anyway."

"You see it, too, huh?" Zach asked, rising and moving toward the main mast.

"What?" George wanted to know. He watched wide-eyed as Ron and the teenagers picked up loose items on the deck, and Zach and Stacey started lowering sails. "See what?"

"Those dark clouds ahead," Ron said as he passed by.

"Everything's dark. Everywhere."

"Not as dark as those clouds in front of us." Ron stopped and pointed ahead. "See those dashes of white on that thick black line under the clouds?"

George strained to see it. "Maybe. A little. I suppose."

"Unfortunately, there won't be any 'maybes' or 'I supposes' before long. That black line is water being pushed by high winds, and the white dashes are whitecaps. It'll be on top of us very soon."

"What will be on top of us?" George asked, but was afraid he knew the answer.

"Judging by what it looks like at this distance, that's one heckuva storm, and we're right in its path."

Chapter 27

RON, Glen, Denise, and Millie went below to put what they had collected on deck into storage bins and lock or tie everything down.

"What can I do?" George asked.

"Open the starboard side storage bin near where you're standing," Zach said from where he was strapping the back part of the mainsail to the boom. "There's a twenty-five foot cable with snap hooks at either end stored there. We need that and two of the four harnesses stored with it. Bring out the two harnesses with the shorter lead lines."

Stronger waves were already hitting the *La Sirena* from the front and the boat was beginning to rise and fall more sharply than it had been only minutes earlier. Stacey activated the electric windlass that controlled the jib sail, rolling it up. When she got the sail at the front of the boat rolled up, she headed back to the cockpit. George brought out the cable, and she took one end to the forward mast to hook it to an eye bolt attached to the mast two-and-one-half feet above the deck.

"There's an eye-bolt like this one on the mizzen mast!" She yelled loud enough to be heard above the howling sounds the winds. "Attach the other end of the cable to it."

George went back and attached it. He had to pull hard on the cable to get the hook into the eye bolt because the cable was just long enough to fit tautly between the two masts.

Zach finished tying the mainsail down so that about one-fourth of it was showing above the boom. He took one of the harnesses from George and strapped it on, then hooked the snap hook at the end of the lead line to the cable Stacey and George had connected to the masts. He pulled on the cable to make sure it was taut. After yanking hard on the line to be sure it was fastened securely, he went back to tie down the mizzen sail the same way he had tied down the mainsail. The line from the harness to the cable was just long enough to allow him to work at the far end of the mizzen boom.

When the mizzen sail was tied down like the main sail, he returned to the cockpit and turned on the engine. "Ron and Denise," he called down to the salon, "you need to join us up here."

When they joined him, along with Stacey and George, in the cockpit, Zach discussed the "game plan" for the upcoming storm. "I judge it to be a big one. It looks like it's coming right at us from the east, so we can head right into it and maybe not be blown too far off course. We might even make some headway."

Ron laughed. "That's about the brightest spin I've ever heard anyone put on a bad situation like this."

"It's bad, no question about it," Zach admitted, "but we need to keep our wits about us. We'll keep the engine on and head straight into it. I've kept as much sail up as I dare, and that should help stabilize us. If any more sail is exposed, it will probably be ripped to shreds. From now on, everybody wears a harness when above decks. We have four, but unless there's an emergency, there will never be more than two people on deck at any one time. The other two harnesses are in this storage cabinet here." He pointed to the bin where George had retrieved the cable and harnesses.

He held up the harness he wasn't wearing. "This one and the one I have on have shorter lines. As you can see, we've come up with a cable that is attached to both masts. We snap the hooks to the cable and they can slide freely from one end to the other. That way, we can move almost from one end of the boat to the other, but if we slip and head to the side, the cable is taut enough and the lines are short enough to stop us from going overboard."

Ron studied the line for a second, and then looked forward. "That's all well and good, but if something happens at the front of the bowsprit or with the dinghy, are the leads on the other harnesses long enough for that?"

"Yes, but if somebody goes over the side in the weather we're expecting, even wearing a harness that's attached to the boat may not save them. They will be in the water, and it may be too difficult to bring them in. Even if we can, it may take too long to get them out of the water before they drown. Losing a dinghy or part of a bowsprit is not worth risking lives, so we will only use the harnesses with the shorter lines unless there is a dire emergency. There will be two people on deck at all times, both in the cockpit most of the time. One will be on the wheel and the other will be watching for emergencies. Everyone else will be below."

"Doing what?" Ron asked.

"Hanging on for dear life, I expect," George tried to joke.

"Not too far off the mark," Stacey replied. "And I'm glad you have a sense of humor about it. You are going to need it during the next day or two. We'll take turns sleeping below and make sure we pick things up if they're shaken loose from their place. And, of course, we'll try to take turns using the head."

"The head?"

"When a boat is thrown around the way this one is going to be, even the most seasoned sailors have a hard time keeping things in their stomach," Zach told him. "When it happens to you, don't be ashamed. You won't be the only one. But, George, right now I'd like you to stay up here and take the first watch with me." He opened the storage bin on the other side of the cockpit and pulled out a raincoat and pants. "It's going to be wet from now on, so we'll all wear rain gear. Put those on, then that other harness, and attach the harness to the cable."

When George was ready, Zach had him take the wheel while he put on his rain gear.

"Okay, we're all set. You've all seen what we're doing, so do the same thing when you're on watch. There are two more sets of rain gear in a clothes locker below. Ron, Stacey will show you where they are. You and Stacey take the next watch. We will do two-hour watches during the storm. As captain and mate, me and Stacey will be doing double duty. We won't get much sleep, which isn't such a big deal. I'll do the third watch with Denise, and Stacey can do the next one with George. Then, I'll do one with Ron."

He directed the next comment directly at Ron. "Either Stacey or I will always be with you."

"I have no problem with that," Ron replied easily. "Up until this storm hit, being a prisoner with this group has been enjoyable."

"Glad you feel that way, but don't forget that's what you are. One more thing. Glen and Millie will stay below to take care of provisions. Is everything clear?"

After everyone nodded, Zach turned back to George. "All set?" The hotel man checked once more to make sure his harness was strapped on tight and that it was connected to the cable. He nodded.

"Good," Zach said, checking his own gear. When he was satisfied, he turned to his wife. "Stacey, you and Ron better get below now and try to get some rest."

Stacey started down the ladder to the salon, turning to go down using the handgrips at the side of the ladder. When she turned, she was facing the cockpit. As she took the first step, she looked over Zach's shoulder at the ocean behind them. She stopped dead, a look of concern on her face.

"What is it?" asked her husband.

Pointing over Zach's shoulder, she said, "I thought I saw a light back there."

They all turned, but none of them saw anything except dark waves.

"It might have been lightning," Zach offered. "It doesn't make much difference right now, anyway. If there is another boat out there, it will be blown miles away by the time the storm passes. Now get below."

Stacey went down the ladder quickly, with Ron right behind her. When they were below, they grabbed onto handholds where they could find them as Stacey headed to the aft cabin and Ron to the bunk on the starboard side of the salon. Glen and Millie had just finished securing plastic dishes in a locked bin, and they, too, headed for their bunks.

In the cockpit, Zach slid the hatch cover closed as the rain started to fall. It was small drops at first but quickly became bigger, and the wind pushed them at an angle so that the faces and raingear of the men on deck were soon wet.

The boat rocked more and more, and George held firmly to the wheel. Zach grabbed the taut cable the harnesses were attached to for support. Feeling the storm, both of them looked up and gripped even tighter, bracing for the shock that was about to hit them.

All they could see ahead was a wall of water as the storm's first massive wave raced at them.

Chapter 28

THE thirty-foot wave lifted the more than sixteen-ton *La Sirena* like it was a toy. Luckily, the comber wasn't breaking yet, so it didn't toss the sailboat backward in a frothy deluge. The bow shot up, the sharp movement throwing anyone not holding on to something solid around like a rag doll.

At the crest, the boat leveled off for a second or two, and then slid down the other side of the rapidly moving wave. The bowsprit dug into the water for a moment, but the stern dropped down as the wave passed and the bow bobbed up, water streaming off on all sides.

"That," George observed at a full shout over the sounds of screaming winds and crashing waters, "was, ah, exciting." He fell to his knees and the wheel turned a little, but he still held onto it.

Zach rose from his seat and re-tied a bungee cord that had come loose on the mainsail boom, eyeing the compass as he worked. "Try to keep it as close to forty-five degrees as you can," he called to George over the noise of the storm. "But always head directly into a wave when you see it coming."

Below, in the V-berth, Denise grabbed Millie's arm when the older woman started to fall out of bed. "Hold on to something at all times in a storm, Millie," she advised.

"How long is this going to go on?" the white-haired woman asked.

"Hate to say it, but a long time, I'm afraid."

"One good thing is my hair can't get any whiter worrying about it."

"I don't think worrying would do any good, anyway."

"Never does," the wizened woman of more than eighty years observed. "You're smart to figure it out when you're young. Follow that line of thought and you'll avoid a lot of unnecessary heartache in years to come." A smile crept to the edge of her lips. "It'll keep your hair blond, too."

The concept of years to come caused both to think about the situation they were in now. The bow of the boat started to rise again, and their thoughts returned to the more immediate situation. Holding on was the only concept either of them cared about at that moment.

On deck, George strained to turn the wheel. By the time the next wave hit, they were on course and drove directly into it. The boat shuddered and the bow again turned up into the swell, but this time George didn't allow the wheel to turn as the boat plunged into the watery valley between that wave and the next. He soon learned how to stand, legs apart and leaning into the wheel, so as not to fall. He fought to maintain control, so as not to allow the raging storm to toss the boat around at will.

He learned that allowing a wave to hit the boat broadside was dangerous and often capsized boats. It was true any time, and in these circumstances, with waves as big as those that were pounding them right now, it would probably be the end of them all. If one of these monsters turned the boat over, getting righted in a sea as turbulent as this one would be impossible. He needed no further prodding to keep the boat heading directly into the waves.

The wind and waves continued to grow stronger. After twenty minutes, Zach relieved George at the wheel. For the remainder of the two hours, they traded places every twenty minutes. When Zach wasn't at the wheel, he moved as best he could around the boat to ensure everything was tied down.

Despite the battering the boat was taking, everything, including the diesel fuel barrels tied to the aft rail, were holding. By the time Stacey and Ron relieved them, Zach was convinced that everything on deck was as secure as possible. He knew that until the storm let up, it was best if the crew's only chore was to keep the boat, and themselves, above water.

"I'm in total agreement," Stacey responded when Zach shared his thoughts with her. George took off his harness and handed it to her. She put it on and relieved him at the wheel. He immediately slipped around the side of the wheel and headed for the ladder to the salon. Zach and Ron were right behind Stacey. Even though they were within three feet of one another, they had to yell to be heard over the storm. "It's getting too dangerous to leave the cockpit," Stacey added.

Ron, a seasoned seaman, also agreed. "Even here, anyone without a harness might go overboard."

"So, you'd better take mine," Zach said. He removed the harness and handed it to Ron. As Ron was putting it on, Zach started to follow George. He looked up and saw that another bungee cord that held the main sail to the boom had come loose. In order to reach around the boom and sail to retie the cord, he stepped up onto a seat that was the cover of one of the storage bins at the side of the cockpit.

It was something he had done dozens of times. This time, though, a gust of wind and a rogue wave hit the boat from the port side as he was reaching his arm up. That knocked him ahead a little, toward the middle of the boat and he grabbed for the boom. The force against the port side of the boat caused it to lean to starboard, and Zach's feet slipped on the wet seat. He started to fall, and his arm couldn't get all the way around the boom and sail. He reached desperately for the boom or sail, anything that he could latch onto, but everything was wet and slippery.

Zach's hand made contact with the polyester sail, but the durable fabric was slippery, and he couldn't grasp it. He made one last try as he toppled over the side of the cockpit, but by then, the boom was too far away, and his own body weight was his nemesis.

They hit an oncoming wave and the bow shot upward. Arms flailing, Zach stumbled toward the starboard rail. The sharp, changing motion of the vessel sent him backwards as well. He fell toward the aft deck. Landing on the wet teak, he slid uncontrollably toward the stern.

In those few seconds, the storm forced the starboard stern down low, several feet into the water. Sloshing, unrelenting water swirled crazily around the deck, ensnaring whatever it encountered with powerful, frothy tentacles, taking everything with it as it rushed to return to the sea.

Chapter 29

ZACH knew that if he continued to slide into the maelstrom that was already snatching with watery claws at his feet, he was doomed. He grabbed frantically for a handhold on top of the aft cabin as he passed but his hand couldn't get a grip on the wet wood. His fingers slipped away and, still grabbing for something, anything that would save him, he skidded closer and closer to the turbulent waters that engulfed the ship's stern.

He lunged one more time for a handhold, and his fingers tentatively grasped a wooden rail. He could feel his fingers slipping away again, and he tried to grip harder. He brought his other hand up in an attempt to get a firmer grip.

Before it found something to grab onto, a hand reached down and grabbed the wrist of that arm. He looked up to see that Ron, his harness attached to the cable that ran from mast to mast, had maneuvered as far aft as the restraining lines allowed. It was just enough to get him to Zach. With Ron pulling him by the arm, and Zach crawling, now with a firm grip on the handrail with his other hand, they moved toward the cockpit.

When they got there, Zach rolled onto the cockpit deck, which gave him over three feet of "wall" on all sides to protect him from the wind and water that were battering the boat. Safe at last, lying behind his wife, who was at the wheel, he gasped for breath. Stacey, who had to stay at the wheel to keep the boat under control, now relinquished it to Ron and dropped to her knees to be by her husband. They were jostled by the boat's constant rocking, but held on to one another.

"Sweetheart," she uttered loudly over the sounds of the storm, "that was too close. We can't lose you!"

Still breathing hard, Zach berated himself. "What a fool I was! Me, the captain, is first to violate the rule about always being harnessed while on deck." He reached up and tugged at the sleeve of Ron's raincoat. When their "prisoner" looked down, Zach said, "Ron, I owe you my life. If it wasn't for you, I would have gone overboard."

"Oh, you would have found a way to save yourself," Ron replied. It appeared he didn't want to continue the conversation, and couldn't have even if he wanted to because another big wave hit the boat hard from the port side. He struggled to keep the wheel from turning as the frenzied current banged at the rudder. It took all his strength to keep it from turning.

Stacey, her harness securely strapped to her body and connected to the cable, held her husband as the boat lifted, and dropped. "You better get below and get some dry clothes on," she advised him when there was a moment of relative calm.

"Thanks, I will. Denise and I will be up to relieve you for the next watch," he said before he crawled forward, around the wheel and continued on to the ladder leading to the salon.

* * * * *

The storm beat at the sailboat with relentless fury well into the next day. Daybreak brought a little light but the sun was not visible through the clouds and rain. The winds, at times, hit near hurricane force and refused to relent.

The crew stayed in the cockpit while on duty, one on the wheel and the other constantly on the lookout for emergency situations. The violent weather punished the boat mercilessly and, without near superhuman effort by those on watch, would have sent it to the bottom of the ocean. It often took two to stop the wheel from turning as the churning waters tried to turn the rudder and send the boat sideways into crashing waves.

No one slept, and it was impossible to cook meals. Bread and bottled water sustained them.

Finally, a little before midnight on the second night, the winds slackened. By four the next morning, the seas were calm. Denise and George managed to get some sleep in those hours and went on watch at four o'clock. At Zach's direction, they kept the motor running. He wanted to check everything out in the daylight to make sure nothing was broken or dangerously weakened before hoisting the sails.

Most of the crew was back on deck shortly after daybreak. They all ate a hearty breakfast during which Zach told everyone about the mistake he had made. Recalling how he came close to being lost at sea, he stressed the importance of the harnesses while on watch during stormy weather.

"Seriously, Dad, did you almost get washed overboard?" Denise queried, her face wrinkled so that her nose seemed scrunched up inside her cheeks.

"Yes," he replied, "and if it wasn't for Ron, "I wouldn't be here right now."

They all looked at Ron, who knew Zach was making a point and this time didn't attempt to minimize his part in saving the man. He made no comment about the incident, but held up a harness to emphasize Zach's words. "These harnesses are critical for your safety," he said.

After breakfast, Zach, Clon, and Stacey checked the sails and all the rigging to be sure everything was safe to use. Denise stepped down into the cockpit and put on the harness Ron had used to demonstrate the importance of the safety device. She pulled to make sure the line was snuggly attached to the cable that was still hooked up between the two masts.

The boat was on autopilot, but George was at the wheel, standing several feet behind Denise. "You don't need that in this calm weather," he advised the girl.

"After my father went to such great lengths just to make a point," she joked, smiling at her father, who was stepping into the cockpit to check out the main boom, it seems to me that I ought to."

"That's awfully flip. . . " George started to say in reproach, but Zach put a finger to his lips.

He leaned over and whispered to George. "Denise has a good sense of humor," he said. "And it almost always serves a useful purpose. Right now, it's keeping her from dwelling on what she had to do back in Hilo. Believe me, a little flippancy is better than having her dwell on shooting a man and watching as we blew up a boat with four men aboard."

George signaled his understanding with a slight nod, and Zach undid some lines and bungee cords to get a look at the sail and the boom to which it was connected. When things looked okay there, he went forward to the mast. He was about to start climbing the mast steps to take a look at the spreaders that extended out about three-fourths of the way up, but stopped and looked back.

George had reduced the engine speed to idle and took it out of gear.

"Why are you stopping?" he called back to George.

George pointed ahead.

Zach and all the others looked forward in amazement. A submarine was surfacing less than seventy-five yards ahead of them. It stopped dead ahead. Well over two hundred feet long, it had an oblong conning tower that was longer at the top than on the part that was between it and the craft's hull. There were square objects that looked like windows at the front of the rounded section at the top.

Glen pulled two pairs of binoculars from the storage bin in the cockpit, handing one to his father. He offered the other pair to Ron, who waved it off.

"I don't need them to know that's a Ming Class sub."

"Ming Class?" said Glen.

"Red Chinese."

As they watched, twelve Chinese sailors climbed down from the conning tower onto the sub's deck.

All were armed with automatic weapons.

Chapter 30

"WHAT do you think they're up to?" Glen asked.

"I have no idea, son," Zach replied. "If they wanted to kill us, they could have done that with a torpedo."

"Maybe they didn't want to waste one on a boat as small as this," George offered.

"I suppose that could be it but I don't think so. They're armed. At this distance, they could easily pick us off with those rifles. They're not shooting for a reason."

"The Ming Class subs are older, and diesel powered," Ron said. "I'd suggest they're after your extra barrels, but that wouldn't take them two miles."

"How is it that you know so much about Chinese submarines?" Zach asked.

"I was in the U.S. Navy for eight years in the Pacific waters. It was my job to know."

"Any idea what they're up to?"

"Not a clue."

"Look, Dad, they're lowering a boat," Glen said, pointing.

They could see that several of the men had lowered an inflatable boat, and three people were getting in it. One looked like an officer. He held a piece of white cloth in his hand. None of the men in the inflatable were armed.

"They want to talk," George said. "Does anyone speak Chinese?"

They all shrugged and looked at Ron.

"Sorry," he confessed, "we were always at sea in Asia, so I didn't learn a word."

"Maybe talk is all they want," Zach said, "but we need to be ready for anything. Based on what we learned from Commander Kotchel, we're officially at war with these people. Stacey, I think you and Glen should go below and bring up the AK-47s. Hand them out to everyone except me. I've got the .38 in my pocket."

"Does that include Ron?" she asked.

"Yes," he answered. He smiled at Ron. "I guess that means that, as of now, you officially cease being a prisoner."

"Thanks," Ron said. "Although being a prisoner in these circumstances wasn't all that bad."

The inflatable rowed over, giving the crew aboard the *La Sirena* time to secure their weapons and find suitable locations to ward off an attack.

The man, who was obviously in charge of the inflatable, watched the sailboat with stoic interest as they approached. He looked to be in his early forties. The other two were younger, probably in their twenties. All three appeared to be in good physical condition. When they came alongside the starboard beam, he appeared to be looking for a suitable place to latch on to the sailboat. Seeing that and anticipating that the visitors had no way of asking for help, Zach found a line and tossed it over the side for one of the rowers to grab.

A man grabbed hold of the line, pulled the inflatable close to the sailboat, and stabilized it. Then the man in charge stood.

"Greetings," he said in perfect English.

Chapter 31

"YOU speak English?" Zach gasped in a tone of obvious surprise.

"I graduated from the California State University at Santa Barbara. It was a most enjoyable time in my life. May I please come aboard, captain?"

"Yes, of course." Zach turned to Denise, who was near the stern. "Denise, would you bring the boarding ladder over to this side, please?"

Denise slung her AK-47 over her shoulder and went over to untie the ladder from the stern rail, where they had tied it down before the storm hit. She took it to her father, who hooked it over the side where the inflatable was bobbing. The Chinese naval officer reached up on either side of the ladder and took a cautious step upward.

The inflatable started to move away from the sailboat, but the man holding the line pulled them in again. Once the officer stepped clear of the inflatable, he was able to move freely and climbed quickly up the ladder. Zach helped him over the rail.

On board, the Chinese officer saluted Zach. "I am Captain Chou Wang of the People's Liberation Navy. Please forgive us for stopping you, but I felt we should talk. We hoped to catch you earlier, but the storm came upon us, so we waited until it was over to make contact."

"Were you behind us the night the storm started?" Stacey asked.

"Yes, but we submerged when we saw what was coming."

"Well, at least that's one mystery solved," she said.

"Perhaps I will be able to clear up more".

"I certainly hope so. I am Zach Arthur. The first mystery that needs clearing up is why you are here. And, of course, what it is you want to talk about."

"You are captain of this vessel, are you not?"

"I am."

"Do you mind if I ask, is this your family?"

Zach thought it strange that the captain of a warship, one that was presumably in the middle of a war, would be interested in things such as family. He looked over at the submarine, which had not moved. The armed men were still on deck, but they were sitting around in a rather leisurely mode and showed no signs of being hostile.

His children had come in close to listen to the conversation. "This is my wife, Stacey, my son, Glen, and daughter, Denise. The others are George, Millie, and Ron, who are traveling with us." Ron had also moved in close, but Millie and George stayed at a distance. All still held their automatic weapons. When Zach turned back to the visiting officer, he saw a momentary tinge of sorrow in the man's eyes.

"It is good that you have your family with you," Captain Wang said. "It shall make for a pleasant journey."

"I agree, and I do not mean to be abrupt, but I am still waiting for an explanation."

"Yes, of course. Forgive me for interjecting a moment of nostalgia at a time when so many things are of such grave consequence. I have a simple request."

Zach was not sure what the "moment of nostalgia" meant, but when the captain of a vessel that could blow his boat out of the water in seconds said he had a request, he would listen. "Please tell me what it is we can do for you."

"We have been following you for days, and by determining your course, based on the median of your tacks, I believe you are headed for the Central California Coast. I would like you to allow us to travel along with you."

Zach had not given any thought to what the request might be, but if he made a thousand guesses, that would not be one of them. His first reaction was an objection. "Captain, I have only recently become aware of what has happened in the world, but from what I've heard, your country and mine are at war. That means that, for all intents and purposes, we are enemies."

"I know what you say is true; however, our world is now in a situation that is without precedent. No government in the world is what it was two weeks ago. Almost all are gone forever. For all intents and purposes, to use your terminology, the war between us is over. No truce has been called only because there are no authorities in either country who have the power to call such a truce."

Zach looked to Stacey and then to Ron. Both shrugged. He looked back at the Chinese officer. "Why do you want to go to California?"

"I know California."

"You know China even better."

"That is true, but the United States had more nuclear weapons than did China. My home and the homes of all of those aboard were decimated. They no longer exist. Nuclear missiles hit every population center. It will be many years before the radioactivity is eradicated from huge areas of China. On the other hand, nuclear missiles struck only sparingly in California. Please forgive my use of the term, 'only.' I know that your country, too, was devastated, and I use the word simply as a term of relativity. The San Francisco Bay Area, Los Angeles, and San Diego were hit with nuclear missiles. While there is radioactivity in those areas, it is quite possible that the central part of California is relatively free of major contamination."

"Your family?" said Stacey.

They saw the same look they saw earlier flash painfully across his eyes, and the reason for his use of the word "nostalgia" became clear. "All our families were in the areas hit hardest," he said.

Zach's heart went out to the man, but he

knew he couldn't let sentiment get in the way of reason. He considered what the man said about Central California and remembered what Commander Kotchel had said. The Chinese officer might very well be right. But, there were still questions.

"You may have a point about the contamination," he admitted, "but you don't need us. Without us, in fact, you could get there a great deal faster. Why would you want to triple your travel time?"

"Many who see us will consider us enemies and will want to fight with us. We do not want to fight."

"Are you saying that you want to become our prisoners?"

Chapter 32

THE officer was taken aback by the suggestion, but recovered quickly. "I can see how my words could be construed in that manner," he said. "However, because I believe we are no longer at war, and my honor would not permit surrender if we were, I suggest a more amicable arrangement."

"We would be mutual protection for one another. As I said, we have observed you for some time and are aware that you have been attacked by marauders. There are many more out there, and they might want to do the same. None, however, will do so if you are guarded by a fully armed warship."

Zach looked around. No one spoke but it was clear that the thought of not having to worry about being attacked sat well with the others. And with him. "Yes, that would be beneficial to us," he told the submariner. "However, we're a small boat. We can't offer you any protection."

"To the contrary," he responded, "it is quite possible you will be able to be of even greater benefit to us. It is not the marauders that concern us, but that of your country's warships. Before the communications systems went down, we caught several conversations between some of them. As with our navy, most of the U.S. force is gone, but a few of your ships are still afloat. They are now operating only on orders they received more than a week ago, when battles raged. If they see a Chinese submarine, they are likely to attack. As your movie people say, they will shoot first and ask questions later. That would force us to respond, and no good purpose would be served by our killing one another at this point in time."

"How do we know you won't attack them?" Ron asked.

"Ron," Stacey objected.

"That is all right, ma'am," the officer said. "He has stated a legitimate concern. I can only respond by telling you that we had every chance to sink the aircraft carrier you met with before you went to Hawaii, but we did not. It was without the escorts that normally travel with a carrier, protecting it from attack by submarines and others. It was as easy a target as any combatant could ask for, and if I had considered us to be at war, I would have been obliged to sink it. As a matter of fact, sinking an aircraft carrier is a dream come true for a submariner. In this case, though, we instead watched from a distance and saw they were ridding the world of the pirates who prey upon the innocent and unarmed. It is a good thing that they are doing, and so we gave them a wide berth, and avoided contact."

"You've been following us since then?" Zach asked in amazement.

"It was then that I came up with this idea. It would be impossible for us to set up this conversation directly with the commander of a warship, which is why I did not attempt to contact the captain of the aircraft carrier. I am sure he would have felt obliged to fight us. It, however, is quite reasonable for you, the captain of a private boat, to do so. You did, in fact, talk with them. As I watched you, I saw the name of a town on the back of your boat. I am aware that it is common to paint the name of the home port on a boat's transom along with the boat's name. San Diego is your home port. It is not where we want to go, but it is in California, and I thought if we stayed with you for most of the trip, it would get us close to our chosen destination. So I decided to observe you closely. As you can imagine, I was elated when I saw that your course was farther north toward Central California, which is the same area as we want to go."

"What makes you think that they'll believe me if I tell them that you are not a combatant or that I even believe it myself."

"I understand your concerns. I don't ask that you do anything that you feel will compromise your beliefs or that you think might put you or your compatriots in harm's way. Just tell them what you know of me and my crew and what I have said to you. Let them decide if they are willing to talk with me. I believe they will. You see, for most of my adult life, I have dealt with military people from several countries. Most, like me, prefer peace to war. That feeling must be compounded a thousand times now, after what has happened. That is all I ask... that you simply tell them all I want to do is talk, and I believe they will then 'ask questions before they shoot'."

"Wait here," said Zach, and he motioned for the others to follow him to the bow, where George and Millie were standing.

Zach got them in a huddle and asked, "What do you think?"

"I think he's sincere," Stacey replied.

"It seems to me it's a rather, ah, unorthodox request," George said.

"True," Ron responded, "but we're living in a very unorthodox world right now."

"You said you're ex-navy," Zach said. "What do you think?"

"Not speaking to whether I trust him or not," Ron answered, "but his logic holds up. If I commanded a warship, I'd try to sink him, but I would talk with you."

"And so, speaking to whether or not you trust him?"

"I was afraid you'd ask that. I don't really know, but I believe it's possible that he is being straight with us. One thing you might do is agree to allow them to go alongside us and see if we can figure it out by the time we have to do something about it."

"I realize I'm just an interloper here," Millie said, "but it seems logical to me, especially being as they can go alongside us even if we say no, and there's not a blasted thing we can do about it."

"Kids?" Stacey asked.

"I think Millie's right," Glen said. "Besides, it would sure be good to have a big guy around to help if we run into a bully."

"Ditto," said Denise.

Stacey agreed.

"Okay, that's what I'll tell him." Zach went back to talk with Captain Wang. The others followed.

"We accept your suggestion," the sailboat captain told the Chinese officer.

"I am pleased that is so. If it is all right with you, we will stay on the surface most of the time."

"It will be good to know where you are," Zach agreed. "But keep in mind that we do not sail a straight course."

"I went sailing with friends several times when I was in Santa Barbara," Captain Wang told him. "I am familiar with how sailboats maneuver to catch the wind, so I will be sure to stay out of your way when you change directions."

"You said you would be on the surface most of the time, which tells me you plan on submerging some other times. Is that when you will go under water, when we cross over into your path?"

"No, we can stay out of your way easily enough on the surface just by changing speeds. However, if we pick up a large ship with our sonar, or a plane comes into view, we will submerge until we are sure it is safe."

"That sounds fair."

Captain Wang saluted Zach, and then shook hands all around. He got back in the inflatable, and the three Chinese mariners returned to their submarine. The crew of the *La Sirena* hoisted their sails.

Thus, they resumed their journey to California, the sailboat tacking and the submarine motoring straight ahead at a very slow speed.

Chapter 33

THE first day and night were pleasant but unremarkable. The weather was sunny and the seas relatively calm, with enough wind to push the boat along at over six knots. The submarine stayed close and was never an obstruction.

On the second morning, Captain Wang had the sub brought alongside the sailboat. Cupping his hands at the sides of his mouth, he called over to the sailboat, asking Zach if he could stop and talk.

Zach agreed, and the crew dropped the sails. When the sailboat slowed to a stop, they dropped six rubber fenders over the side and the submarine edged up alongside. They tied one to the other. Once they were sure the fenders would prevent damage to the sailboat's fiberglass hull, the submarine's crew extended a "gangplank" between the vessels. The submarine was higher than the La Sirena, so Captain Wang walked carefully down the improvised walkway, which his crew had fashioned out of metal used for flooring on their vessel. He saluted and asked permission to go aboard before actually stepping onto the sailboat.

"Thank you for stopping, captain," the Chinese officer said, directing it at Zach, but looking around to let everyone know he intended it for all of them. "I have another request."

"Yes?" Zach said, waiting cautiously.

"With your permission, I would like to have members of my crew ride along with you so that they might learn things about your country."

Zach thought for a second before responding. "I'm sorry, but that seems like a rather odd request. Why would you want that?"

"No need to be sorry. You have every right to know why.   Having lived in the United States, I know something about the people and how the country functions. Your combination of democracy and capitalism has resulted in a unique society. As I am sure you are aware, our attempt at straight communism resulted in abject poverty for a vast majority of our people.

"I am a military person and not political, but I was happy when we changed to a capitalistic economy. It brought a form of wealth to many that we had never before seen. We did not change our form of government, however, and my crewmembers do not know the feeling of being able to make the choices that will govern their lives in a free society. If we are successful at getting to live in your country for a time, it would be very useful for them to know something about how you think and talk."

"For a time? Does that mean you plan on returning to China?"

"I am Chinese. It is my country. Yes, if it is possible when the air is again fit to breath and the water fit to drink, I will return."

"And take democracy with you?"

"As I said, I am not a political person. I like democracy but I shall try to fit into whatever system the people choose."

Zach looked the man in the eye. He wasn't fool enough to think he could determine if someone was telling the truth or not, but liars often gave themselves away by either shifting their eyes or attempting to focus them unusually straight at a person. Captain Wang's eyes did neither. He didn't try to convince him that he was going to promote democracy when he had the chance, either. Someone trying to pull something would do that to build confidence, wouldn't they? On the other hand, a smart operator might use that as a ploy.

Zach had the same concerns he had with Ron, that the Chinese could use the opportunity to learn how to sail the boat. But, why? They already had a two-hundred-fifty foot boat of their own. Besides, Captain Wang already knew something about sailing, and the others could see them plainly from the deck of the submarine, which was going to be on top of the water most of the time. They could learn simply by observing for a few weeks.

He decided to get more information. "How many do you have aboard?"

"Thirty-seven men, five of whom are officers, including myself."

Ron, who was standing close behind Zach, commented, "That sounds like very few for a boat that size,"

Captain Wang looked appreciatively over Zach's shoulder at the ex-navy man. "You know about navy craft, I see. You are quite correct. The normal complement is fifty-five men, nine of whom are officers. However, before we left the South China Sea, we were involved in several skirmishes with the kinds of marauders your aircraft carrier is now hunting down. We rid the world of many bad people, but we lost eighteen men doing it."

"Thirty-seven is still a lot," Zach observed, "and I don't believe any of us speak any form of Chinese," Zach replied, looking at the newest members of the crew. Millie, George, and Ron all shook their heads.

"I would suggest only two or three at a time," the Chinese officer said. "One of my officers and one of the enlisted men speak very good English. Two others have a working knowledge. I would also, with your permission, take a turn aboard to translate." That last statement came as a bit of a surprise given the Commanding Officer's lead role and responsibility.

Zach looked around. The others, like himself, had considered the consequences. Stacey, Glen, and Denise nodded weakly. They didn't have any specific objections but their expressions indicated there were reservations.

"As a guest, I probably don't have a say," Millie observed, "but I would say yes, if I did."

"If there are unfortunate consequences, you will suffer them the same as us," Zach replied, "so, as far as I am concerned, in this process, you do have a say."

"Then I suppose I have a say, also," George said. "I have doubts about it, so if you allow them to come aboard, I suggest we watch them closely." He turned to the submarine captain. "No offense, but we've had some bad times recently."

"No offense taken. There are members of my crew who are just as suspicious. It is to be expected in times such as these."

"Very well," Zach concluded, "we can take three at a time. There isn't room for more. Does eight a.m. to six p.m. sound okay?"

"That sounds very good. As we will be having lunch with you, we will bring food."

"I hadn't given any thought to that," Zach admitted. "What do you have?"

"Rice," said the Chinese officer.

"Oh," said Zach with little enthusiasm in his voice.

The Chinese officer laughed. "It is my attempt at a joke. Having watched Americans eat for over five years in Santa Barbara, I am aware that rice is seldom on the menu. We have vegetables and meat. And we catch fish."

"We sometimes eat rice," said Stacey, "but we don't have any at the moment. Maybe we could use some."

Glen tried to be helpful. "I like rice pilaf well enough. Remember when we ate it at that restaurant in Mission Bay?"

Denise made a face.

"I will see what our cook can come up with," said Captain Wang, smiling.

Having decided to start immediately, the submariner captain brought one man who spoke English very well and one who spoke none at all over to the sailboat and introduced them to all those aboard. The two were obviously ill at ease in this strange situation, but the one who spoke English repeated the names of each of the Americans as they were introduced. He never forgot any of them. The other said nothing.

Shortly afterward, a man came over with a large cardboard box. "This is our lunch," said Captain Wang. He smiled. "It is mostly rice. However, there is one large portion of Cantonese Rice. That is flavored rice mixed with vegetables and various kinds of meats. My cook is very well known for that dish. There is enough for each of you to try for lunch today."

"Hey, that smells good!" Glen exclaimed, edging up close to the Chinese men.

"I hope you will find that it tastes even better than it smells." said the officer.

Zach took the box and handed it down to Millie. Put this in the refrigerator, please. We can microwave it later."

"You have a microwave?" Captain Wang asked.

"Yes." Zach pointed to two large solar panels on the roof of the main cabin. "We have both solar power and a diesel generator. As long as we don't overdo it, we have a good supply of electricity."

At lunch that day, they decided to drop the sails and cut the engine to enjoy a leisurely meal and conversation.

"I remember that Americans can be very cosmopolitan," commented the submarine captain.

"You have many kinds of restaurants in your country."

"Did you get used to eating American food, or did you just eat rice?" asked Denise.

"When I was there, I ate mostly American cuisine and became quite fond of it."

"Oh?" said Stacey. "What was your favorite American dish?"

"Tacos."

Chapter 34

THE Chinese officer and the Americans burst out laughing at his remark, astonishing the other two submariners. When he was able to control his mirth, Wang told his speechless compatriots about the vast cultural diversity in the United States.

"Every country has its own specialized dishes," he said after explaining that every country in the world is represented in the U.S. population, some so heavily they make up a majority in areas. "There are restaurants serving dishes from everywhere around the world," he continued. "In some areas, Mexican restaurants outnumber all others. The taco is actually a Mexican dish but there are so many served, a stranger would assume they are a native U.S. dish."

After the man who brought the food returned to the submarine and the "gangplank" was removed and stored, the Chinese ship moved away from the *La Sirena*. The sailboat's crew worked around their "guests" as they hoisted the sails so they could resume their trip. As the Americans talked, the two Chinese who spoke English translated for their shipmate.

When lunch was served, the rice dishes were warmed up in the ship's microwave. The Chinese were again surprised when Zach, Stacey, and George used chopsticks to eat their Cantonese Rice.

"Yes, the United States must have a very diverse society," the second English-speaking submariner concluded, a hint of awe in his voice.

Just as surprising to the Americans, Captain Wang used a fork. "Easier to eat with," he said, although he did resort to chopsticks to pick up smaller items.

After the first day, the submarine pulled up next to the sailboat every morning to drop off three of their crew, and again in the evening to allow them to return. There was always one English-speaking sailor among them. They listened to the Americans talk and asked questions about life in the United States. There was interest in family life, work, entertainment, and shopping but political issues were usually the main topic. The Chinese were amazed that there were different political parties and philosophies, but what seemed to baffle them most was that people openly questioned the actions of their leaders.

The submarine was always in sight, and some members of its crew were always on deck. They worked out, an exercise that looked like yoga to the Americans. When not doing that, they either studied, or fished, using poles at times, but mostly using nets. They caught enough to feed themselves regularly and had enough left over to give to the Americans. They also provided their hosts with a variety of foods from their storage area, which consisted of mostly rice and noodles or a variety of cut portions of meats and vegetables from their freezer. Because of the gifts of food, the Americans used barely half of their own stores during the more than three weeks they were at sea with the submarine.

The crew of the *La Sirena* got used to having the Chinese on board during the day and equally accepted having the submarine nearby at all times. Although they would not characterize their relationship with their "guests" as friendship, it became comfortable for most of them. George kept his distance.

Several of the Chinese were suspicious of the Americans, as well. They weren't openly hostile but neither did they attempt to get close, their eyes constantly on guard. Ninety percent of the submariners, though, exhibited no hostility and used the opportunity to learn all they could. Like the majority of the Americans, they became comfortable with the arrangement.

Three weeks passed, and they didn't see another boat as they approached the waters outside California. There was one plane, which was headed west. It was off in the distance and flying at more than thirty thousand feet altitude, so they had no way of knowing what kind of plane it was, where it came from or where it was going. It was unlikely anyone on the plane would have seen them. Two months earlier, on the trip west from California to the

South Pacific, they had seen fifteen boats, and at least fifty planes passed by overhead. Things had changed drastically.

As Captain Wang and two members of his crew started to leave the sailboat one evening, they spotted a small clump of loose kelp floating nearby. The officer pointed it out to the sailing crew and called back to them, "We're near a kelp forest. We should see land by morning."

A member of the Chinese crew snagged the brownish sea plant with a gaff; a large hook attached to a long pole, and pulled it aboard the sub.

"Great for wrapping some of my cook's rice dishes," the captain yelled to the *La Sirena* crew as he watched his men take the kelp below. "He uses it in soups, too. Great food source."

*   *   *   *   *

As dawn broke the next morning, Glen, whose shoulder had healed well enough that he could again stand his watch, saw the California coast ahead. "Hey, everyone," he called to those below, "we're home."

Denise was the first to make her way to the cockpit, followed by Stacey and Zach. The other three soon joined them.

"In eighty plus years," Millie stated exuberantly when she saw the hills of the Central California coast, "I've never been more pleased to see anything than I am to see dry land."

"Believe me, Millie," Stacey told her, "even us 'old salts' are just as happy to see it. We love the ocean, but walking on a surface that doesn't move is going to be a joy."

"I wonder how the submariners feel about it." said Zach.

They all turned to see if the submarine crew was on deck to watch as they closed the distance to land.

They saw nothing but ocean where the submarine usually was. It had disappeared.

Chapter 35

ZACH turned on the radar. "That thing doesn't pick up underwater objects, does it?" George asked.

"No. I'm just looking to see if there is a large ship around. If Captain Wang thought there was an American warship nearby, he'd take his submarine into hiding."

"Or, now that we've given them safe passage, they're going to do what they came for, which probably isn't something they want us to see."

"You have a suspicious mind, George, but I admit we can't discount that possibility. We'll just have to play it by ear."

"See anything on the radar?" Ron asked.

"Nope," Zach replied. "No boats, large or small, but that does not mean there aren't some around. This radar has a limit of fifteen miles. His sonar is a lot more powerful, so he can see things we won't know about for an hour or more. We'll keep going."

"Where are we?" Millie asked.

"Trusting that Ron's navigation is right on," Zach said, "Santa Barbara is dead ahead."

"That's definitely Santa Barbara," Ron said. "What's the plan when we get there?"

"Originally, we were going to dock the boat and find transportation to Santa Maria, where my parents live. After what we ran into in Hilo, though, it's doubtful that we would have a boat when we got back. Stacey and I have talked about it, and if it's all right with the rest of you, I'll have her drop me and Denise off in Santa Barbara. Then you can bring the boat back out to sea and wait for us on the water. It's a lot safer out here than in port."

"It would be dangerous for the two of you going alone," George said. "I'll go with you."

"I appreciate that, George, but it is our family. There's no need for you to risk your life for them."

"My life has been at risk since the day this all started. We're all in this together."

"I should go, too," Ron added. "If California has become anything like what happened to Hawaii, you'll need every gun you can get."

"I'm overwhelmed," Zach turned to look at his wife, "but Stacey and Glen could use help, too."

"You keep forgetting about me," complained Millie. "I'm a long way from being useless."

George agreed. "I'd take her at her word if I were you. Millie can outwork people half her age and can hit a fly at fifty paces with her .357 magnum."

"Millie and Glen are all I'll need," Stacey advised her husband.

Zach turned back to George and Ron. "Very well, then, I'll take the two of you up on your offers. So, let's lay out a plan."

They gathered at the back of the cockpit to talk about it. None of them had ever sailed into Santa Barbara before, so they would have to depend solely on charts. There was no way of knowing where the party could safely go ashore until they were there. All they could do was check out the charts for logical spots. Without knowing the local landscape and possible hiding places, it would all be guesswork. Bad guys could be anywhere, and they wouldn't know it until they were ambushed.

"We may have a bigger puzzle to solve than that one before we even get to the harbor," Stacey told them as they were gathering up the charts. "A blip came up on the radar screen a little while ago. It's southeast of us, and it looks like whoever it is plans on intercepting us."

Denise went to the front of the boat with a pair of binoculars. She scanned the area to the southeast, then stopped and concentrated on one small area. "I see it," she called back. "It looks pretty big, and Mom's right. It's hard to tell at this distance, but it sure looks like they'll run right into us in an hour or so if they stay on the course they're on."

As they got closer to land, the wind changed. They were soon "running" with the wind behind them. Once the sails were set, they were able to sail directly toward the harbor entrance without tacking. From time to time, they "took in" or "let out" a sail, but otherwise it was a fairly leisurely sail.

Which gave them many opportunities to watch as the bigger ship got nearer. It was still the only one on the radar. Denise had been right; it was larger than the usual small craft seen close to shore.

"If I'm not mistaken," Ron told the others, "that's a U. S. Coast Guard cutter."

"I hope you're right," Stacey replied. "We could stand to run into some good guys."

As the ship neared, the configuration of its hull and superstructure became clearer and they could see markings on its hull. "It's definitely Coast Guard," Ron confirmed. "A buoy tender, I think."

"They have big ships just to look after buoys?" Glen asked.

Ron laughed. "They actually do tend buoys, I think. But most of their time is probably spent on the lookout for bad guys – drug smugglers and any other kind of smugglers, including those bringing in illegal immigrants. They'd also be interested in a submarine from an enemy country, I suspect."

"And well they should be," George asserted.

"They won't be interested in us, then," Denise decided.

"Why not?" queried Glen.

"We're obviously just a family out sailing," his sister responded.

"Yeah, but how do they know we're not someone smuggling gold, or guns, or something like that?"

"Denise could be right," Zach reasoned. "But, if they don't stop us, we'll try to stop them. We need information, and they need to know about

Captain Wang and the submarine."

"Should we go below and get our weapons?" Millie wondered.

"We'd better keep them out of sight," Zach determined. "We don't want a friendly military crew thinking we're itching for a fight. It would be better for us to welcome them with a few cheery hellos."

As the one-hundred-seventy-five foot cutter approached, they all went to the rail to wave at whomever they saw. Denise even whistled. It was all for naught. Not a single person was visible aboard the cutter.

When the cutter was thirty yards away, a loudspeaker activated. "Heave to," a loud voice commanded.

An instant later, over twenty members of the cutter's crew appeared at strategic locations. All were armed. This was different from when the Chinese seamen held their weapons loosely at their sides under similar circumstances several weeks earlier. These people had their weapons trained directly on the sailboat's crew.

Chapter 36

WHILE the crew dropped the sails, Zach started the engine and put it in reverse to stop the sailboat's forward motion. The cutter's engines were also now in reverse to stop the ship. It had a unique thruster system that allowed it to return quickly to where the sailboat was.

When the two vessels were side by side, pointing in opposite directions, an officer from the cutter went to the rail and called, "Who are you and what is your business here?"

"We're a family trying to reach my parents," Zach called back.

The officer talked briefly into a small device that looked like a cell phone, and then turned back to the sailboat. "We need to board you for an inspection. Please put a ladder over the side."

Zach nodded to Denise, who once again got the ladder. Zach hung it over the side as the cutter's crew put an eighteen-foot skiff in the water. The officer and six armed men got in the skiff and motored the twenty yards from their boat to the *La Sirena*. The Coast Guard crewmembers who remained on the cutter still had their weapons pointed at the people on the sailboat.

The officer stood when the skiff got to the sailboat. He saluted. "Permission to come aboard," he said.

Zach knew they were going to board with or without permission. In truth, even with the guns pointed at them, he was happy they were here. He saluted back. "Permission granted."

Two of the armed men boarded first. They took positions behind members of the crew. The officer then boarded followed by two more armed men. The two others remained on the skiff, watching carefully.

The officer scanned the group, his gaze finally stopping at Zach, who was standing in front of him. "You responded to me. Can I assume you are the owner of this boat?"

"It is my family's boat," said Zach. "I'm Zach Arthur, and this is my wife, Stacey, and children, Glen and Denise. Millie, George, and Ron are traveling with us. We were sailing in the South Pacific, and when we learned what happened, we came back to check on my parents."

"My name is Commander Richard Beam, United States Coast Guard. Please excuse what might appear to be overkill, but we must search all vessels entering and leaving waters of the United States."

"There's still a United States?" asked Stacey.

The Coast Guard officer was deliberate in his answer. "Yes, there is still a United States. It is not what it was a month ago but it does exist. We believe it will once again be what it was before. In the meantime, those of us left who still have some authority will continue to act on our country's behalf in whatever way we can. That is what we are doing now."

"Tell your men to go ahead and search," Zach told him, "but make sure they put everything back where it was. Our survival isn't just based on having what we need; it's also dependent on our knowing where it is if we need it in a hurry."

"A sensible practice," the commander agreed. He turned to the Coast Guardsman at his side. "Take two men and proceed with the search, and if you have to move anything, put it back the way it was."

The man motioned to two of the men, and they went below. George followed.

"He's a very careful man," Millie explained to Commander Beam when he looked quizzically at George going down the ladder after his men. "He wants to be sure everything is done right."

The commander smiled. "And, I presume, to make sure everything is still there when we leave."

"That, too," Millie admitted.

"A reasonable precaution. I'd probably do the same." He turned to Zach. "Were you at sea very long?"

It appeared to be a way of making conversation, but Zach knew it was a more casual means of gaining information. "Let me tell you the whole story," he said, "beginning with why we were in the South Pacific to start with." He told the Coast Guard officer about their taking a long vacation and sailing to the Marshall Islands. He mentioned their stay on the little island and how communications had gone out while they were there. He was telling him about the trip to Hawaii, and was about at the part of the story where the aircraft carrier almost ran them down when the man in charge of the search came up the ladder from the salon.

He was carrying one of the AK-47s. "Look what we found, Commander," he said. "There are five more like them down there, plus some small arms."

"How do you explain those?" the commander asked Zach.

"That's what I was just getting to," Zach told him. He described how the aircraft carrier almost ran them down and how they caught up to it the next day. "They sent a boat out to blow up a pirate that was on our tail. Then, they came over to talk to us."

"The automatic weapons?" the commander asked impatiently. "That's what I need to know about."

"I understand that, and that's what happened when they came over to talk." Zach's tone was almost as impatient as the commander's. "The executive officer of the carrier, Commander Kotchel..."

"What did you say?" Beam exclaimed.

"I was explaining how we got supplies, including the weapons."

"No, I mean the name you mentioned."

"Commander Kotchel?"

"Yes, that's what I thought you said. Joe Kotchel?"

"I'm pretty sure he called himself Joseph."

"Excuse me for a minute." The commander seemed excited. He took out his phone and punched in a number.

When it was answered, he said, "Captain, this is Dick. We have a situation here."

He listened for a moment. "Yes, it's something I would normally handle on my own," he said in response to what his captain said. "But I think you'll want to get personally involved in this one."

After he clicked off, he turned to Zach. "We'll carry on with this when the captain arrives."

Chapter 37

THE Coast Guard Commander sent the skiff back to the cutter, and a few minutes later, it returned with the captain, a trim man of about forty. He requested permission to come aboard. Moments later, he was on the deck, standing next to the commander. Even though the Arthurs had not seen him before, he looked familiar.

"Captain Arthur," Commander Beam said, "I'd like you to meet my commanding officer, Captain James Kotchel."

The Coast Guard captain extended a hand.

Taken aback by the name, Zach stared at the captain and was slow in extending his hand. "Did he say Kotchel?"

"Yes," confirmed the captain. "What is so strange about Kotchel?"

"It's not strange; it's just that I met Commander Joseph Kotchel a month ago south of Hawaii. That's how we got..."

"Joe?" exclaimed the captain, his face transforming from that of a stern captain to one of a man feeling sheer joy. "You talked to Joe? He's alive?"

"That's why I thought you needed to come over, Jim," the commander said, all formality at bay for the moment. "From what I've heard so far, they have quite a story, and your brother is part of it."

"He was very much alive, when we saw him. He and his carrier were doing somewhat the same thing you're doing here."

"And, Joe? How did he look?"

"In good health. I can't say happy, but he seemed in good enough spirits considering the situation."

"It's hard for anyone to be happy at the moment," judged the captain. "But, I'm thrilled to hear he's alive and well."

"I take it you're not in communication with ships in that area."

"There's very little in the way of communications anywhere right now. We have people trying to get things back in working order, but we haven't heard much of anything from anyone in over a month. The last word we got was that almost all our ships were lost in Asia. I feared the worst."

"Well, I'm glad I was able to bring you a bit of good news. I imagine there isn't much of that these days."

"Virtually none, but what you've told me today helps fill a big void. My younger brother and I are very close. If it's all right with you, I'd like to talk to you more about Joe later. Right now, we had better get back to business. I'm sorry, in my excitement, I forgot your name."

"Zach Arthur." He again introduced the others. He told the captain the story, beginning with the carrier almost running over them.

When he got to the part about the submarine officer asking to go along, the Coast Guard captain stopped him. "Wait a minute," he said. "Are you telling me there's a Chinese submarine with you?"

"Yes, at least it was until this morning when we got close to land. It disappeared, and we haven't seen it since. Now I don't know if they really want to talk or not."

"Talk?"

"Yes, that's what I was about to tell you. Captain Wang..."

"Captain Wang? You know him?"

"Yes. He speaks excellent English and spent quite a bit of time aboard with us. He says that, as far as he is concerned, the war is over. Instead of fighting, he wants to talk. Now that the sub has disappeared, though..." His voice trailed off.

"They must have submerged when their sonar picked up our ship"

"Probably, but things have been so discombobulated, I quit trying to make judgments."

"I can understand that," said Captain Kotchel. He turned to Commander Beam. "That must explain that odd sonar reading."

"That's what I was thinking." said the commander.

Zach and the others looked questioningly at the two U.S. Coast Guard officers.

"This morning," Captain Kotchel said in response to their unasked question, "one of our sonar techs detected a moving object on the sonar. It stopped, and he hasn't seen any movement since."

"The timing sounds right," Zach said. "What he picked up must be the sub. Did he track it?"

"Yes, as best he could before it stopped moving. Now, it is part of the ocean floor, although he does have a stationary object pinpointed that he's sure is it."

"Where is it?" Denise couldn't contain her curiosity.

"Not too far from here, as I recall." said the captain. He turned to the commander. "Dick, call the lion..." He stopped to explain the unusual name to the *La Sirena* crew. "He's a big Detroit Lions football fan." Returning his attention to Commander Beam, he said, "See if he has a more precise location."

The commander punched in a number on his phone and asked "the lion" for coordinates. "What?" he said excitedly after listening for a few seconds. "When? Where?"

While still trying to listen to "the lion" on the phone, the commander told the captain, "He was about to call us. The object was only a mile from us, and it started moving less than a minute ago. It's headed right at us."

"Call an alert," Captain Kotchel ordered. "Everyone to battle stations."

"Do you have depth charges?" Ron asked.

"We're not equipped for combat with a big sub, but I've armed our boat to deal with the small boats being used by the criminals who are out there these days, so we're not helpless. If it's a fight they want, they've come to the right place."

Before the cutter's crew was able to get to battle stations, the bow of a submarine shot into the air.

The Chinese warship was directly between the cutter and the sailboat.

Chapter 38

A S THE Coast Guard crew scrambled to get into position, the warship rose to the surface, its props screaming in full reverse to stop its forward progress.

It came to a stop, almost swamping the skiff that brought the Coast Guard crewmembers over to the sailboat.

Captain Wang was the first to open the conning tower hatch and step out into fresh air. He looked around. He saw that the men on the cutter were in position and had every weapon at their disposal trained on him and the other submariners who were climbing out onto the conning tower. He ignored the threat. Seeing the officers on the sailboat, he turned to them and came to attention.

He saluted.

The Coast Guard officers saw that the Chinese sailors were unarmed. Being as they were standing, anyway, they returned the salute.

Captain Wang called over. "Sorry for the dramatic entrance, but I was worried that you might attack. Can we talk?"

On the sailboat, Captain Kotchel looked at Commander Beam, who shrugged. He turned to Zach. "Was this how he approached you?"

"Pretty much, except the sub wasn't this close, so it wasn't quite as dramatic. And, he showed us a white flag."

"I suppose he considers you his white flag," Kotchel surmised. "He's not armed, and they can't shoot a torpedo at us pointed the way they are, so talking might be a good thing." He called back to the sub. "I'll send our skiff over to pick you up."

He told the man in the skiff, which by then had settled down, to fetch the Chinese captain from the sub. It was less than twenty feet away. There was a ladder leading from the sub's deck to the water, so Captain Wang climbed down from the conning tower, and then went over to climb down. The skiff wobbled when he stepped aboard, but the Coastguardsman steadied it. Wang remained standing for the short distance back to the sailboat. They reached the *La Sirena* a minute later, and Wang climbed aboard.

The officers once again saluted when facing each other directly on the sailboat's deck.

Wang turned to address Zach and Stacey. "Captain Arthur, Mrs. Arthur, it is good to see you again." He then faced Captain Kotchel. "I am Chou Wang of the People's Liberation Navy. I am captain of the submarine that just surfaced between this boat and your ship."

"I see that, Captain," said Kotchel in acknowledgement. "I am Captain James Kotchel, United States Coast Guard. This is Commander Richard Beam."

The officers shook hands.

"Now, Captain Wang, what is it you want to talk about?"

The Chinese officer retold the story he had told the *La Sirena*'s crew almost a month earlier.

Kotchel and Beam listened carefully to what the man had to say. The sailboat's crew watched their faces, but couldn't read anything into their expressions as they listened.

After Wang had his say, Kotchel asked the very question Zach had asked several weeks before... "Are you saying you want to become our prisoners?"

"No, captain. I am not. I do not believe we are still at war."

"I have received no such information from any authority," said Kotchel.

"That is only because there is no authority available to deliver such information," said Wang.

The Coast Guard officer considered that for a moment, then said, "That is not quite accurate. We have virtually no communications at this time, but our Congress will be put back together in time, and what military we still have is functional."

"As I suspected," said Wang, "the damage to the United States was less than what happened to China."

"My God," said Kotchel, "can that be? Less than twenty percent of our people are still alive, and more are dying every day. Our infrastructure is virtually gone."

"Even before we left," said Wang, "The only people left in China were in the western hinterlands. I cannot guess what sicknesses have spread to them by now."

Pain etched Kotchel's face. "I am sorry," he said, allowing himself a moment of reflection. "How could this have happened?"

"I cannot answer that," said the Chinese officer. "I can only hope that it is over and does not ever happen again."

"It isn't over by a long shot," Kotchel moaned. "Gangs and terrorists are killing innocent people everywhere we go. There is still radioactivity in major areas, and a plague is sweeping across the continent."

"That is also so in Asia, and I am sure on all continents," Wang agreed. "However, the wars between countries must be over. Perhaps those of us who still have weapons capable of killing large numbers of people can refrain from using them against one another. It would be better that we cooperate with each other. My men and I will work in any way to help, even if it is in the fields, picking crops."

Kotchel studied the Chinese captain's face and didn't answer right away. After several seconds, he said, "I agree that we have enough on our hands without continuing to fight one another. However, as long as there is no truce, joining forces might be going too far. If you believe in peaceful coexistence, though, I can agree to that. Stay in these waters as long as you like, and we won't interfere with you."

"Our provisions will run out soon," said

Captain Wang. "We must go ashore for more, and we have no local currency to use."

"You can't go ashore," the Coast Guard officer told him.

"Because we are red Chinese?"

"More because it is too dangerous. You don't know anything about this country, and there are thousands of people who will kill anyone they see if they think it will gain them even a morsel of food."

"Captain, I lived in Santa Barbara for five years, so I know this part of the country."

"You lived in Santa Barbara?"

"Graduated *cum laude* from the university there."

"Well, I'll be. Still, it's much too dangerous. In fact, even at sea it would be best if you weren't seen, so you should stay under water most of the time." Captain Kotchel thought for a moment. "We have access to food, and can meet you from time to time and supply you."

"You'd do that?" Wang appeared genuinely grateful.

"Putting a world that is in total disarray back together is going to take a lot of cooperation. It might as well start here."

"Thank you." Wang started to say something more, but hesitated.

"Yes?" asked Kotchel.

"I don't want to, how do you say, push it?" the Chinese captain said, "but we will be running out of fuel soon, too."

Kotchel looked over and studied the submarine for a minute. "Diesel?"

"Yes."

"We can supply some of that, too, but don't think about taking any long trips."

"Just to the supermarket and back," said Wang, smiling.

Kotchel laughed. "I've never heard a cutter referred to as a store before, but I guess it fits."

"Not much in this world is as it was," said Wang, with tinge of sadness in his voice.

Chapter 39

THE Coast Guard skiff took Captain Wang back to his submarine, and the Chinese warship submerged as soon as he was aboard.

Kotchel asked the crew of the *La Sirena* to gather around the cockpit. "We haven't had a chance to discuss your plans, but you need to know that what I told Captain Wang was all true. The destruction caused by this war has resulted in the worst possible situation imaginable. People are dying everywhere, some from sicknesses, and some from starvation. Others are being killed by people that a little over a month ago, they considered friends. Some of the killers were bad to start with, of course. Most, though, have only recently turned that way. They seem to think that the only, or at least the fastest, way of getting sustenance is to take it from others."

"More immediately, gangs of looters are running rampant throughout Santa Barbara. There is hardly an area that hasn't been overrun by what has become the worst criminal element ever seen in this country. It is much too dangerous for you to go ashore there. Fortunately, you don't have to. The reason we have access to food is because there is a settlement on Catalina Island. We helped them set up, and stop there regularly. We've taken some people there because it is still peaceful."

"At Avalon?" Stacey asked. "That's a nice little town."

"No, I'm afraid Avalon has been taken over by the same kinds of hooligans that are terrorizing Santa Barbara. The settlement is at the other end of the island, the area called Two Harbors, or The Isthmus."

"The Isthmus is a great spot to spend a few peaceful days," Zach allowed, "but there's not much there."

"Before now, just a store, a restaurant, and a small hotel. There's also a little schoolhouse, which will be getting plenty of use. The people have been able to live there without interference because there isn't much there for people to steal. The thugs haven't bothered to invade them like they did Avalon. Not yet, anyway. There were about a hundred and fifty people there to start with, and they accepted the newcomers without qualms when they learned a little about them.

"You see, the people we took there are survivalists. They had to leave their homes because they lived in areas that either were destroyed by bombs or were overrun by terrorists. They are tough, but the numbers were stacked too heavily against them and they had to get away. We came across them on the docks of Port Hueneme after they fought their way there. They'd come in vans and pickups, so they managed to bring most of the supplies they had stored with them. The people that were already at The Isthmus are not survivalists in the strict definition of the term, but people living in an isolated area like that are natural survivors.

"We figured The Isthmus was a logical match for those people. Fortunately, the people already there saw it the same way. What the newcomers brought with them, plus what the locals had on hand, has allowed them to live rather comfortably so far, and those supplies should carry them for another few months. There's no sign of any radioactivity getting out that far, so the fishing is good, and they have buffalo."

"Buffalo?" commented Ron. "On an island?"

"Yes," said Kotchel. "Most people don't know it, but a herd was started there many years ago. So, they have fish and meat, and the newcomers immediately planted crops. They're in pretty good shape."

"As I remember, it's too hilly and dry there for crops," said Zach.

"We took them tractors, so they're cultivating the hills. As far as water goes, there are a couple of wells, and we gave them a water supply by towing a badly damaged guided missile cruiser out there. It is no longer useful militarily, but the desalinization plant is working just fine. We have an almost unlimited supply of diesel, so we can keep things going indefinitely."

"You said the new people were at the docks of Port Hueneme," Zach recalled. "That's a navy base. Wasn't it hit hard?"

"Yes, by missiles, but they were conventional. The base was wiped out, several docks were totaled, and all the gasoline tanks blew. However, there is enough dock space left for our use, and four diesel tanks are intact and full. One small naval craft and we are the only ships using the docks and the fuel, so what is there is more than sufficient. We collected all the surviving naval personnel we could find and set them up there. They're guarding the facility."

Kotchel ended his summary by saying, "That's pretty much the situation as it stands. I'm telling you all this because we have an agreement with them. When we find compatible people, we take them there. That's where you need to go."

"Eventually, we will," Zach told him. "But, first I need to get to Santa Maria."

"I told you," Captain Kotchel said emphatically, "it's too dangerous."

"I heard you, but that's where I'm going," Zach stated flatly.

Chapter 40

"WHAT'S so all fired important in Santa Maria that you'd risk your life for it?" Kotchel wanted to know.

"My parents," said Zach, not backing down in the slightest.

"Are they still alive?"

"With no communications, I don't know for sure. But if enemy attacks didn't kill them, then I'm sure they are."

Kotchel tried not to sound too fatalistic but he didn't beat around the bush. "It's likely they would have run out of food weeks ago. Besides, they can't be young, and there are many tough young hoodlums out there. An older couple wouldn't stand much of a chance if they were attacked."

"My parents would," Zach argued. "And, they wouldn't have run out of food; they are survivalists. They have twelve months worth of food and water on hand at all times."

"The very thing gangs go after," Kotchel pointed out.

"In this case, at the risk of their own lives. My dad and mom keep weapons on hand at all times, too. I've seen my father hit a running coyote at a hundred yards. My mom is just about as good."

"It'll be people after their food, not coyotes."

"He was in the thick of things in Viet Nam. If anyone can protect himself and his loved ones, it's my dad."

Kotchel sized Zach up. "And he raised a son who's just as tough."

"I wouldn't say that, but I'm just as determined."

The Coast Guard officer sighed. "I can't stop you, but I still advise against it." He could see that Zach would not be taking his advice, so he asked, "Are you going by yourself?"

Ron spoke up. "I'm going with him."

"Me, too," added George.

"Me, three," said Denise.

"In view of what the captain told us, we may have to rethink your going," Stacey said to her daughter.

"It's because of what he said that it's important that I go," argued Denise. "I'm the best shot on this boat."

"I'm a pretty good shot," Ron said.

Denise put her hands on her hips and stared him down. "I'm better."

"She probably is, Ron," Zach told him. "She'd be a terrific back-up for us."

He turned to Stacey. The two communicated in the silent way couples do after years together, even in a situation as unprecedented as this. Stacey bit her lip but nodded.

"No going off on one of your wild goose chases, Denise," her mother said to the girl, reluctantly relenting.

"I understand the situation, Mom. I'll be right by Dad's side at all times."

"I don't know if this is a family of 'survival-ists'," Kotchel said, "but it's obvious you're a group of survivors."

"We face situations squarely," said Stacey.

"Okay, at least accept some advice. Forget Santa Barbara. Go up the coast twenty miles or so. You can go ashore at the area between Santa Barbara and where Vandenberg Air Force Base was before it was destroyed. Gaviota State Park. I would normally suggest even farther north, where you would be closer to Santa Maria when you went ashore, but we've seen some bad looking characters along the beaches there, so I wouldn't recommend that. From the sea, it looked like Gaviota was deserted when we passed by last week. There is not much beach there, but there is a spot where we could get you in close and you might go ashore unnoticed. Don't try it with that little dinghy you have hanging back there, though. We're heading north, anyway, so we'll go with you, and I'll have a man take you to shore on our skiff."

"That's very thoughtful of you, captain," Zach said sincerely.

"I'm not just being thoughtful. If you're willing, I'd like you to do something for the people at The Isthmus."

"What do they need?"

"Seeds. They planted everything they had, but we keep adding people. They need a lot more vegetables. Large portions of the state are contaminated, so we can't get seeds in those places. Santa Maria escaped radiation, and I don't believe any of the rampant diseases have hit there yet."

"As I recall, there are several nurseries there. If any are still in existence and still have seeds, we'll find a way to get them."

"I thought as much."

"Anything else?"

"Yes. Advice on how to travel. You will be closer to Santa Maria from where we drop you off than from Santa Barbara, but walking will take too much time. You'll need to drive. I see you have those barrels of diesel back there, so look for a vehicle that uses diesel. Most gasoline tanks blew, and so did a lot of diesel tanks, so there is little fuel available. Having your own is the safest bet.

"How do we get a vehicle?"

"There are cars and trucks abandoned everywhere. For the most part, the owners were killed either in the attacks or by carjackers since. The thugs drive the vehicles until they run out of fuel, and then they just leave them by the side of the road. If you can find a four-wheel drive, so much the better but you'll probably have to take the first diesel vehicle you find. Do you have small cans to haul fuel?"

"Yes, a two-gallon can."

"That won't be enough. We'll supply you with a couple of five-gallon cans."

"I really appreciate that, captain. I think

one is enough, but these aren't normal circumstances. Based on what we've run into so far,
and from what you've told us, it's better to have
the extra can, just in case."

"Expect the unexpected is the motto we live
by these days."

Chapter 41

THEY reasoned that most of the people they had to watch out for were probably night owls. The thugs would probably be marauding until the wee hours of the morning and wouldn't start up again until early afternoon. Therefore, it made sense to hit the beach just before sunrise. That should give Zach and his small crew time to find a vehicle and get to Santa Maria before the bad guys went on the prowl. Not having to fight their way to Zach parents' house would be a relief after what they'd been through so far.

The cutter sailed north the afternoon before to check activities in the waters there. While they were gone, the *La Sirena* sailed to a position about a thousand yards offshore at a spot they reckoned was where they could go ashore safely. The place appeared to be easily accessible by sea, but not so easy to get to by land. Even in peacetime, it was unlikely that anyone used the tiny beach much. Now, they hoped, it wasn't being used at all.

As planned, the cutter came back from its northerly tour and arrived at their location at four-thirty in the morning. Zach, Denise, Ron, and George boarded the skiff the cutter sent over. Each of them wore one of the backpacks the Arthur family used for outings. Each had enough food and water for two days. All four people wore jackets, but they carried no extra clothes. Zach had a few toilet supplies and his mother's herbs in his pack, George carried medical supplies, and Denise carried the 8 X 35mm binoculars. They all had AK-47s slung over their shoulders and carried fifty rounds of ammunition in their packs. They had filled the two five gallon cans with diesel the night before and loaded those onto the skiff. Ron carried the nozzle they would use to put the diesel into whatever vehicle they found. He also carried a flashlight.

The cutter was going to be back in the area at midnight, and the plan was for them to signal with the flashlight. It wasn't a strong light, but it would almost surely be the only light in the area at night. If they weren't there, the cutter would return the following night. If they weren't there the second night – well, in view of the precarious situation they were going into, they figured there was no point in planning beyond the second night.

The skiff moved toward shore with the motor running at low rpms to avoid excess noise, so it took almost ten minutes to get there. The sun was still well hidden behind the eastern land-

scape, but the before-sunrise light was enough
for them to see shapes and forms. The spot they
chose was a small beach bordered on either side
by low, rocky cliffs. By putting the motor in
reverse gear at the lowest possible rpms, the
pilot was able to keep the skiff a little behind
where the waves were breaking until the four
were in position to jump. When they were ready,
he put it in neutral and let a wave carry them
part way. The second the four went over the bow,
the pilot shoved it in reverse and accelerated,
backing it away before a breaking wave hit the
boat and shoved it ahead, which almost certainly
would have beached it.

The four jumped at the same instant. They
landed in thigh-deep water. The footing underneath was rocky, but the rocks were small
and didn't hinder their progress. Zach and Ron
carried the five-gallon cans as they jumped into
the roiling waters, but George lost his balance
when he landed in the turbulence.   As he
struggled against the current, Zach grabbed his
arm to keep him upright as they half ran and
half carried him to the beach.

"Thanks for..." George started to say, but cut
it off when Zach put a finger to his lips. The
skiff's engine got loud, but by then it turned
and headed slowly, almost silently, back to the
cutter.

The four sloshed out of the water and onto
a beach that was mostly dirt and rocks. It
sloped up to a rise that was just high enough to
hide the activities of the group. Zach looked at
Denise and cupped his hands around his eyes,
indicating that he wanted the binoculars. He

motioned for the others to stay where they were while he crawled up to look around. If there was anyone looking at the little rise, they would probably see four heads pop up, but it would be unlikely that they would see one if he didn't make any quick movements.

The slightly improving light allowed him to make out a few things in the distance, mostly trees and low hills. Off to the right was the main area of the park, where people would likely be if there were any around. It was still too dark for the binoculars to allow him to see anything in detail, but by steadily training them on a single spot for several seconds, he would be able to determine if there was any movement there.

He concentrated on many spots over a period of five minutes, mostly in that main area. There was no movement while he studied the area but he needed confirmation. He motioned for the others to join him. They crawled to the top of the rise. By pointing, he indicated what area each should scan. After an additional three minutes, they were convinced they were probably alone on this part of the coast. If anyone else was around, they were asleep. For the time being, that served the same purpose.

They stood and walked over the rocky terrain toward the main part of the park. There was now enough light to allow them to skirt around objects. By not kicking rocks and branches, they were able to move almost silently. They crossed under a trestle supporting a railroad bridge and made their way up a slope leading to the park's center. In twenty minutes, they came to a narrow roadway. There were no vehicles on it, suggesting that it was rarely used. But it angled off in a northeasterly direction, and Zach was sure it would lead to highway 101. If the captain was right, they would likely find many abandoned cars on that highway.

Expecting to hear a disturbing silence, they were instead greeted by a few birds chirping and some small animals scurrying about. They heard the hum of insects and the soft croaking of frogs. Although the park was named for the gaviota, the Spanish word for seagull, there were not many of them around. They assumed that was because the ocean current that passed by offshore was from the north, and San Francisco had been nuked. Radioactivity would have killed off most of the fish the seagulls feasted upon. There was no hum of electric wires and no sounds of traffic in the distance.

They trudged on for half an hour before reaching the main highway. The cutter's captain was right. There were cars abandoned all along the roadway. They didn't see any people. The tenth car they came to, a twenty-year-old Mercedes Benz sedan, had a diesel engine. The key was in the ignition. The tires were worn, it was dirty, and it wasn't a four-wheel drive vehicle, but it suited their purposes well enough. They put a little diesel in the tank to make sure the engine was in working condition before putting in more. It took a couple of minutes, but the fuel finally reached the engine, and it started.

"Shall I put it all in?" asked Ron.

"Put all of that one can in. This is probably going to be our transportation all the way to

Santa Maria and back, and we don't want to run out on the way. We will keep the second can in reserve. This old car may guzzle fuel pretty fast, so we may need it for the return trip."

They loaded the cans in the trunk but kept their backpacks and weapons in hand as they started on their way to Santa Maria. Having driven that road before, Zach took the wheel. When driving his family to Santa Maria in the past, he often took Routes 1 and 135 so they could enjoy the scenery, but this time he stayed on the 101. There were abandoned vehicles all along the way, often in the middle of the highway. At times, they had to pull over to the shoulder to get around and twice had to push cars out of the way in order to get through.

As the morning wore on, they saw several people off to the sides of the road. All looked thin and discouraged. It appeared there was longing in their eyes as they watched the Mercedes pass. A couple of the men started running toward the highway when they saw the car coming but it passed by them before they could get to the road. Those in the car didn't dare stop.

On the outskirts of Santa Maria, two motorcycles pulled onto the highway from a side street and caught up to the car quickly.

"Pull over," a large, tattooed man with a patch over one eye ordered as he began to inch closer to the driver's side door.

"Don't have time," Zach called back.

The man took his right hand off the controls and reached into his pocket for a gun. When Zach saw the gun, he hit the gas pedal hard and sped away. The man started shooting as soon as he pointed the gun at the car, but by then the Mercedes had pulled ahead. Bullets hit the back window, but missed the people in the car.

Denise, in the back seat behind the driver, rolled down the window, leaned out, and opened fire with the AK-47 on automatic. She aimed low and her bullets bounced off the highway, but in seconds, the front tires of both bikes blew. One flipped and the other skidded along the highway until it came to a stop. Those in the car had no way of knowing if the drivers survived, but if they did or didn't, they were no longer a threat.

"Were you trying to hit the tires?" Ron asked.

"I thought it best that they didn't have anything to chase us with," she responded matter-of-factly.

"You were right," he said, impressed.

"About the tires?"

"About being a better shot than me," he told her. "And, about the tires. Even if I had time to get a shot off, I wouldn't have thought to incapacitate the vehicles."

"I'm more than just a pretty face," she joked, grinning.

They all laughed, although it was a guarded moment of levity. Zach turned off the highway and they drove through a residential neighborhood that had an eerie look to it. Windows were broken and cars were parked at crazy angles, some up on lawns that looked like they had probably been well maintained until recently. Doors were ajar and several roofs were caved in. Fire had gutted some houses.

"It's around the corner," Zach said before he

turned right onto a street that still had a look of peacefulness to it. It was on the outskirts of town, and the houses on the right side backed up to open fields.

They soon learned that the seemingly peacefulness was a deception. Gunfire echoed down the empty street, emanating from an area ahead of them. Zach slammed on the brakes when he saw two men using an overturned car to rest rifles on. They were shooting at a house on the other side of the street, the right side.

"That's my parents' house they're shooting at," he yelled as he grabbed his weapon and jumped from the Mercedes.

Chapter 42

THE cutter sailed south as soon as the skiff returned from taking Zach and his team ashore. They planned on checking out the area south to Port Hueneme until time to return to pick up the four they had just dropped off.

Stacey and her crew of two hoisted sails and headed the *La Sirena* out to sea as soon as the four had boarded the skiff. Their plan was to stay far enough away from shore to avoid prying eyes until it was dark and time to return for the pickup of their boat mates. When they were fifteen miles out to sea, they dropped the sails and let the boat drift. They sat in the cockpit, resting as the rippling water gently rocked the boat.

"I'll sure be glad to get to that Isthmus place," Millie offered as she reclined on one of the cushions that covered the storage bins at the sides of the cockpit. "A month of walking on water is more than enough for me."

"I like it," said Glen. He and Stacey sat on the cushion on the other side of the cockpit.

"Oh, I like it, too," admitted Millie. "Any time you want to take me out for a leisurely sail on a Sunday afternoon, you've got a willing crewmember. But, these old bones are better suited to a more stable flooring."

"Does that mean you aren't going to ask us to take you back to your hotel?" Stacey asked. She immediately regretted saying it.

Millie's face fell and she sighed. "I have to face facts. My hotel is gone, and it is unlikely I'll ever get back to rebuild it." Then she brightened. "I heard the captain say there's a small hotel on that place called The Isthmus, so I'll see what I can do to help build it up. If more people are going to be staying there, they're going to need an experienced hotel person."

Stacey studied the eighty-year-old woman with respect. "I get the feeling it takes a lot to keep you down,"

"A lot? So far, nothing has, and I don't intend to start getting feeble just yet, either."

"Could you get up a minute, Millie?" Glen asked.

"What? Are you going to test me to see if I can still stand on my own two feet?"

Embarrassed, he stammered, "Ah, er, no, that isn't it. No, I, ah, you see, I saw something on the water north of us, and I want to get the 8x50mm binoculars so I can see what it is."

Millie jumped to her feet. "See," she said, winking at him.

The young man grinned. He decided that she was kidding but wasn't sure how fitting it was for a teenager to joke around with a woman that much older. He lifted the top of the bin and found the binoculars. He replaced the cushion and straightened it for her.

"Stacey," Millie said to his mother, "you're raising a real gentleman here, but I think he needs to lighten up a little sometimes."

"Denise is our jokester," Stacey replied. "Glen has a sense of humor, but he's mostly serious."

"At the moment," he interjected, "and usually for good reason." He removed the binoculars from his eyes and handed them to his mother. "Here, take a look."

Stacey trained the glasses on the location Glen pointed out. After studying the spot for a full thirty seconds, she lowered the glasses and asked her son, "What do you make of it?"

"It's big, but it doesn't look military," he responded. "I thought it looked like a cargo ship, probably one of those container ships." He took the binoculars back and studied it a little more. "It's riding high, so it's empty." He watched it for several minutes. "It looks like it's moving pretty fast for a big ship. It's closer than it should be."

"My fault," Stacey lamented. "We would have seen it sooner if I'd set up watches."

"Wouldn't have made any difference," Millie consoled her. "If we'd seen it an hour ago, how far could we have run? And where to?"

"How long before it gets here, do you think?" Stacey asked Glen.

"Hard to tell. I would guess about two hours. For all I know, though, it might pass by five miles away from us."

"Your best guess?"

"I think it's going to come a lot closer than five miles."

"We'll keep our eye on it and when it gets close, I'll get the engine going, for all the good that will do us."

Glen went forward and positioned himself near the bow. He kept the binoculars trained on the ship. An hour later, he went back to the cockpit. "It's a container ship, all right," he told the women, "but there's something strange about it. It's kinda like it's – armed."

"Armed?" the women said in unison.

"Yeah, but not like a military ship. It has some military tanks and a helicopter on the deck. It has some other stuff, too. Smaller stuff. I can't be sure, but it looks like rocket launchers or something."

Stacey took the binoculars and looked at the ship, then handed the glasses to Millie.

Millie whistled. "Say, these binocs are pretty powerful. I can actually see stuff in detail. Those are tanks, all right. Everything else you said, too."

"Do you see any people?" Stacey asked.

"Everything is really small at this distance, but some things are moving around on the deck."

"Is it possible they're military?" Stacey wondered. "Maybe some army people needed to move some weapons to another location and there was no military transportation available."

"Hold that thought," said Millie.

Forty-five minutes later, there was little reason to hold the thought any longer. Unless military uniforms now consisted of dirty jeans, torn tee-shirts and arm-length tattoos, the people aboard the container ship did not represent any government authority. They did have a bevy of armaments aboard, however. Visible were three tanks, a helicopter, twenty missile launchers and even some old bazookas. Who knew what might be below in the cargo holds.

"What could they want from us?" Stacey wondered. "We can't possibly have anything that would benefit them."

"People like that don't reason things out," said Millie. "It's why they never have much and are always on the prowl."

The big ship's course was not directly at the sailboat. Stacey had the engine running and was prepared to try evasion tactics, but as the container ship approached, it was over a mile-and-a-half further out to sea than the *La Sirena*. It began to slow down, causing the three aboard the sailboat to grab their weapons. The ship was well distant, but they nonetheless eyed it suspiciously.

The container vessel never came to a complete stop. It was close to being at a standstill when it was as close as it would ever be to them, but then its engines revved up and it moved ahead again.

"What was that all about?" Millie asked, not expecting an answer.

She got one. "That," said Glen, pointing toward the stern of the container ship.

The big ship had lowered a forty-foot launch on its seaward side, out of sight of those on the sailboat. When the mother ship had passed, the launch moved directly toward the *La Sirena*, leaving a trail of swirling water in its wake.

With the binoculars, Glen could see that there were six determined looking men aboard. Four had automatic weapons at the ready. One of the others had a bazooka on his shoulder, pointing it in their direction. The launch got closer and, even without the binoculars, they could all see that the sixth had a shell ready to shove into the bazooka's tube.

Chapter 43

Z ACH started shooting while he was still thirty
yards away from the men behind the overturned car. His bullets sprayed the area, and
one hit a man in the arm. He fell to the ground
and grabbed his arm, trying to stop the bleeding.
The other man shuffled around to the front of
the car to get out of the line of fire.

George, who was in the front passenger seat,
slid behind the wheel, drove the Mercedes up to
the overturned car, and stopped in the middle
of the street. Ron and Denise jumped out as he
braked.

A shot from the house hit the lower right leg
of the man who tried to escape by going to the
front of the car. "Stop shooting, I give up!" he
cried. He tossed his rifle into the middle of the
street, threw his hands in the air, and stumbled
over beside his partner. "I give up! I ain't got
no weapon no more!"

Zach grabbed the second guy, raised him up,

and made him stand against the overturned car, his back up against the rusted frame. The man was still trying to stop the bleeding, but Zach, who had seen a lot worse, was paying no attention to the wound. He had his AK-47 pointed at the man. Denise and Ron came around to cover the other man, who was leaning on the car frame for support.

"What the devil are you two trying to do?" Zach barked.

"Them people got food in that house!" the man with the leg wound growled. "We need it."

"And you'd kill them to get it?"

"We told them to give it to us, but they wouldn't."

"Zach, is that you out there?" came a voice from the house.

"Yeah, Dad, it's me. If it's okay, we're coming in. We have a couple of wounded prisoners."

"They're lucky they're not dead!" his father called back.

Zach looked sternly at the man with the leg wound. "He's right, you know. He could just as easily have put that bullet right between your eyes. C'mon, we're going over to the house. They'll have something to clean and bandage your wounds in there."

"That old geezer'll kill us if we go there."

"If he wanted to kill you, you'd be dead! Let's go."

He pushed the two men ahead and was joined by Denise and Ron, their rifles pointed at the men.

"George called out from the car, "I'll stay here and keep an eye out in case they have friends."

"That's a good idea," Zach agreed. "Thanks, George."

With one man limping badly and the other trying to nurse his arm wound, they marched up to the front door. A man in his late sixties opened the door and let them in. He leaned his rifle against a wall and hugged Denise. "My, my, look at you!" He sized her up. "I bet you're as tall as your mother already."

"Still two inches shorter, but I grow that much in a year."

"It's good seeing you, too, Dad," Zach interjected. "But we have a couple of wounded prisoners here. Where's Mom?"

"She's guarding the back. Sometimes one or two of these yokels try to come at us via the open field back there. I'll go get her."

"Ron, do you mind going with him so you can watch the back while she tends to these two?"

"Be glad to," Ron said, following Zach's father through the living room and onto the back patio.

A minute later, Zach's father came back with his wife. She was carrying a 12-guage shotgun but set it aside so she could give Zach and Denise big hugs.

"Hey," the man with the wound in the leg groused, "I'm wounded over here."

She folded her arms and stared at him. "If it had been me, Bob, you'd be dead, not wounded."

"You know these guys, Mom?"

"We gave them some food and told them where they could get more," his mother said. "But they decided it would be easier to come and steal it from us. Stupid mistake."

"Hey, the food you told us about is more than

a hundred miles away and still in the ground. I ain't no stoop laborer."

"You'll learn to be if you want to eat," said Zach's father.

His mother went out into the garage and came back with first aid medications and bandages. She cleaned and bandaged the wounds while the senior Arthur turned to his son. "We heard there are some crops in a few isolated places in this valley and more in the central valley. They're drying up, so we were going to go get some before these goofballs came by and distracted us. We have enough to last awhile, but we could always use more."

"Dad, you need more than food. You have to think about finding another location."

"We've already decided that. We have the SUV packed with all our food, water, and other supplies. That's why your mother had to go out there for the bandages. What we were going to pick up in the fields would have been given us fresh food until we were on our way to where we were going. We heard of a place that some survivalists set up in the mountains. We figured they'd accept us if we brought extra food."

"Survivalists?" asked Denise, remembering the Coast Guard Captain's warning. "What's the name of the place?"

"Avalon," the elder Arthur said.

"Avalon? No, Grandpa! Hooligans are running it. The captain told us."

"Captain?"

"Just a minute," Zach interjected. "Did you say mountains? The Avalon Denise is talking about is on Catalina Island."

"I know the Avalon on Catalina," the older man said. "Nice place, but not the one I'm talking about. This one is in the high Sierras."

"That's a long way away Dad. We heard of another place, and we're going there from here."

"Oh?"

They were interrupted by Ron yelling from the back. "We have company. "I'm going to need some help."

Zach's mother finished tending to the wounded men, picked up her shotgun, and trained it on the two guys. "You go help that man," she told the others. "I'll keep these two covered."

Before they got to the back porch, the three heard a growing roar.

A motorcycle gang of more than fifty armed thugs was converging on the house through the open field behind it.

Chapter 44

THE boat that was lowered into the water by the container ship was bearing down on the sailboat. Glen watched it nervously. "What are we going to do, Mom? They outnumber us, they have that bazooka thingy, and we can't outrun them."

"The first thing we'll do is find out how good their nerves are," she responded through clenched teeth. "You two lie down on the deck so you won't be easy targets. Shoot at anyone on that boat who makes a move."

"What are you going to do?" Millie asked.

Stacey put the throttle in full ahead and turned the *La Sirena* directly into the path of the other boat. "I'm going to ram them," she said, her eyes boring in on the man piloting the other boat.

"Couldn't have come up with a better plan myself," said Millie. She sprawled out on the deck and, although she didn't have a specific target, she got off a few shots with her .357 magnum.

The other boat was still out of range for accuracy, but the bullets sent the men on it scrambling for cover. The one with the bazooka fell to the deck but got back up immediately. The fellow with the shell also jumped up. He still had the shell in his hand, and he prepared to ram it into the bazooka's tube.

Glen put his AK-47 on automatic and sprayed the area where the bazooka was. He couldn't tell if the bullets hit anyone but both men and the bazooka hit the deck once again. The shell rolled overboard and sank into the ocean.

By this time, the two boats were fifty yards apart. The sailboat was closing in at full speed. The other boat, which had been heading for the sailboat from the start, didn't alter its course. It wasn't at full speed, but half speed was faster than the sailboat's full speed.

In a few seconds, the distance was reduced to thirty yards. Then, twenty and closing.

Stacey's fierce gaze never left the eyes of the man piloting the other boat. He tried to look as determined as she was, but the nearer the boats got to one another, the less he was able to control his emotions. At the last second, he panicked and cranked the wheel hard to port to avoid the head-on collision.

The forward hull of the *La Sirena* scraped the aft part of the powerboat's hull as it turned away, but neither boat was badly damaged. The sailboat's bowsprit shot out over the stern of the power boat as it passed, taking part of the aft rail and a man who had tried to hide there, high in the air. The rail hung from the bowsprit as the boats separated but the man was unable to grab on to either boat. He fell into the ocean, never to be seen again.

Stacey turned away and slowed the engine so she and Glen could check the damage. Glen had already run forward and was looking over the side of the bow that hit the powerboat.

"An ugly scrape," he called back to his mother, "but no holes. The roller furling looks damaged, though."

The roller furling was what let out the jib sail at the front of the boat, but they had no need for it at the moment, so Stacey could concentrate on what they needed to do to stay alive.

The powerboat came to a halt a hundred yards away, and the men aboard checked for damages to their own boat. As was the case with the sailboat, the damages were mostly superficial. But the men aboard were now angry. Whatever their intent was before, their faces now showed that they would settle for nothing less than sinking the sailboat. Their caution increased to the same degree as their anger, however, so they stood behind the main cabin to focus on their target. Even the man piloting the boat stayed low. Everything but his eyes and the top of his head was hidden.

The nearly invisible pilot turned the boat and moved it slowly in the direction of the sailboat. This time, he didn't attempt to get in close. When he felt they were close enough to take a shot with the bazooka, he stopped and peered malevolently over the cabin at the people who attempted to ram his boat.

Stacey saw what the men on the powerboat were doing and was worried. They were too far away for her to try to ram them again, and it was obvious they were going to stay just far enough away to avoid a repeat of their first encounter. She looked futilely around, but there simply wasn't anywhere they could escape to.

She could see the bazooka clearly enough, but the man holding it was mostly hidden by the cabin. His angry face was visible, but it presented too small a target for them to hit with bullets at that distance. Only the tops of their heads and fierce eyes were visible. Except for the man holding the rocket shell. All they could see of him was his hands. The rocket shell itself was all too visible.

In seconds, the shell that would tear a hole in the *La Sirena*'s hull and sink her and her crew would be on its way. There was nothing they could do to stop it.

Chapter 45

"I WAS too busy at the time to notice, but do you have a vehicle?" Zach's father asked as they watched the motorcycles bearing down on them. "There's no way we can fight off that many hoodlums."

"It's out front," said Zach'.

"Good. You have automatic weapons; see if you can slow them down. I'll get your Mom, and we'll get the SUV out of the garage." He rushed back into the house.

The motorcycles were within fifty yards of the house, though the field was bumpy. Zach could see that two were riding double, and he thought he saw that one of the riders on the back was wearing an eye patch.

"I'll take the ones on the right," Ron said.

"Okay, I'll take out those on the left," Zach added. "Denise..."

"The center," she said before he could finish. "I'm going for their tires again."

"Good idea. The more bikes we can take out of action, the better.

They opened fire. Dirt spewed up in front of the motorcycles and none stopped at first. Soon, though, the front tires of the front bikes burst and they went down. One wobbled to a stop, but the others flipped and crashed. Those behind the leaders began hitting the downed bikes or sliding to a stop off to the side.

"Let's go," yelled the elder Arthur from inside the house.

The motorcyclists were in disarray, and none were heading for them at the moment, so the three turned and rushed into the house.

"We're ready," said Zach's mother as the three got to the living room. "Dad's got the SUV started and the garage door open." She started for the door leading to the garage.

"Hey, what about us?" one of the wounded men said. The two of them were sitting on the sofa where Zach's mother had kept them under guard.

"The house is all yours," she called over her shoulder as she left.

"Huh?" the man said, looking around the living room.

"Enjoy it while you can," said Zach as he, Ron and Denise darted out the front door.

The SUV, a four-wheel drive Ford, was on the street next to the Mercedes, which George already had running.

"Where to?" called Zach's mother from within the SUV.

"We need to find a nursery," replied Zach as he opened the front driver's side door to the

Mercedes. George, realizing that the Arthur men would be likely to know each other's moves, relinquished the wheel and slid over to the passenger seat. Ron and Denise jumped in the back.

"Nursery? What for?" Mae Arthur wanted to know.

"Seeds. The people at The Isthmus need them."

"We've got thousands we were taking with us to the mountains."

"Then let's head straight for Highway 101," Zach said.

They hesitated when they heard the roar of motorcycles behind the house start up again. "They'll see we're gone and come after us," Zach's father said. "They'll have to go to the main road and come here, the same way you did. The sounds of their motors are moving in that direction. We need to detour around the back way."

"We'll follow you," said Zach.

"What's happening?" George wanted to know. "It was really quiet out here until the shooting started."

"That's the way it is these days," Zach mused. "We'll explain what happened this time as we go."

They drove in the opposite direction of the main highway, turning left at the first corner.

The two wounded men came out onto the front steps and watched them disappear. A few seconds later, the first of the motorcycles, many of them now carrying two people, turned onto the street.

Pulling up to the curb in front of the house, they looked over at the two men who clearly didn't belong.

"We're looking for the people who have a bunch of food," a large, scraggly-bearded man who was riding on the back of the first motorcycle called out.

"They went that way," the man with the leg wound called back, pointing toward the corner the Arthur family and friends had just turned. "They got the food and all kinds of other stuff with them."

"Other stuff? How about gas? They have any of that?"

"Yeah, they got some full cans in the back of the SUV"

"A bunch of hoarders. Is this their place?"

"No," the wounded man replied, "It's ours."

"Yours?"

"Yep," the man said proudly.

The bearded man and five others pulled out a variety of handguns and peppered the two men on the front step with bullets.

"Ain't no way I'm gonna let people that shoot at me live," the bearded man snarled as he put a last bullet into the man's head. As soon as they were sure the "home owners" were dead, they jumped off their bikes and, stepping over the dead men, went to investigate the house.

A few minutes later, having found nothing to eat and little they wanted to steal in the house, they came out and looked around. The bearded leader said to a man with a patch over one eye, "Blinky, are you sure it's the same people?"

"Same MO," replied Blinky, trying to make it

sound like a certainty. "They shot the tires out from under us on the 101, just like they did back there in the field. Gotta be the same ones."

"Then they'll probably head back to the 101," the leader surmised. He turned back to the man with the eye patch. "You take twenty guys and go watch for them on the 101, south of town. Me and the others will try to catch up to them. Between us, we'll have them pinned down within the hour."

Chapter 46

THERE was no way to stop them from shooting the rocket, but a split second before it fired, Stacey made one last, desperate move. She shoved the throttle full ahead and cranked the wheel hard to starboard. The shell from the bazooka, a small rocket with the power to stop a tank, whistled by, barely missing the stern.

She knew it was a temporary reprieve, at best, but at least they had another minute or two of life. She could see the man with the bazooka zeroing in on the sailboat again. This time, he would be ready for any diversionary tactic she might employ. She was too far away to try to ram them again. They could get off four or five rockets in the time it would take to reach them, and they wouldn't miss a target on a straight course, either.

The *La Sirena* would be sunk long before it had a chance to get near them a second time. Even at that distance, she could see the evil smile on the face of the man with the bazooka. *Great*, she thought, *we've come across one of those fiends who enjoys killing.*

"I'm sorry, Glen," she said. "You, too, Millie. There's nothing more I can do."

"Maybe not, but I can at least try to nail one or two before I die," Millie growled. She began shooting at the distant boat.

Glen followed suit.

The men on the launch were under cover, but instinct told them to duck, so the bazooka was momentarily out of action. The bullets flew by without coming close to hitting anyone.

All the crew on the sailboat had gained was another few seconds.

The smile on the face of the bazooka trigger-man broadened. He trained the weapon on the sailboat and called for a shell to be loaded. The second man picked up a shell and shoved it into the tube.

Before they could get a shot off, the launch raised high in the air, knocking all of the men down and causing the bazooka to fall into the ocean. The nose of a submarine shot up right at the launch's bow, creating a massive wave that lifted it and threw it backward. It rolled over and capsized, throwing all the men into the angry water.

The submarine surfaced, stopped its forward motion, and backed up to where the swamped launch was laying half out of the water; the overturned boat was sinking rapidly. Two of the men were trying desperately to get a small dinghy loose from the davits that attached it to the launch. A third person was swimming around the bow of the boat, trying to get back to them – and away from the sub. There was no sign of the other men.

Captain Wang, joined by two armed crewmembers, climbed onto to the conning tower deck and watched as the bad guys got the nine-foot fiberglass dinghy loose from the davits and climbed aboard. They all watched as the third man managed to get to the dinghy just as the launch sunk into the ocean.

The Chinese captain called to them. "I suggest you head for shore."

If the men were surprised there was a Chinese submarine in California waters, or that the officer in charge spoke English, they didn't show it. They looked out to sea, but the container ship was off in the distance and heading away at a fast pace. They apparently anticipated that would be the case, because their expressions didn't change when they looked back. The only concern they expressed was for the unfortunate situation in which they suddenly found themselves. "We don't have a motor," the man who'd held the bazooka yelled back. "We don't even have oars."

"Well, now, you do have a dilemma, don't you?" Captain Wang was not sympathetic.

"You sunk our boat!" the man screamed.

"Because you were trying to do the same to friends of mine," Wang reasoned. "A fitting response, I'd say." The dinghy drifted close enough for him to get a good look at the men and converse just by talking a little louder than normal. He looked the three men over. None had anything but what they were wearing. "I'll tell you what I'll do. I will tow you ten or fifteen miles from here, far enough away to be sure you can't get back to bother these people again. I will take you to within a mile of shore, and you can paddle with your arms to get the rest of the way in."

"By hand? That will take hours!"

"Exactly."

By that time, the *La Sirena* had motored up alongside the submarine, on the opposite side of where the men sat in the dinghy.

"Captain Wang," Stacey called, "We thank you for saving us."

He went over to the other side of the conning tower. "Ah, Mrs. Arthur, so good to see you again."

"In this case, I can assure you the pleasure is all mine!"

"No, not entirely. It is always a pleasure to see my friends." He explained that he was going to take the three men far away.

"Good! We dropped Zach, Denise, and the other two men off this morning. The three of us are alone out here.

"Yes, I know."

"You know?"

"We have a periscope."

"Which also explains how you knew we were under attack." She voiced in a moment of realization. "It continues to be in our favor that you and your submarine are in the vicinity. What are you going to do after you take those men to an isolated spot?"

"As we agreed to do, we will once again become inconspicuous."

Chapter 47

AFTER making the first left turn following their quick departure from his house, Zach's father turned several more times. Zach understood they were simple evasion tactics and kept pace. Those on the motorcycles were too far back to see any of the moves, so they wouldn't be able to follow easily.

Fifteen minutes and twelve turns later, the elder Arthur pulled over to the side of a quiet street. There were several burned out houses nearby, but it appeared that the damaged happened weeks before, and there was no evidence of any people in the area. They surveyed the houses and the street for several minutes to be sure they were alone, and then they got out of their cars.

"We need a plan," the elder Arthur said when they met on the street.

"Yes, we do," agreed Zach. "But first, we all need to know one another. These are my friends,

George and Ron. George and Ron, meet Glen and Mae Arthur."

"So, that's where young Glen got his name," George observed. "I suspect he's proud."

"I can't say if he is," said the older Glen, "but it's for sure that I'm proud he's my grandson."

"I don't recall your mentioning a George or a Ron in the past," said Mae. "Are these new friends?"

"You're as sharp as ever, Mom. Yes, they are, and let me tell you how we happened to get together." He gave his parents a quick rundown regarding what had taken place in the last month, ending with their trip to Santa Maria. "I'm afraid I recognized one of the motorcycle gang members as one of those that Denise shot the motorcycle out from under," he admitted. "We probably led them to you."

"Don't fret yourself over that," his father told him, "because it isn't true. If they had been following you, they would have come in from the front. That gang has been checking us out from the back of the house for the last couple of days. I think they picked that field because they could spread out and hit us with large numbers. The two of us with our single shot guns couldn't have done what you three did with your automatic weapons. But, even with those weapons, there's just too many to fight off. We knew it was coming, and that's why we were packed and ready to go."

Zach looked over at the SUV. "That looks like a gas powered car," he said. "How'd you get gas? On that note, how are they getting gas for their motorcycles?"

"I don't know about them, but I anticipated there would be a gas shortage, so I filled up the tank and twelve five-gallon cans while there was still a gas station or two intact. I hear that their tanks ran dry the next day, and there are no other ready sources. I haven't driven the car since. I figured I would have enough to get to that survivalist camp in the mountains, and that was about it."

"Exactly where is that place."

"To be honest, I only have a general idea."

"Well, I think you two should come with us."

"I agree," Glen Arthur said. "We should stick together. We're family."

"Which brings us to the plan. The Coast Guard cutter I told you about is scheduled to pick us up tonight at midnight at Gaviota State Park." He looked at his watch. It was almost noon. "We have twelve hours to get there."

"More than enough time," his father said, "if not for that motorcycle gang. Did you come in on the 101?"

"Yes. That's where the two motorcycles tried to ambush us."

"They'll be watching for us there. We can try Highway 135. Hopefully they won't have it under surveillance, too."

"They're doing all this for a little food and some supplies?"

"That's like gold these days. Besides, they've been watching us, so they know we have solar panels, batteries, and even some walkie-talkies. And, now that you're here, they have a chance at getting some slaves."

"Slaves?"

"That's what I've heard they've started doing. People like that don't like working, so they're taking men to do the work for them. They want women around to do their bidding." He looked at Denise, and then turned back to his son. "You need to be darn sure you don't let our little girl here get taken by those thugs."

"Let 'em try," Denise exclaimed, sticking her AK-47 out at arm's length so her grandfather could see that she was ready for them.

Zach grinned. "There'd be a lot of dead ones."

"But," his father opined sadly, "that'd still leave a lot of live ones. What say we not get in that situation? Follow me. I'll take streets alongside Highway 135 and we can stop and check every now and then to see if they have the highway staked out."

They drove through a burned-out business district and on to a stretch of road that fronted the highway. They stopped at the end of the first block on that street, and Zach and his father got out and walked over to the corner of a building to look at the highway. The elder Arthurs took a set of binoculars he had in the SUV, so both men were able to survey the highway.

They saw no activity, so they moved two blocks and repeated the procedure. The fourth time, Zach was first to the corner of a building and, immediately after focusing on the highway, he motioned for his father to use caution. The motorcycle gang was there.

"Any thoughts?" Zach asked after his father had studied the area for a minute or two. Although the bikers were well over a mile away, the ex-army ranger whispered.

"It's them all right," said the elder Arthur. A combat veteran himself, he, too, whispered. "There's not many of them, though."

"Yeah, I saw that... and that's exactly what worries me."

Chapter 48

"WHY?" the elder Arthur asked. "The fewer the bett... ahhh, I get your drift." He pointed to their cars. "Okay then, let's go take a look."

They went back to the cars and trained their binoculars on the street ahead of them. The street angled slightly down, but they could see a couple of helmeted heads in the distance.

"They must have every southbound street covered," said the older man. "What we'll have to do is go back seven or eight blocks and head west to Guadalupe. There are some country roads west of the town that eventually lead to Highway 1. The intersections are far enough south that we should be able to avoid these guys. How are you fixed for fuel?"

"The tank is about empty, but we have another five gallons in the trunk."

"That should be enough," his father said. "I doubt they have binoculars and probably can't see us. But to be on the safe side, let's back up slowly and in a straight line for a few blocks. By that time, the distance and the earth's curvature will definitely have us out of their sight. We can put the fuel in, then head for Guadalupe."

They backed away carefully. If anyone was watching from a distance, they couldn't see the cars move. Fifteen minutes later, the last five gallons of diesel was in the Mercedes, and the two cars were speeding as fast as they could around stalled autos, toward Guadalupe, a small town west of Santa Maria. Again, they saw few people, and most of them were just sitting forlornly along either side of the road.

"Grandpa" Glen took several side streets after they passed through Guadalupe proper, and they ended up on a single lane road that passed through an area of small hills. It took more than three hours for them to get to the outskirts of Orcutt, a town south of Guadalupe. They skirted around the town and finally arrived at Highway 1.

They were several miles south of Santa Maria and were confident they had escaped the motorcycle gang that was after them. The sun was rolling down toward the ocean, its light shining on the highway in front of them. It reflected off the windshields of several vehicles that were blocking the road. After a quick discussion, they agreed that Zach and Ron would drive to the blockade in the Mercedes to find out what was happening. The others remained in the SUV a hundred yards back.

When they arrived, Zach and Ron saw there were six or seven armed men behind the cars.

Taking their weapons with them, they got out of
the car and walked over to the first car. "Why
are you blocking the road?" Zach asked.

"We are the appointed leaders for this area,"
a gruff looking, overweight man of about fifty
said from behind the car. "Where is it you're
going?"

"To Gaviota."

"You may pass, but you have to leave your
vehicles here."

"We can't go on foot," Zach protested. "We
don't have the time, and we have things with
us, plus some elderly people."

"You are not allowed to take anything out of
the area."

"By whose order?"

"I told you, we've been appointed."

"By whom?"

You ask too many questions! Now, go get the
other vehicle and bring it here."

He eyed the AK-47s Zach and Ron were
carrying. All the weapons the men behind the
cars had appeared to be single shot or, at best,
semi-automatic. "Leave your weapons. No one
except us can have weapons."

"By order of. . . ?"

"Just do as I say."

Zach and Ron exchanged glances. They
backed slowly toward the Mercedes.

"Where are you going?" the overweight "leader"
demanded.

"You ordered us to go get the other car."

"Leave those automatic weapons here."

"No can do!" said Zach as he and Ron eased
into the Mercedes.

Several of the men got up, went to the front of the cars, and watched suspiciously as Zach backed the Mercedes away. Unlike the forlorn people they saw off to the sides of the roads, none of these people appeared to be undernourished.

"What was that all about?" Zach's father asked when the Mercedes was alongside the Ford SUV.

"It's not good," Zach told him. "They claim to have some kind of authority, and they want everything we've got."

"All our food?" asked Mae, who'd come over to the car.

"Food, cars, guns, everything."

"Why, that's robbery," she said.

"They look to me to be the same as the guys who stole my boat," said Ron, "except these guys are scamming people instead of outright robbing them."

"I'd have shared food with them if they were in need," Glen Arthur said, "but if that's the kind of people they are, they're not getting a blasted thing from me."

"Well, Dad, that's the kind of people they are," Zach advised him. "So is there another route we can take down to Gaviota?"

"It's the long way, but we can go west into Vandenberg. There are some back roads that will take us near the coast and then south. I'm not all that familiar with the roads, though, and if we run into trouble, we'll have a tough time making your midnight rendezvous."

Zach glanced back at the men at the road-block. Several had taken a few steps toward them and were watching them intently. Several others got in the cars and started them. "Expect trouble," he said.

"Okay, here's what we'll do. I'll start my SUV and turn it around quick. You stay right behind me. If they come after us, they'll have to stop to pick up their buddies, so we'll have a good head start. The sun is going down, but I'm not going to turn on my lights. I'm going to be making a lot of turns, so keep alert."

"I'm with you, Dad."

"One thing first," Glen said as he walked to the back of the Mercedes. He smashed the brake lights and then did the same to the SUV. "No point in our brakes giving us away on the turns."

"Great thinking, Dad," the younger man beamed.

They walked to their cars slowly so as not to give the men at the roadblock a warning that they were planning a quick getaway. As soon as everyone was in their cars, all their movement sped up. Glen started the SUV and in almost the same motion, he shot backwards across the highway, turned and was on his way north in seconds, Zach was right behind him.

It took a few seconds for the startled road-blockers to react, but the cars moved forward to pick up the men who were standing, and then there were four cars in pursuit.

Chapter 49

STACEY, Glen, and Millie sailed the *La Sirena* to within one hundred yards of the beach off Gaviota State Park before eleven p.m. It was just shallow enough to anchor there with the extra length of chain and line they acquired for their summer cruise.

They watched the beach anxiously for the flashlight signal. The plan was for the signal to occur at midnight. Stacey reasoned that the sailboat would be visible in the moonlight to anyone looking for it, so Zach would signal if he was there. There was no signal.

A little before midnight, they saw the ghostly shadow of the cutter arrive and stop a thousand yards further out. They soon heard the soft purr of the skiff's motor heading in their direction. A few minutes later, it pulled up alongside the *La Sirena*.

"Permission to come aboard?" It was Captain Kotchel, himself.

Stacey gave permission and put the boarding ladder over the side for the officer to climb aboard. The seaman piloting the skiff tied it to the boarding ladder and waited there.

When he was aboard, the captain asked Stacey, "Has there been a signal?"

"Not yet." She looked at her watch. "It's just now midnight, so it should come any minute now."

They watched the beach for a few minutes, and then the captain asked, "How was your day on the water?"

"Oh, boy," said Millie. "Tell him, Stacey."

"Oh, it sounds like there's something to tell."

"There definitely is. Glen, you and Millie watch for the signal while I fill the captain in on what happened today. She told Kotchel everything, ending with what the Chinese submarine had done for them.

"That's really amazing, and it justifies our agreeing to supply them. Maybe Captain Wang was being truthful." He thought for a second or two, and then spoke again. "To be honest, however, that container ship has more of my interest right now. Tell me more about it, and remember that even the smallest detail may be useful. We need as much information as possible."

"Glen looked it over thoroughly. Glen, can you tell the captain all that you saw?"

Stacey kept her eye on the beach while Glen gave the Coast Guard officer a full report of everything he saw on board the ship.

Kotchel nodded when Glen mentioned tanks and rocket launchers. It was apparent the captain was committing information to memory, but it also appeared that not all of it was news.

"The rocket launchers... were they the hand held kind, or were they bigger?"

"All I saw were the small ones like the bazooka they tried to hit us with. They had some bigger things, though. I thought those were for missiles, but they might have been for rockets. I'm sorry, but I'm not all that familiar with those types of weapons."

"Don't worry about it, son. Until now, there's been no reason for you to be."

"Now, though..." Glen's voice trailed off.

"Yes, now, though..." The captain knew what was in the teenager's mind, and he put a hand on the young man's shoulder. "Keep in mind, son, that there are still lots of good people out there. In time, it will again be unimportant that young people know things like that."

Millie, who heard the entire conversation, added, "He's right, Glen. There have always been nuts out there to cause wars. This last one was the biggest mess they have made so far. But we've cleaned up their messes before, and we'll clean this one up, too.

"Thanks, both of you," said Glen. "Actually, I've been thinking the same thing."

"You have?" said Kotchel.

"Sure. Most people don't want to live in a world where everyone is shooting at everyone else, so it has to be fixed."

"Simple and logical," the Coast Guard officer responded thoughtfully.

"Absolutely," Millie said, "and I'm sure it will happen in time. But first, let's get back to

262   Albert A. Correia

something a little more current. Captain, I could
tell that you were not surprised by much of what
Glen told you about the big ship. Why?"

"Even though most of our communications
systems were knocked out, we still get snatches
of information here and there by handheld
transceivers – walkie-talkies is probably what
you call them. There have been reports of that
ship hitting both land targets and ships at sea.
They don't seem to have any specific target or
goal, and they steal whatever they can find. It
started in the Pacific Northwest several weeks
ago. As near as we can guess, those people took
over a container ship in a port up in that area.
Seattle is completely gone, so maybe Portland,
which still has a few facilities functioning – more
or less. They stole most of the weapons from a
destroyed army base in Oregon and probably got
their missile launchers off an abandoned navy
ship that foundered off the coast of Northern
California.

"We don't know for sure that's how they got
their missile launchers, but I say that because
we've taken a few off missile cruisers ourselves
for use on our little ship, so it can be done."

Millie asked, "You have missiles on your
boat?"

"We're the biggest U.S. Military ship around
right now. The only other is a little boat the
navy used for ferrying people around. It's armed,
too, but it's smaller than our cutter. We don't
have to tend buoys right away, so we borrowed
some launchers and missiles, and now we're a
warship. Most of what we have are the kind
designed to shoot down aircraft, few of which

are in the air right now, but we managed to get some rocket launchers and a few guns, too. Not a lot, but we're not unarmed.

"Anyway, they used the weapons they stole to make a warship out of the cargo carrier. And, a lethal one at that. We heard that they hit Santa Cruz last week, killing dozens and stealing all the food and fuel that was still there. Now, they're here."

"Do you think the people are military?" asked Millie.

"No. Word has it that there are a couple of ex-merchant marines piloting the ship, but most of the others are dock workers, boaters, or petty thieves. They must have someone who can fly a helicopter and a few who can drive tanks; otherwise, they don't seem to have any military people. Not well-trained ones, anyway. From what we've heard, their aim is terrible. I hear they just point guns, rocket launchers, or whatever, in the general direction and shoot."

"That would be scary enough," said Millie.

"Yes, and when they're in close, they have enough weapons to hit anything in their path just by the sheer volume of shells they unleash. Apparently, they stole tons of ammunition and have an almost unlimited supply. They sunk two ships that we know of, and Santa Cruz wasn't the first land target they hit.

"Now, for the part of the story that most affects you. They loaded more than a dozen small craft aboard and used one of them to attack you today. They needed a lot of help to load all that equipment and ammunition, so they made deals with the no-goods hanging around the docks. For their help, they are rewarded with the spoils they get off small boats. Three were hit before you, and one of those boats ran aground. As you can imagine, not all these guys are great sailors. We captured one of them. He says they drew lots and every time they spot a small boat, six guys go attack that target.

"You were the only ones to get away, and that was because you had a guardian angel of sorts looking after you. You can't depend on that luck holding out. You need to get to The Isthmus and out of harm's way posthaste."

Stacey, who overheard most of the conversation while watching for the signal, said, "I'm with you on that. As soon as we pick up our people, we can be on our way."

"Right now wouldn't be too soon," said the captain. He looked at his watch. "Speaking of time, they're almost half an hour late."

"I'm sure they'll be here," she said. Her eyes scanned the beach area hopefully.

"It had better be quick," said the officer. "We have a lot on our agenda, and you need to head for Catalina. With or without them... we're leaving in an hour."

Chapter 50

THERE was no way that Zach and the others would get to the beach within the hour. Stacey, Glen, and Millie waited near the beach at Gaviota, while Zach and his group hid behind the remains of a missile silo on what once was part of Vandenberg Air Force Base. That was at least an hour away in ideal conditions, even if they could leave immediately. The conditions were far from ideal, so in all likelihood it would be hours before they could get away.

The senior Arthur's tactic of heading for Vandenberg and keeping the vehicles' lights off had worked well in getting away from their pursuers. By angling north off the main westerly road, then slipping unseen onto a side road he knew, they had ditched the four cars following them. They quickly slowed to a stop on the side road and heard the cars speed west on the main road. They knew there were still men and cars at the roadblock, so going back was not an option.

Neither was going back to Santa Maria because it was almost certain the motorcycle gang would still have spies out.

That left a single workable alternative. They stayed on the side road that led into Vandenberg near its northern border. They turned southwest on a utility road, and planned to follow it all the way south until they were back in civilian territory. If there were no hitches, they would have ample time to get to the beach long before midnight.

But, of course, there were hitches. As they approached the southern border of the base, they saw lights on the road ahead. The men from the roadblock weren't smart enough to turn their lights off, but they were savvy enough to guard at least one of the roads leading south.

The crew from the *La Sirena* backtracked and checked another road. Again, there was a car waiting.

"How many roads are there that go south from here?" Zach asked his dad after they once again backtracked and were out of earshot of the men blocking the road.

"Three."

"And they have four cars to cover them." Zach checked his watch. "Even if the motorcycle gang is gone from Highway 1, it's too late for us to go that way and get to Gaviota on time."

"Maybe Stacey and the Coast Guard will wait," Mae said, hopefully.

"For a little while," her husband replied, "but they can't wait for long."

"Why not? What could they have to do that is more important than saving people?"

"Mom, with the world in the condition it's in right now, those people have more to do than they can ever get to. That includes saving people, by the way. Other people – hundreds, not just a few. Besides, they'll be there again tomorrow night."

"You're sure?"

"I don't have a doubt in the world."

"What will we do until then?"

"Two very important things."

"What?"

"First, figure out how we can get to Gaviota State Park on time."

"And, second?"

"Stay alive."

* * * * *

The people on the boat waited another hour, but saw no signal.

"Okay," said Captain Kotchel, "that's it. We have to leave."

"They're only an hour and a half late," Stacey pleaded. "They're still alive, I know it."

"Look, your husband and Ron are ex-military, Mrs. Arthur. If they..."

"And grandpa," Glen exclaimed.

"What?"

"My grandfather is also ex-military," Glen said with determination in his voice.

"Okay, so if he's with them, there are three ex-military. They know how it works. We said if they couldn't make it this night, we would try again in twenty-four hours. If they're going to make it, it will be then. We, and by 'we' I mean my cutter and myself, will be here."

"And so will we," said Stacey.

"Mrs. Arthur, the longer you stay in open waters, the more dangerous it will be. You have to leave for Catalina, and you need to leave right now!"

"I am not leaving without my husband and daughter."

"Mrs. Arthur, as far as I'm concerned, we are officially still in a state of war. I am ordering your boat to The Isthmus."

"The boat may go, but I won't."

"Mrs. Arthur, you are going. . . "

The captain watched in amazement as Stacey ran over to the side and dove into the chilly Pacific Ocean.

He looked questioningly at Glen and Millie. "Is she going where I think she's going?"

"To go wait for her family on the beach would be my guess," said Millie.

Kotchel rolled his eyes. He walked over to the other side and climbed into the skiff. "Let's go get her," he said to the waiting seaman.

They pulled around the sailboat, passed Stacey, and then turned the boat so they were between her and the beach. She stopped just short of the skiff

"Mrs. Arthur," Kotchel said, "we can't let you go ashore like this. It would probably be suicide for you."

"I said I'm not leaving without my husband and daughter."

"I didn't have time to tell you this before you fled, but that container ship tried to attack our people at Port Hueneme yesterday. When they met strong resistance, they retreated and headed south. They will no doubt look for targets between Los Angeles and San Diego. When they find that everything in that area is destroyed, they will come back. However, that will take a couple of days. It is the perfect chance – probably the only chance – you will have to get your boat and your son safely to Catalina."

Treading water, Stacey considered that. Relenting a little, she said, "Very well, the boat and Glen can go. There is plenty of fuel, so he can motor to Catalina with Millie's help. It will be faster than sailing, especially if the roller furling is out of action. I, however, am staying."

"Mrs. Arthur, please be reasonable. I cannot let you go ashore."

"What I do is none of your business. Please get your skiff out of my way."

"Okay, okay, you win," he said, the exasperation clear in his voice. "But I still can't let you go ashore. You can stay aboard the cutter until we come back here tomorrow for our alternative pickup appointment. Maybe they'll be here then."

"Th... they will be," she assured him, her voice shuddering as she swam over to the skiff. The water, flowing down from Alaska, was icy cold.

I really doubt it, he thought, *but my life will sure be simpler if they are.*

Chapter 51

A S THE sun rose, Mae prepared breakfast – cold sandwiches, which at that point tasted as good as the famed Eggs Benedict at Brennan's in New Orleans.

"The ice in the cooler has about melted," she told the others. "I figure the mustard and mayonnaise will be a little less tasty by this afternoon."

"Maybe by then we can barbeque steaks on the beach instead of eating sandwiches," George joked.

"Wouldn't taste any better than this," was Denise's opinion.

"And," Glen Arthur sighed, "we may have a difficult time getting to the beach by then. Those cars would have passed by that street over there if they left, and not a one did. If they keep blocking the streets all day, we're either going to have to stay here, or fight our way through."

"I have no respect for those people," said

Zach, "but I don't want to kill anyone I don't have to."

"Maybe we can try Santa Maria and Highway 101 again," Ron suggested. "It's been thirteen or fourteen hours since we left our motorcycle friends. Those kinds of dudes aren't exactly known for their patience, so they may be long gone by now."

"It's a possibility," Zach agreed, "but there are two problems with it. First, we add distance by going back, and there may not be enough diesel in the Mercedes to reach Gaviota if we go that way. Second, the motorcycle guys have us outnumbered ten to one. We could beat these locals if it came to a fight, but ten to one odds are too heavy to overcome."

"Your last shot at being picked up is at midnight, right?"

"Yes, Dad."

"Then we have time. If those guys give up the roadblock sometime during the day, we just head south as planned and we'll be in Gaviota hours ahead of time. If not, at mid-afternoon we decide whether we knock off a couple of guys on one of the roads south, or we take a chance the motorcycles are gone and double back to Santa Maria. If you run out of fuel, you can hop into the SUV and we'll haul you the rest of the way."

"Dad, the SUV is full."

"There's room for one in the front seat, and one can squeeze in between the supplies. I've got luggage racks on the roof, so two of you – you and Ron would be my suggestion – can ride up there." He laughed. "I know it's against the law, but these are extenuating circumstances, and at the moment you don't have to worry about the highway patrol nailing you."

"You have supplies up there, too."

"It's a darn good thing you both have watched your weight. You can squeeze in nicely."

That settled, they filled the SUV with gas in anticipation of their next attempt to get to Gaviota. Then, they all took advantage of the down time to clean their weapons. Each had a road to watch, looking to see if the cars were leaving the roadblocks, or if any others were out searching for them. It was boring, but boredom was suddenly a welcome relief.

* * * * *

The skiff took Stacey back to the *La Sirena* so she could change into dry clothes and pick up a few things to take with her on the cutter.

When told he was going to be responsible for sailing the boat to Catalina, Glen said, "Mom, what about Dad and Denise? The boat will have to be here for them."

Stacey explained the timing problem the container ship had created. She added, "Don't worry; the cutter will be here to take us to Catalina when we pick the others up tonight."

"What if they're not there again?"

"In the first place, they will be. In the second place, I do not intend to leave until we have them on board. Settle in at The Isthmus and wait for us. We'll be there a couple of days after you, at most."

"I'm having word relayed via our antiquated, but right now very useful, communications system for those at The Isthmus to be expecting you," said Captain Kotchel. "Go around to the second harbor, the one on the southwest side. There's good anchorage there and, unlike the one on the northeast side, it is well protected from the weather – and is hidden from view."

Stacey and the captain got back on the skiff, and Glen and Millie started out for Catalina, using only the diesel engine for power.

"I didn't say anything at the time," the Coast Guard captain said to Stacey as they motored toward the cutter, "but you weren't entirely honest with your son."

"In what way?"

"We are making a last run north now, and will return tonight to watch for your husband's signal. After that, we have to go south to intercept that container ship. The way you expressed it to your son, we would wait for your husband and daughter no matter what. Obviously, that isn't true. We can't wait. If they aren't there to signal us, we have to go."

"They'll be there. If not right at midnight, then within an hour or two, I'm sure."

"If you're so sure, then you'll have no qualms about promising not to jump in the water again if they're not."

"I know Zach and his parents. They'll show."

"But, on the unlikely possibility that they are unable to. . ."

Stacey grimaced and hesitated. Whispering through gritted teeth in a throaty growl, "Okay, yes, I promise!"

"Good," said the captain. "This time, I'll give them a two hour leeway. Not a minute more.

Those people on that container ship are ruthless, killing everyone and everything in their path. We have to stop them, no matter what the cost. We will leave at two a.m. whether your people are there or not."

Chapter 52

NOTHING had changed in the area around Vandenberg by noon. Nor had it changed at one p.m., or two, or three. It seemed certain there would be no change the rest of the day, so the elder Glen Arthur conducted a quick poll of everyone.

They all felt they stood a better chance of avoiding bloodshed if they doubled back through Santa Maria. They decided to leave at five p.m., which would give them ample time, almost an extra five hours, to get to Gaviota. They could make it by midnight even if they ran into minor problems. They could not gauge how much time a major problem might cost them.

At five, they motored cautiously out from behind the missile silo. Nothing moved around them as they drove east toward Santa Maria. They were all thankful that, at least at that point, they were alone.

* * * * *

By the time the SUV and Mercedes approached Santa Maria, the Coast Guard cutter was turning back from their northern cruise. They were told that there was a vessel in distress in the waters off Pismo Beach, but after searching the ocean in that area for several hours, they didn't see a single vessel... much less one in distress.

The contact on shore that relayed the distress message to the cutter at one in the morning, said he heard nothing further and had seen nothing in the water all day. They concluded that it had to be a nuisance call or the boat had sunk.

There was nothing to prevent the cutter from arriving at the pickup point on time.

* * * * *

The senior Arthur, still in the lead, made stops along a side street so they could check the 101 for motorcycles with their binoculars. After only two stops, they spotted several bikes on the highway. There were also bikers still blocking the side streets.

"There's only two or three on each street, so we could easily bust through," Zach reasoned. "The problem with that, of course, is that the others will hear and be on our tails in seconds. There will be less risk in going back to Vandenberg and blasting our way past the fewer locals."

"There is one other alternative," said his father. "I didn't bring it up before because it's long and risky."

"What is it?" Zach asked. All the others looked at the older man expectantly.

"We could go east on the 166. It's not too far from here."

"The highway to Bakersfield?"

"It could take us there if we wanted, but I was thinking about the turnoffs. If we take the right one and make the right connections when doubling back this way, we will end back on the 101 north of Gaviota, but south of here."

"That explains the 'long.' And the risk?"

"That I can remember which is the right turnoff and what are the right connections. And, of course, that the roads haven't been destroyed."

"What are the chances you'll remember the roads?" asked George.

"I haven't gotten us lost yet, have I?"

"If you find the right roads, and they're still there," asked Zach, "how long will it take?"

"If all works perfectly, probably about five hours."

Zach looked at his watch. "That would get us there a little before eleven. If we run into trouble, we will only have an hour to solve the problem." He looked around.

"It beats having to kill some people," George opined.

They all nodded, some reluctantly,

"It's our best course of action," Mae stated flatly. She looked directly at the two men. "If anyone questions whether or not my husband's faculties have diminished," she said pointedly, "I'll match him against any of you in a memory contest."

No one took her up on it. As they started toward their vehicles, they heard someone yelling off in the distance. Moments later they heard motorcycles engines starting up in the same area.

They had been spotted.

"The 166, Dad!" Zach called as they jumped into their vehicles. They turned the cars around and sped north toward the highway that led to the hills between the coast and California's vast Central Valley.

Somewhere along that highway was a turnoff that would lead them back to Gaviota... if they could evade the motorcycle gang... and if Glen Arthur could remember the way.

The motorcycles congregated from all the side streets. There were men on over thirty bikes, and they had the SUV and Mercedes in their sights.

They were less than a mile behind and gaining fast.

Chapter 53

B Y THE time they reached the highway, the lead motorcycles were within five hundred yards of the vehicles. They could see there were not as many bikes as before, but thirty was more than enough to worry them. The gap got smaller and smaller as they sped toward the hills.

It had started to rain – unusual for that time of the year, but they assumed the global weather patterns had changed along with everything else. Neither those in the cars nor those on the motorcycles changed their actions because of the weather. The situation was too intense to let up in any way.

When the bikes got close, Zach caught up to the Ford SUV and drove alongside it, filling both lanes. When a biker tried to encroach on the narrow spaces between them or on the shoulders of the highway to get close shots at the drivers, one car or the other moved over to block the way. Those in the car were running low on ammo, so they didn't shoot as long as the bikers were kept at bay behind them. They could only guess that the bikers were not firing away from behind for the same reason.

Driving alongside one another worked until they came across an abandoned car in the road. One of the vehicles had to drop back and then speed up again to keep ahead of the bikes.

Several bikers tried to get ahead by taking frontage roads, but they were soon blocked by stalled vehicles on the roadway, and they had to double back and return to the chase on the highway.

When the bikers finally realized they were never going to get alongside to get shots at the drivers on that stretch of the highway, they lost their patience and opened fire. When they did, Denise leaned out and shot at the tires of the leading bikes. She hit two, and they flipped, taking three more with them as they slid along pavement slickened by the rain.

The other bikers slowed for a minute but were urged on by a fallen biker who survived his crash. Most were right on the tails of the cars again. Several had inexplicably stopped, two behind the fallen bikes, and one stopped right after passing them.

Denise was out of ammo, so Ron and George leaned out and tried to shoot the tires out from under the closest bikes. They got rid of a few, but there were still almost twenty bikers after them. Ron soon ran out of ammunition, as well. George kept shooting for a while to keep the bikes at bay, but he, too, ran out of ammo. The only weapons they had left with bullets were

Zach's AK-47 and the single shot weapons his parents had.

Up ahead, they could see that the highway widened. Once they were completely out of ammo, there was going to be no way to stop the bikes from moving to the sides of the cars and shooting the drivers. The rain was coming down harder, but the determined bikers kept coming.

Zach handed his AK-47 back to Denise. "Keep them away from this side as long as you can," he instructed her. They were left of the SUV, so the bikers would be able to get close to the driver's side window when the road widened. "To save ammo, put it on single shot and don't shoot until they come alongside."

Mae had her window rolled down and her shotgun at the ready on the right side of the highway.

The bikes moved over to the sides of the highway as they approached the side section so they could get in position to surge ahead for shots at the drivers. Denise got a bead on the one in front on the left side, but it slowed down, slowing the others. They could see it pull over to let the others by. It stopped in the middle of the highway. Then, another slowed and stopped. One did pull up, and Denise shot the front tire out from under it.

On the other side, Mae shot the lead biker, and his bike turned into the SUV and bounced off. The caroming bike tripped up two more that were following it.

Looking back, they could see that the remaining bikes were slowing. Several more stopped. Six others kept after the cars at first, but when they realized they were alone, they, too, stopped.

The cars kept going for ten miles with the passengers looking back anxiously and the drivers keeping their eyes on the rear view mirrors. When it was clear they were alone, they slowed to a stop alongside one another in the middle of the highway.

"What was that all about?" George asked the senior Arthur, who was directly across from him. He spoke loudly over the sounds of the falling rain. "Why did they stop?"

"I'm not sure, but I have an idea," the elder man replied.

"Me, too," said Zach, "and I bet it's the same one. He was looking at his dashboard gauges. "We're about empty."

"That's what I was thinking," his father agreed. "They're out of gas. That is why there were fewer of them and why they were so blasted persistent. And patient enough to wait for us all night. They saw the extra gas and were bound and determined to get it."

"They'd kill people just for gasoline?" Denise wanted to know, perplexed at the thought of how ruthless that was.

"Those kinds of people would kill for any reason," her grandfather told her. "But in this case it was a really big reason. They need their bikes, and there may not be gas for hundreds of miles. That's probably why those cars didn't move from their roadblocks, too."

"What now, Dad? I'll be running out of fuel myself pretty soon."

"The turnoff is about ten miles ahead," he replied. "Keep going as long as you can. When you run out, all of you hop in the SUV. It will be a little crowded, but without those bikers and local thugs to hassle us, we'll reach Gaviota in plenty of time."

Chapter 54

THE Mercedes ran out of fuel five minutes later, so the four occupants moved their backpacks and weapons to the SUV. Because of the rain, they moved more of the goods to the roof and they all squeezed into the SUV.

It was after dark when they found the turnoff. They decided the risk of being ambushed in that open area was less than having an accident, so the senior Arthur turned on his headlights. They only saw two people as they traveled along, and neither of them appeared threatening. After two wrong turns, they ended up on a road Glen was certain was the right one. It was ten p.m.

"It's not much over an hour from here," he said. "We should be there with time to spare."

The rain was coming down in a torrent by the time they reached the final crossroads before they arrived at Highway 101. They turned right and headed west.

Fifteen minutes later, the rain had dwindled to a light drizzle. Looking ahead, the senior Arthur hit his brakes hard and the SUV skidded from side to side on the wet road, finally coming to a stop with its front tires at the edge of a steep precipice.

Pushing away the cans, blankets, and boxes that had crushed him against the side of the vehicle during the frenzied braking, Zach cried, "Dad, what is it?"

"The bridge."

"What about the bridge?"

"It's gone."

The SUV's lights shined out over a thirty-foot gully that was dry most of the year; but at that moment, it was full of rushing water. There was a concrete foundation, pilings, and portions of twisted metal girders half in and half out of the water, but no bridge.

Glen backed the SUV up a few feet and set the parking brake. He reached behind the front seat and pulled out a flashlight, then got out of the car. The others followed. Zach had the flashlight they were going to use to signal the cutter. They aimed the lights onto the water in both directions; it was easily ten to fifteen feet wide as far as they could see. They couldn't tell how deep it was just by looking, but they knew it had to be deep enough to make it impassable. The current was too strong for them to try to ford it there.

"Is there another bridge?" Zach asked.

"There's probably one somewhere, but I have no idea where, or how far," his father replied. "Hop in and we'll look."

Having just come from the north, they knew there wasn't one there, so they drove south. After driving half an hour with no luck, Zach suggested they stop.

"I saw some spots as we passed that looked more or less level," he said. "Do you know of any place shallow enough for us to drive across?"

"I have no idea," his dad replied. "I've never seen water in that gully before."

The rain had stopped, and while the water was rushing at a slower rate, it was still far from calm. They got out of the vehicle and again shined the lights on the water as they walked along the edge. They came to a spot where the water widened to almost thirty feet.

Zach walked across and the water never got higher than his lower thighs. In the places he walked, the ground underneath was covered with rounded rocks. Spread out over thirty feet instead of ten or fifteen, the current was not too strong. It barely threatened to move him downstream, so it shouldn't push the SUV at all. He looked at his father. "Do you think you can cross here?"

"Not knowing much about what the ground is like below the water, it's a risk," his father said. "But, it's the only chance we have of getting there on time. And, what the heck, this is what a four-wheel-drive is for!" He got behind the wheel of the SUV and, while the others walked alongside, he drove into the water.

The tires gripped the rocks underneath and the vehicle moved along well at first. When it was half way across, one front tire hit sand. The front of the vehicle on that side dropped several inches, but it kept moving. When the back wheel hit the sand, the back also dropped. The vehicle kept moving, but slower. Then, both front tires hit a soft spot and the entire front dropped almost six inches.

The vehicle almost came to a standstill. Glen pushed down a little harder on the accelerator, and it began to move a little faster. The front tires found some gravel and the car moved ahead. They were now within ten feet of the other side.

Then, both the front and the back tires hit soft ground. The whole vehicle dropped six inches. Glen again pushed down on the accelerator, but the wheels spun and the car sunk deeper. It stopped moving.

"Get behind and push," Glen called out.

While the others got behind and pushed, Glen handled the steering wheel and the accelerator. No matter how hard they pushed, or how hard Glen pushed down on the accelerator, the only direction the SUV moved was deeper into the muck.

It was hopelessly stuck.

Chapter 55

"IT'S TWO A.M., Mrs. Arthur," Commander Beam told Stacey. "We have to go now."

The captain had sent the commander with strict orders to leave at two a.m. – no matter what. The captain wasn't there because he knew Stacey would try to persuade him to change his mind. The commander could not disobey an order.

They were one hundred yards off the beach at Gaviota. The rain had stopped hours before and the moon, along with a few stars, sneaked out from behind the clouds.

She looked sadly at the dark beach in the distance, feeling much further away than she knew it actually was.

"You promised the captain you wouldn't jump in again," he reminded her.

She smiled grimly, a thin look that had no mirth in it. She had promised, and she knew he had his orders.

The seaman at the controls turned the skiff toward the cutter and motored toward it.

"I've seen your husband and the others," the commander said. "They are all very capable. If they're alive, they will find a way to get to you on Catalina Island."

"A minute longer without your loved ones is a minute too long," she retorted.

"I agree," he said, turning his head away.

She realized that he, and probably everyone else on board the cutter, had lost loved ones in the terrible war that had claimed billions of lives. She slumped against a rail and she, too, looked away.

When they were on board the cutter, Commander Beam said to Kotchel, "Sorry, but they were a no-show. We can head south and look for that container ship now."

"We'll have to delay that," the captain replied. "We just got a call about another boat in distress north of here. We need to take a look before we head south."

"Do you think it's the same as before? Another false alarm? That container ship has put several pirate boats out there."

"Yes, that could very well be what it is," Kotchel conceded. "Whoever made the distress call didn't give our contact on shore a description of their boat or its name. They just said they lost power and immediately went off the air. Sounds fishy, but we have to check it out."

* * * * *

Zach and Ron went looking for another abandoned vehicle, and at three a.m., they returned to where the others were waiting on a bank of the gully near the SUV. By that time, the water had subsided considerably. But the SUV was so far down in the muck, there was no way they were going to get it out.

"We couldn't find a four-wheel drive, but we did find a pickup," Zach advised the group. "There's a gravel road about a hundred feet from here that leads to the highway, so I can take a can of gas out to the pickup and bring it that close. The pickup bed is big enough that we can transfer all the supplies to it and still have room for all of us. It will take a little time, and we're still an hour away from Gaviota. We should be there by seven or eight."

"They were expecting us at midnight," his mother reminded him.

"Maybe they waited," Denise cut in, looking hopeful.

"I don't think so," said her grandfather. "They're military, and they have a lot to do."

"Stacey can be very persuasive," Zach responded with a bit more emotion in his voice than even he expected.

"They're military," his father repeated. He didn't feel he needed to elaborate with his son.

"True," Zach conceded, "but we have to do all we can – and hope for the best."

* * * * *

Kotchel and Beam worked out a plan to capture the "pirate," if that was who had sent the two distress calls. They reasoned that if the boat that made the first call was a pirate, it probably had radar strong enough to spot the cutter before the cutter could pick up their small blip. If that was what happened, the pirates would know that the blip was too big for it to be a small boat, the kind they targeted. They would have sped north and got in close to shore. They could hide near rocks and not be seen by the Coast Guard ship or by the people on land.

The Coast Guard officers determined that if that happened, the pirates would attempt to do the same thing again. The way to thwart that tactic was for the cutter to stay close to shore and speed north, blocking off the pirate's escape route.

It turned out that it was a pirate, and by the time the men on the small boat spotted the cutter this time, it was too late. They tried to make it to shore by heading northeast, but this time the cutter had them on their radar, and it was between them and land.

Using their powerful loudspeaker, the Coast Guard ordered the boat to stop. Instead of surrendering, the pirates opened fire with bazookas. The weapons were ineffective against the larger ship, but the shells could do great harm to the Coast Guard personnel. The light generated by the pirates' bazooka fire gave the cutter's shooters an easy target. They sunk the smaller boat in minutes.

"Fools," said Kotchel as he watched the blip on his radar disappear. Turning to Commander Beam, he added, "Okay, let's head south and look for bigger game."

* * * * *

The cutter was more than a mile offshore as it approached the Gaviota area. The sun was up and land was clearly visible.

"Are you going to go in and look?" Stacey asked the captain.

"We'll move in a little closer. If they're there, we can see them easily with binoculars."

They sailed to within a few hundred yards of the beach. Four Coast Guard personnel scanned the land looking for the crew of the *La Sirena*. Captain Kotchel handed his binoculars to Stacey so she could confirm their findings. No one was on that little beach or anywhere else along the shore. Not the *La Sirena* crew; not anyone.

The ship continued south.

Chapter 56

IT WAS a little before eight when Glen Arthur, who was behind the wheel of the pickup, drove into Gaviota State Park. He stayed on paved roads as he maneuvered toward the beach. When those ran out, he sought gravel roads, winding through the area.

Denise, who was in the front seat with Glen and Mae, suddenly pointed out the road she and the three others had used leaving the beach two days earlier. It was a dirt road, but the area was rocky, so it wasn't all mud. The rain from the night before was the first in six months, and most of the water had soaked into the dry ground. There were puddles, but it was passable. The tires slipped and spun without gaining traction in spots. The riders got out and pushed. The pickup kept moving forward.

Ten minutes later, they had gone as far as the pickup could take them. They were thirty yards from the bank that led to the beach on which they had landed. The four crewmembers jumped from the pickup and ran to the hill. When they got to the top, they could see the cutter off in the distance.

It was too far away for anyone aboard to hear, if they called out. They couldn't even hear gunshots.

Glen and Mae joined them on the hill.

Zach turned to his father. "Dad, are those walkie-talkies handy?"

"I remember seeing them on the top of the pile, near the front," the older man responded, directing the comment to Denise, who was at the bottom of the hill. She darted toward the pickup.

He cupped his hands around his mouth and called, "In a black plastic case," as she neared the vehicle.

"The problem is," he confided to Zach, "I have no idea what frequency they're using. I doubt we'll be able to make contact."

"True, but we need to try everything we can."

When he had the walkie-talkies in hand, the senior Arthur tried to make contact. He tried numerous settings, but never got a response.

"No use," he admitted. "I might never hit it, and we're running out of time. Do you think Stacey is aboard that Coast Guard ship?"

"The *La Sirena* isn't around, and I doubt she'd leave without us, so there's a good chance she is."

"She knows the way you used to signal us when you were a kid, right? I've heard the two of you joking about it."

"Dad, that couldn't. . . "

Glen put up a hand. "You said yourself that we need to try all we can and hope for the best."

Zach rolled his eyes, but nodded. "Couldn't be sillier than trying to ford a muddy river in a rainstorm." He called out, "Denise, Ron, gather all the driest limbs, twigs, and leaves you can. George, do me a favor and bring one of those cans of gasoline up here, will you?"

Mae said, "I'll get a blanket."

* * * * *

Stacey sat near the stern of the cutter, still watching the area behind them. Although it was hazy on the sea ahead, the rain had cleared the skies over land. There were a few cottony clouds up high, brightened by the sun that rose over the coastal range of mountains.

Her eyes never left the area that she had watched so hopefully for two nights. There was a little cloud there. Unlike the ones up high, this one was dark. And very low. She watched it rise.

Rise? A cloud was rising? She leaned forward, as though getting an extra foot or two closer would give her a better view of an area miles away. Another small, dark cloud appeared. It seemed to be rising from the ground. She continued to watch. Two minutes later, there was another.

She jumped up and started to run forward, stopping abruptly when she ran headlong into the captain.

"Whoa, whoa," he said, grabbing her arm to keep her from falling. "I was coming back to see how you're doing, but if you're on your way somewhere. . ."

"I was on my way to find you," she exclaimed excitedly. "They're there! They're there!"

"What do you mean, 'they're there'? Who's where?"

"Zach is on the beach. And the others, too, I'm certain."

He looked toward the distant beach. "How could you possibly know that?"

"He's signaling. Look." She pointed to what was left of the dark "clouds," most of which had dissipated as they rose in the air. Another began to rise at that moment. "Look," she cried, again pointing.

He looked again. Confusion rather than enlightenment registered on his face. He saw something that looked like a little dark cloud, but had no idea if that was what she was talking about or what it meant if it was. "What am I looking at?"

"Smoke signals."

"Smoke signals? You're joking."

"No, I'm not. When Zach was young, he used to go on long hikes in the country. He sent up smoke signals when it was time for his folks to pick him up. It was some kind of game he and his dad dreamed up. Cheaper than phone calls, they said. Look!" She took his arm and pointed once more. "That's definitely a smoke signal."

He studied the beach area, but before he could respond, there was a buzz in his pocket. He put up a finger and took a little communi-cation device out of that pocket. "Yes?" he said into the device.

He nodded. "What do you think?" he asked. He listened again. "Yes, I have an opinion. It might be them."

He listened another second. "Yes, that's them." He listened for a few more seconds, and then responded, "Yes, but that container ship will still be there if we show up a little later than planned. Turn us around."

"That was Commander Beam," he told Stacey. "The radio man picked up some weak signals coming from land. He couldn't get a fix on it, but thinks someone with a handheld transceiver is trying to make contact. I'm like a cop; I don't believe in coincidences. We're going to check on that smoke you're so fixated on."

He shook his head, but a smile played on the corners of his lips. "Smoke signals! What could possibly be next?"

Chapter 57

STACEY jumped into the water and swam to shore before the skiff slowed to a stop, technically breaking her promise. No one faulted her for it. Zach and Denise rushed out to greet her before she reached shore and the three engaged in a very wet hugging spree.

Captain Kotchel waited on the skiff beyond where the waves started to break. He allowed the Arthurs a few moments to greet one another, and then called out, "Good to see you, Captain Arthur."

"And I, you," Zach responded happily. "We weren't sure you would see our signal."

"Were those really smoke signals?" the curious Coast Guard officer wanted to know.

"I found that if you pour gasoline on wet wood and leaves, and then put a match to it," Zach advised the captain, "you get a lot of really dark smoke. I'm glad you saw the signals."

"Stacey saw them."

Zach hugged his wife again.

"Ready to go to Catalina?" Captain Kotchel asked, a grin on his face.

"Absolutely," said Zach. He pointed at Glen and Mae. "My parents were doing just fine, by the way, and they're coming with us."

"I will never underestimate the survival ability of anyone in your family again!"

"Speaking of which, we also have the seeds you asked for."

"Didn't doubt it for a minute."

"And a lot of other supplies. When we saw the ship turn back, we brought them here to the beach, so all we need to do is load them."

The captain had brought an inflatable along, just in case they needed it. They inflated it and loaded Glen and Mae Arthur's supplies on board. Zach, Ron, and George pulled it past the breaking waves to the skiff. The same seaman who had dropped them off was piloting the small vessel. He maneuvered the controls to keep the craft as near as possible to shore, but always behind where the waves broke.

Twenty minutes passed, and they were on their way to the Coast Guard buoy tender. Those who had been ashore were pleased to learn that it was now an armed United States military ship.

In another twenty minutes, the Coast Guard cutter had again turned south, now with six additional passengers aboard. It was ten a.m. The cutter's top speed was fourteen miles per hour in neutral water, but faster with the current behind. They would be at The Isthmus before six p.m. That would give the Coast Guard two daylight hours to drop off their passengers and then hunt for the container ship.

* * * * *

Two hours later, they were in a light fog. It reduced their visibility, but they could see almost three miles ahead, so they sailed unimpeded toward Catalina at full speed.

The passengers found places toward the back of the ship to recline and talk. In those two hours, Zach and the others learned what had happened at sea during the last two days, and Stacey learned what took place on land. The most obvious lesson they learned was that life in this new world was dangerous, no matter where a person was. They hoped The Isthmus would be an exception.

"Hard to imagine a container ship equipped as a warship," Zach commented. "I would have thought it was too cumbersome to be effective."

Captain Kotchel overheard Zach's comment. "That would have been true two months ago," he agreed. "Now, it's like the big, cumbersome kid bullying the other kids on the playground. He doesn't have to be well coordinated if he's twice the size of the others."

"And the container ship is twice the size of your ship?" Stacey asked.

"A lot more than that," Kotchel replied, his voice thoughtful.

"How are you going to handle that?" Zach asked.

"We'll find out soon enough," the Coast Guard officer reported. "That's what I came back to tell you. We just got word that they've attacked Avalon on Catalina Island. We're still headed in that direction, but we're changing course to go to Avalon."

"Didn't you say Avalon was taken over by hooligans?"

"Yes, and I got word last night that they've learned about the settlement at The Isthmus. They went there yesterday and demanded food and fuel."

"That sounds familiar," said Zach. "What happened?"

"The leaders at The Isthmus pretty much told them they could have what they worked for and nothing more."

"Good for them," Zach said. "But, I imagine that didn't go over too well with the hooligans."

"They said they would be back with a small army to take what they wanted."

"Maybe the container ship is doing everyone a favor," Zach suggested.

"I can't fault your logic," said the captain, "but right now, we're sort of like cops. We can't pick and choose who we protect. When bad guys attack someone, we have to go stop them, and that's what we're going to do."

* * * * *

At a little after five," the Arthurs noticed the ship altered its coarse from almost due south to southwest.

"What do you think it means?" Stacey asked her husband.

"This will take us to The Isthmus instead of Avalon. That should be good news, but I don't have a good feeling about it."

They, along with Glen and Mae, went looking for Captain Kotchel. They found him on the forward deck where the weapons were. Some had been bolted down and others were loose on deck. Ron was there, talking to several of the Coast Guardsmen.

"What's happening?" Zach asked.

"Ron was on a missile cruiser when he was in the navy," Kotchel said. "We've had a little training this past month, but he's filling us in on what we missed."

Glen spotted five bazookas lying on the deck off to one side. He went over and picked one up. After he examined it, he said to Kotchel. "Where did you get these?"

"A fellow brought those five and several hundred shells in from some old armory out in the desert. They looked pretty lethal, so we traded some diesel for all he had. Are you familiar with them?"

"Sure," said the old vet. "You made a good deal. These are M20s, 'Super Bazookas.' Haven't seen one in years, but we used them a lot in Viet Nam. You're right; it is lethal. It'll penetrate six inches of steel, easily."

"Do you remember how to use it?"

"Yep. I used to knock out vehicles at five hundred yards with one of these."

"Do you feel like training some people?"

"It will be my pleasure!"

Zach stood by as patiently as he could while his father and the vessel's captain talked but cut in when there was a lull in the conversation. "It sounds like the training is going to be top notch," he said, "but what I meant was, why are we headed for The Isthmus instead of Avalon?"

"Necessity," said Kotchel. "The container ship apparently finished doing what it set out to do at Avalon. They left there and headed northwest. That can only mean The Isthmus."

"My son is there!" Stacey exclaimed.

"I know."

"How long before we get there?" Zach asked.

"About half an hour."

"Can we beat them there?" Stacey wanted to know.

Kotchel looked her in the eye. "I don't think so. The problem is that we don't know exactly when they left Avalon. It could have been up to an hour ago, which means..."

"Which means they may be near The Isthmus already." She finished his sentence, and her voice dropped in her final words.

They all looked ahead, straining to see their destination. The fog was thinning. Although they got glimpses of land at times, they never saw anything for more than a few seconds.

The loud sounds of big guns going off brought total silence among those at the bow of the cutter. They still couldn't see what was dead ahead, but there was no doubt that the sounds emanated from there.

The Isthmus was under attack.

Chapter 58

THE modern-day pirates on the makeshift container-warship, fresh from demolishing the picturesque tourist town of Avalon, were having a marvelous time at The Isthmus. They had uncovered a stash of liquor in a ruined restaurant in Avalon that the ruffians who had previously taken over the town evidently overlooked.

The pirates were depleting their newfound stash at a rapid clip. The alcohol magnified their already prevalent penchant to destroy. All three tanks and all the missile and rocket launchers pointed in the direction of the little settlement.

They were just under two hundred yards offshore. Although they would have liked to move in closer to increase their chances of hitting their targets, the huge ship had a draft of almost forty feet, and they were as close as they could get.

Because many of their targets were set lower than the deck level of the monster ship, all the weapons were near the bow. Ten men kneeled next to the tanks with small rocket launchers on their shoulders. Even in that normally stable stance, they tended to stagger. Nevertheless, they did get off shots between drinks. Most of their shots were hitting hills with nothing but plants.

The men, staggering as they shot, were having a difficult time. The twenty men shooting missiles from the other side of the tanks weren't doing much better. Having clear shots from the bow wasn't much help at first, but that didn't bother them. They were getting closer with each shot, and they seemed to believe they had unlimited ammo and time.

The helicopter pilot was inside his craft. He still had four missiles loaded into the launchers attached to the sides, but he didn't need them for such a small job. He just drank and enjoyed the show.

Although almost all the shooters' first volley went wild, they did knock out one roof and started a small fire. The residents immediately went about putting out the small fires. Several shots went well wide of the buildings and traveled through the little "valley" between the two harbors, hitting and sinking two of the more than twenty boats anchored there. The hits were the results of bad aims, but those who fired the shots pointed proudly at their accomplishments. The sinking of the Bismarck in WWII probably engendered a less raucous outburst from their shipmates. They were having a great time.

The pirates knew they would eventually kill everyone there, so they continued to drink and shoot. The captains of the ship, two ex-merchant mariners, watched from the ship's bridge, which they called the wheelhouse. They did nothing to interfere with the men. Working with a crew such as theirs required patience. They, too, knew they had unlimited time and ammunition... and, virtually no opposition. The people on land had a voluntary "militia" of more than forty, but all they had were small arms, which were useless against the massive ship, tanks, rockets and missiles.

The fog was lifting, and the pirate ship would have at least two hours of sunlight to accomplish their task. As bad as the shooters were, they would demolish the settlement in a quarter of that time.

* * * * *

After they heard the initial gunfire, the few minutes it took for the cutter to break through the last of the fog seemed like hours. Those aboard were in awe of the size of the container ship when it finally came into view.

"That's huge!" said Ron.

Kotchel, who was looking at it through binoculars, said, "Well, it's smaller than it might have been."

"Smaller? That's got to be eight, nine hundred feet long."

"Over nine hundred I'd say. But some of the new ones are up to twelve hundred feet. At least now I have a better idea of exactly what we're up against."

"You were right," Stacey said. "It's more than twice the size of the cutter. I bet it's four times as big."

Kotchel shook his head. "I wish. Counting overall dimensions and weight, it's twenty times our size."

They all took another look at it.

"The bigger they are, the harder they fall," said Glen Arthur.

"Think so?" asked the captain

At that moment, the improvised warship was setting off another volley of tank, missile, and rocket fire.

"I can hit it easily with one of those super bazookas," Arthur said.

The captain didn't hesitate. "Do it!"

Moving with a speed that belied his age, Zach's father picked up the bazooka he looked at earlier. A nearby crewmember overhead the two men and grabbed a rocket shell. As the senior Arthur aimed, the crewman loaded the shell and a few seconds later, it was on its way.

At the same time, the cutter sounded its siren in an attempt to create confusion.

Moments later, they could see an explosion half way up in the container ship's super-structure, which was located in the middle of the vessel. The explosion looked small from a distance, but they knew it had done some damage.

And it got the attention of the big ship. All the guns on the container-warship stopped firing.

The blast knocked the two ex-merchant mariners down. While it didn't do any damage to the bridge itself, it shook the whole superstructure.

The two got off the floor looking quizzically at one another. "What the heck was that, Hank?" said one.

The other looked out the back window. "Looks like there's a ship coming toward us, and that sounds like a Coast Guard siren."

"Coast Guard ships aren't armed like that," the first one snapped.

"Neither are container ships, Joe," his partner reminded him. He picked up a pair of binoculars and studied the other ship. "It's not very big. I'm going to turn our ship around and we'll hit it with everything we have. We'll sink it in ten minutes. I'll go down and tell Marty to get the helicopter ready. Once we're turned around, he can go over and disable it while we get in close. Then we'll finish the job."

Before Hank could leave, they felt another jolt. This hit was aft and far away from the superstructure. They could barely feel it there, and had no idea an armor-piercing shell had penetrated their stern below the water line. Hank shrugged. "Not sure what that was, but it couldn't have done much damage."

As he started down the outside steps leading to the deck, several of the gunners were starting up. "We've got it under control," Hank called down to them. "Get back to your posts. I'm going to turn around and get close in so you can have fun knocking out a pipsqueak military wanna be ship. Then we'll come back and finish off those dudes on land."

The gunners went back to their weapons and their drinks. Hank continued down to the deck and over to the helicopter. After he talked to the pilot, he went back up to the bridge and started the slow process of turning the huge ship around.

The war had been good to him. He finally had the power he always knew he deserved. Those petty military jerks who always looked down on him would soon get a taste of that power. He was about to send them to the bottom of the sea.

Chapter 59

A S THE big ship turned, the senior Arthur hit its stern with a rocket – a hit those in the bridge barely felt. Then, while it was still turning, he shot three more times at the starboard side. He aimed all the shots below the water line. He saw splashes after each shot and was confident they were all hits. The shells were powerful enough to penetrate thick metal, but there was no way of knowing how much damage the big ship suffered.

By the time the ship turned around and headed toward the cutter, the Coast Guard ship had closed in, and the two were no more than a half mile apart.

Captain Kotchel heard how poor the marksmanship of the thugs aboard the cargo ship was... an advantage they needed to exploit. "Those guys couldn't hit the broad side of a barn at this distance," he told the crew, "so they're planning on getting in close. We can beat them if we knock out their guns before they get so near they can't miss. That's your mission. Don't hold anything back."

"Okay," said Glen, "but first I'm going to put a shell into either side of that wide bow of theirs." He got off the two shots, and they saw water splash in front of the big ship, first on its starboard side, and then on its port side. He then raised the super bazooka and concentrated on the tanks.

There hadn't been time enough for the Coast-guardsmen to train extensively, but they knew how to aim and shoot. There were people on all the weapons, including the four men and three women connected to the *La Sirena*. Ron was in charge of a missile pod, and Zach and George had handheld rocket launchers similar to the one Zach's father was using. Stacey and Denise had their AK-47s. They were still too far away for the assault weapons to be lethal, but the container ship was getting closer. Mae looked doubtfully at her shotgun, set it aside, and picked up Zach's AK-47. That was better.

Glen took out a tank right away, and he saw that the man next to him destroyed a missile launcher. He looked over to congratulate the shooter, and realized it was Zach. "I guess that Ranger training took," he said, smiling broadly at his son.

"Just a chip off the old block, Dad!"

Not long after that, they saw two more missile launchers go down. With each hit, they saw men on the big ship fall. At least six men with rocket launchers were out of action.

Although the shooters on the big ship were

as bad as Captain Kotchel said they were, there were so many of them, and they had so much ammunition, they couldn't miss every time.

One small missile tore a large hole in the cutter's bow on the starboard side, just under the deck. It knocked some men down temporarily, but in seconds they were up and firing again. The radar acquisition antennae on top of the superstructure was blasted away.

Four more missile launchers and six more men with rocket launchers on the larger ship went down. Individually, the people on the cutter were doing far more damage than their counterparts on the container vessel. The odds were going down but still favored the bigger adversary. It still had two functioning tanks and more than a dozen missile and rocket launchers.

More importantly, they had the helicopter, which lifted off in the midst of the battle. By itself, it could wipe out all of the shooters on the deck of the cutter before they could kill any more of the pirates. It headed straight for the cutter's bow, where all the combatants stood.

Ron was the first to see it coming straight at them. He saw that the craft's missile pods on one side were loaded and ready to fire. He only hoped the pilot would wait until he was close enough to be sure of his shots. Ron was trained for this, and he acted quickly.

Calculating the speed and altitude of the helicopter, he zeroed in on it in a matter of seconds. Just before the helicopter pilot was ready to fire, four missiles came flying at him.

Three hit his helicopter. They didn't down the craft immediately, but tore away one side and set it on fire. It zigzagged out of control but kept heading toward the cutter. Then it lifted, dropped, and turned around and around. With one side completely open, they could see the pilot when the craft was above them. He was alive and looked wild-eyed at them as the flame-infested whirlybird bucked by. Flames licked at him from every side. Just past the cutter, the copter bucked one last time, then exploded.

The explosion fired off the craft's missiles. Three shot harmlessly into the water, but a fourth hit one of the cutter's propellers, shattering it. A piece of that prop shot across and hit the shaft of the other, bending it and rendering that prop useless, as well.

With both props out of action, there was nothing to propel the ship. It slowed to a halt, still heading in the direction of the container vessel.

* * * * *

The men at the controls of the big ship watched in dismay as the helicopter, their most fearsome weapon, went down. Angered, Hank went out and called down to the men below. "Knock them out, you fools! Kill them all!"

When he went back in, Joe was clicking off from an intra-ship call. "That was the engine room. We're taking on water."

"That idiot! Tell him to stop wasting time and close off the leaky compartment!" Hank shot back. "It's watertight, so it's no big deal if it takes on a little water."

"That's just it. He did close it off, but there's water flooding into the next one, too."

"That's the problem with taking guys off the docks like we did; you end up with a bunch of incompetents. Watch the controls, and continue heading right at that cutter so we can get close enough for our guys to actually hit something. I'm going below to straighten out this flooding situation."

While he was gone, another tank and ten missile launchers were destroyed by fire from the cutter. Now, they were not only taking missile and rocket fire, but there was small arms fire coming from the cutter, too. The bullets were finding targets. Two more men were killed, and the others were looking for places to hide. More than forty men were already down.

When Hank rushed back up the steps to the bridge, there was a look of panic on his face.

"What's the situation?" Joe asked.

"There's flooding forward, aft, and everywhere in between." Hank groaned and slumped into a chair. "Those rats hit us below the water line five or six times."

"What does that mean?"

"It means we're sinking, you fool. We need to finish off that ship and get to shore."

"Finish them off? Did you see the mess down there?"

Hank went over to look at the foredeck. There were almost no missile or rocket launchers still operational, and the single tank that was operational was stuck behind the two that were knocked out. They were turned sideways, pushing the one good tank to the side of the bow.

The inoperable tanks were so close to the bow, there was no room for the functional tank to get around them for a clear shot at the cutter.

"Push them over," Hank screamed down at the men.

"There are men inside," one of the men holding a rocket launcher called back.

"This is war. Push them over now. That's an order!"

The man jumped up on the tank and relayed the order. The tank driver opened the hatch, stood, and looked up.

"Push them over if you want to get out of this alive!" screamed Hank.

The man didn't argue. He stayed where he was, his head above the top of the tank so that he had a clear view of all around him. He moved his tank forward, pushing one disabled tank ahead of it. A minute later, the wrecked tank toppled off the deck. It bounced off the bow hull twice as the boat moved ahead, then hit near the ship's bottom one more time as it sunk into the sea.

Just as the driver started to slide into the tank to stop it, a bullet from the cutter hit him in the neck, and he slumped over. The tank continued on, going over the side and replicated the previous tank's voyage to the bottom of the sea.

Getting close was no longer a plus for the container ship. Well over ninety percent of their firepower and most of their men were gone. The closer they got, the more hits the gunners on the Coast Guard ship were registering.

There was no place for the pirates to go. The

ship was slowly sinking, and the few gunmen left were being killed at a rapid pace.

"They've beaten us," said Joe.

"No they haven't," argued Hank.

"We have no more weapons."

"Oh yes, we do," growled Hank. "We've got the biggest weapon left in the world."

"You mean...?"

"I'm going to run that dinky little boat down. I'm going to crush it. As of this minute, they're all dead!"

* * * * *

"We licked them," said Denise.

The Coast Guard crew and those from the *La Sirena* were standing at the cutter's bow, watching the container ship approach. There was no gunfire coming from the big ship.

"We outfought them," Kotchel agreed, but shook his head. "It doesn't look like they're licked, though. They're headed right at us."

"I punched half a dozen holes it its bottom," Glen Arthur said. "Why isn't it sinking?"

"I'm sure it is," the captain told him, "but a ship that size has multiple holds. It could take hours for it to go under."

"And, we're dead in the water," George moaned. He looked anxiously at the captain, hoping to hear he was wrong.

The look on Captain Kotchel's face did nothing to sooth George's fears. "I don't like your terminology," he said, but I can't quarrel with the reality of it. We can't get out of their way and, in a few minutes, they'll crush this ship like it was a sardine can."

"How much time?" asked Zach.

"Three minutes at most."

"Not near enough time to lower the life boats and get away," Zach reasoned.

"No," sighed the captain sighed. "There will barely be time enough for each of us to have one last word with whoever we consider our maker."

Chapter 60

THE massive explosions were so violent they shook the ground at The Isthmus settlement and even shattered a few windows. The container ship was cut in half with the first blast, and the second, which came less than a second later, blew both halves to pieces. The hole in the water the explosions caused sent forty-foot waves out in a wide, turbulent circle.

Large parts of decks, hulls, superstructure, and an engine flew hundreds of feet in the air. Smaller pieces of shrapnel and metal shards shot out much farther, hitting the only thing left on the water – the Coast Guard cutter.

Several aboard the cutter, which oscillated wildly when the explosion-born wave swept past, were hit by flying debris. A piece of shrapnel hit Denise's right arm, cutting through flesh and breaking the bone. The thirteen-year-old was wounded for a second time in the wake of a global war in which everyone lost.

Even before the cutter stopped rocking, the questions began. "What happened?" cried George as he got to his feet.

"I'm not sure," replied Captain Kotchel, who was lying nearby, "except for the obvious. That ship blew up before it got to us."

"I know," said Stacey. She was using a rail to get to her feet, scanning the area around the ship.

"You know what?" asked Zach, who used the same rail to get off the deck.

"Yeah, I know what happened," she replied, smiling.

"You think?" asked the captain, now on his feet next to her. "Yes, of course. It has to be."

"They've been watching us all along and came to our rescue once before."

"Ah," said Zach, "you're talking about Captain Wang and his sub. I bet you're right."

While the water was settling, the ship's medic started treating the wounded. It was only then that Zach and Stacey found out that their daughter was wounded... again.

"I'm so sorry, Denise!" Stacey held her daughter tightly.

"Mom, I'm alive. Three minutes ago, I didn't think I would be, so everything is fine." She giggled. "Except you're hurting my arm."

Stacey let go, and the family laughed.

When the wave action settled into small whitecaps around the explosion area, the Chinese submarine surfaced and motored over to the cutter. As always, Captain Wang was the first to climb up to the conning tower. He saluted. "Captain Kotchel," he said.

The Coast Guard captain returned the salute. "Captain Wang. I offer you our most heartfelt thanks for torpedoing that ship."

"We shot four simultaneously just to be certain. We couldn't let them sink our source of food and fuel, now could we? The way it exploded, though, one would have been enough."

"They had a huge amount of ordnance in their holds," Kotchel explained. A torpedo must have hit the ammo, and it all erupted at once."

"Live by the sword," said the Chinese officer.

Stacey said, "I couldn't think of a more fitting epitaph for a bloodthirsty bunch of pirates."

"Mrs. Arthur... it is good to see you once again,"

"And, once again Captain Wang, I say the pleasure is definitely more mine than yours."

He acknowledged the remark with a slight nod, and then turned back to Kotchel. "Is there anything more I can do for you folks before we again become invisible?"

"I think it's time for us to rethink your being inconspicuous," said Kotchel. "Among other things, I'd appreciate a tow to Port Hueneme where I hope I can find some propellers and shafts that fit."

"Among other things?" said Captain Wang.

"If you're going to be part of this community, and I believe you have proven reasons to legitimize such thinking, it would be odd if you were always invisible."

Captain Wang smiled in response.

* * * * *

Before the Chinese and Coast Guard left for the mainland, Captain Kotchel took the *La Sirena* group ashore on the skiff. They took Captain Wang and two of his men along so they could be introduced to the people on the island. They also took all the supplies Glen and Mae had brought from Santa Maria.

The Arthurs offered to share all the supplies with the islanders, and Captain Kotchel relayed that information to them via the transceivers they used for communicating with one another. After the transfer was made, the Chinese crew became a topic of conversation.

The movable dock used at The Isthmus was sloshed up near shore by the explosion's shock waves, so the people on shore moved it back out toward the bay. Once it was in place, fifteen of the settlement's population walked out on the dock to meet the people from the boat. Zach was the first off the skiff. He tied its line to a cleat and went over to introduce himself to the people. The others stepped off the skiff and joined them.

"Welcome to The Isthmus, all of you," one of the leaders said. He turned to Wang. "Captain Kotchel has told us about you. He says you and your men want to help around here."

"We do," said Captain Wang. "It is our hope to become an integral part of your settlement."

"If you each do your share, you will," the man said. He turned to Glen and Mae. "We originally planned on telling you to keep your supplies for yourself. However, we lost some things during the attack, so we will accept the things we need."

"Whatever you need is yours," said Glen.

As the settlers looked through the supplies, young Glen hobbled out on the dock, accompanied by a woman in her late twenties. All the Arthurs rushed to greet him.

After hugs all around, Zach asked why his son was limping.

"He banged his knee saving my three-year-old daughter," the woman told him. "A shell started a small landslide, and he dove into the middle of it and pulled her out. Your son is a real hero."

The fifteen-year-old acted as though it was nothing out of the ordinary, which his family understood. A small landslide wasn't hard to deal with after a bullet wound, being shot at by bazooka-bearing madmen, and surviving more than one storm at sea.

"He just wanted to have some kind of wound so I wouldn't be ahead of him," said Denise, She moved her arm out as far as the sling would allow so he could see it.

He pulled up one leg of his pants to show off a bandaged knee. "I bet mine is bigger than yours."

The two laughed and walked together, him limping and her favoring her arm, toward the settlement.

"Okay," said Millie as they all walked toward the few buildings that were part of the settlement, "where's the hotel?"

"What's left of it is over here behind the store," a man said. "Not really fit for guests at the moment, though."

"It will be," she informed him.

* * * * *

Ron and the elder Glen went with the Coast Guard officer and the Chinese when they towed the cutter away. Both men would spend the next few weeks in extended training of the cutter's crew on the use of their weapons. Ron accepted Captain Kotchel's offer to stay aboard as an officer. He eyed the crops growing on the sides of hills with envy, but the sea was his first love. The older man planned to return to The Isthmus with the Chinese to begin a new chapter in a life that had seen many changes.

Millie and George stayed in the area where the buildings sat. The restaurant wasn't touched by the tank and missile onslaught, and two buildings, including the small hotel, were only partially destroyed. They were already in deep discussions with the hotel's owner. They anticipated it might be a while before a hotel was needed – as a hotel – but they were determined that it would be available quickly for whatever use it could be to the settlement.

The Arthurs walked to the far end of the second harbor where the *La Sirena* was anchored. It took two trips in their small dinghy to get them all out to the sailboat, but they were settled in by sunset.

They could see the heads of buffalo and goats over the hills to the north. The animals had fled from the gunfire to the northwest corner of the island but were returning in the quiet of the evening to look curiously at the humans below them.

There was no fog and only a few clouds over

the Pacific west of the island. The Arthurs, now five in number, sat in the cockpit, watching the sun as it settled in. The reflection shimmered in an almost straight line toward their boat. The few clouds in the sky captured a rainbow's pallet of color from the setting sun. Neither the sun, nor the sky, nor the expansive dark blue ocean, appeared to have been changed by what humans had done to the world.

"It's beautiful here," said Mae. "No wonder you all like boating so much."

"How are you feeling, Mom?" asked Zach.

"Just fine, son, just fine. Feeling a little tired, though. I brought some seeds in hopes I could get my herbs to grow wherever we landed, but I'm out of them for the moment."

"Gosh, Mom, with all the turmoil I forgot all about it. We brought herbs from Hawaii for you... wait here." He climbed down into the cabin and retrieved the herbs from the backpack he had with him since he first landed at Gaviota.

The last sliver of sun disappeared as he returned to the cockpit. "Here, Mom. Do you take them with anything?"

Mae smelled the herbs and looked at them lovingly. "I heat them in water, like tea. I'll do that in a little while. Right now, I just want to sit here. This was so thoughtful of all of you. I hope you didn't go to any trouble getting them for me."

The four looked knowingly at one another, recalling what took place that fateful night in Hilo and all that had happened since. A big smile broke out on Denise's face. Glen started to chuckle. Then, they all burst into laughter.

"What's so darned funny about that?" Mae begged to know.

Zach hugged his mother. "Nothing, Mom. Or, everything. We're just happy to be here!"

The End

Get a sneak peek at
Al Correia's
anticipated sequel in

"The Seeking Saga"

SEEKING
— *a* —
SANE
SOCIETY

The Arthur family enjoys their first peaceful night's sleep on beautiful Catalina Island, only to be confronted the next morning by demands for "taxes." They, along with all the other residents of Catalina, learn that a former state legislator – who happens to be a former state prison inmate – has installed himself as governor of California.

Catalina and Tracy, a small Central California town, are among the few habitable areas still in existence, but they must fight to survive. Each area has to find its own way of combating an illicit government, and its militia, a cutthroat gang of hardened criminals

Expected in the Fall of 2016

Chapter 1

ZACH, a fit and trim man in his early forties, caught a glimpse of movement behind a tree as soon as he climbed up to the cockpit of their sailboat, the *La Sirena*. The tree was off to the left of where they were anchored in the Two Harbors area of Catalina Island. He set his morning coffee down and sat next to his wife, Stacey, never taking his eyes off the tree.

"What is it," she asked, looking off in the direction he was looking.

"There's someone behind one of the trees near the buildings over there," he replied, nodding toward the northeastern side of the harbor.

She tried to get a better look. The rising sun was low and the trees and buildings in the area cast shadows over the landscape. "Which tree?" she asked. "I don't see anyone."

"Whoever is there is hiding," he said.

Stacey didn't doubt him. Her ex-army ranger husband saw things most people missed. She couldn't figure out why anyone would be hiding out on this island. She had to ask, "Hiding from what?"

"From us, I think," he told her. "A head peeks around every now and then, looking our way. We're being spied on, so I need to go check it out." He took a sip of coffee before getting up and going to the back of the boat to lower their dinghy into the water.

"I'd hoped we were finally going to get some peace and quiet now that we're here," she told him.

"Peace and quiet?" Zach replied. He thought that over for a second or two. "We may have that as time goes on, but in a world gone crazy, it's a relative condition." He climbed through the hatch that led down to their aft cabin. There, he opened a cabinet on the starboard side, taking out a .38 caliber revolver. He checked to make sure it was loaded, then stuck it in his belt at his back. He untucked his shirt so that it would hang loose and cover the gun. He started to leave, then turned back and picked up a .22 caliber Beretta. He shoved that in his front pants pocket.

When he went back up on deck, Stacey met him near the ladder leading down to where the dinghy was now floating in the gently rippling water. She carried both their coffees. "I'm going with you, and I see no reason why we should miss out on our morning coffee just because of a snooper."

Stacey was in her late thirties, but she was in as good physical shape as her husband and was often taken as being in her twenties. She looked around and shrugged. "It's not like they're shooting at us."

He started to reply, but stopped when he heard someone moving around in the main cabin. "Mom?" he called.

"Good morning to you two," Mae Arthur responded. "I'm going to fix hot chocolate for Glen and Denise."

"Thanks," Stacey called out. "That will get them off to a good start this morning. There's hot coffee in the pot if you want some."

"I already poured myself a cup," the older woman replied.

"We're going over to talk with the people in charge," Zach advised his mother. "We should be back soon, and then we can discuss what we're going to do on our first day here." He climbed down into the dinghy first, then steadied the small craft by holding onto the ladder as Stacey climbed down. As soon as she was seated, he shoved the dinghy away from the sailboat. He inserted two small oars into the oarlocks and began rowing. It took just a couple of minutes to reach shore in the narrow harbor. Zach jumped out and dragged the dinghy onto dry land.

Stacey got out and handed Zach his coffee. "Are you expecting trouble?" she asked.

"Not really," he responded after taking a sip of coffee. "Captain Kotchel said these were good, reliable people. I think we can trust them."

"I saw the bulge at your back when you climbed into the dinghy. I figured it had to be a gun, so I was wondering."

"It's like drawing up a contract when doing business with friends and relatives. You have faith in them without the contract, but feel a lot better when you know you have protection."

"Did you bring one for me?"

"Of course," he answered, pulling the Beretta from his front pocket and handing it to her.

She slipped it into her own front pocket, then took a sip of coffee. "Okay, now I feel better, too."

"Good," he replied, taking her hand. "So, let's go find out who is being nosy."

Their boat had been the last one into the harbor, so it was the one nearest the mouth, and therefore the farthest from the settlement's buildings. As they strolled toward the other end, the occupants of the other sixteen boats anchored in that harbor were beginning to stir. Several were already on deck and waved at Zach and Stacey as they passed.

As they walked, Zach caught glimpses of a red shirt as a man crawled from the tree he'd been hiding behind to a large bush. Apparently believing he was concealed by the bush, the man stood and walked quickly to a building, entering through a side door.

The building was where they were headed.

Chapter 2

A S THEY walked toward the buildings, the Arthurs passed a tractor that had small cultivating discs that could be lowered and raised hydraulically attached at its rear. Two men and two women were walking alongside the tractor. They carried gunny sacks, and were dressed in the kinds of casual clothes people wear on weekends. They all waved friendly acknowledgments to the newcomers.

"We're heading toward the hill over there to plant the seeds you brought yesterday," the tractor driver called out, pointing to a low hill south of where their boat was anchored.

Zach and Stacey waved back in response. Speaking softly so only he could hear, she said to Zach, "None of them look like spies."

"True," he agreed, "but my understanding is that spies make a point of not looking like spies."

She turned to look at them again as they moved toward the hill. "In that case, they're doing a bang up job of fooling us if they really are spies." She laughed lightly. "They don't look the slightest bit like farmers, either."

"I doubt that any of them were farmers before the war. Now, survival will depend on a lot of people who never even imagined doing it before learning to farm."

They came to the end of the harbor and began walking across the narrow land mass between the two harbors at the northwestern end of Catalina Island. The buildings used by the people who had lived there year around before the war, and now the survivalists who had come there to live, were on the edge of the harbor they were coming to, Isthmus Cove. The buildings were near that harbor because it was the one facing the mainland, making it the easiest harbor to get to for boaters. It was also where ferry boats dropped off curious tourists. Two Harbors hadn't been a location for a large number of overnighters before the war. The small hotel located there was usually full and boaters slept aboard, but otherwise it was only the one hundred fifty permanent residents and a few campers who slept there.

Now, Two Harbors, also known as The Isthmus, was the headquarters for a new settlement and the population was steadily growing. There were still few buildings, but some temporary shelters had been constructed and ground was being prepared for more permanent structures. The most prominent building there was the one the red-shirted man had disappeared into.

Zach and Stacey spotted Harry Peckham, the man who had been introduced to them the night before as the acting "mayor" of the settlement. He was sitting alone, having coffee at a table in front of that building. It had been the chandlery and general store for the area until a little over a month before. It still served those purposes, but now was also the repository for all critical goods.

Peckham, a slightly heavy-set man of about forty, called them over. He stood and shook hands with them. "I see you already have coffee," he said. "Here, sit." He indicated two of the vacant chairs at the table.

Zach and Stacey eyed the placement of the chairs. They were facing the building, so they would not have their backs to the man in the red shirt if they sat there. Neither had any real concerns about their safety, but they'd learned to use caution at all times. Zach pulled a chair out for Stacey to sit, then pulled one out for himself.

"Did you have a good sleep?" Peckham asked once the Arthurs were seated.

"Yes, it was good to sleep in calm waters and not worry about what awaited us," Stacey said. She fixed her eyes on Peckham's. "It was a bit of a shock, though, to find out we were being spied on as soon we woke up."

A look of mild surprise came over Peckham's face, but there was no evidence of alarm.

Zach had been watching Peckham's reaction. "You don't seem concerned," he noted.

"Oh, I'm concerned all right," said Peckham. "Warren shouldn't have been caught so easily. Certainly not in the first five minutes."

"You knew about it?" Stacey asked. "You have people spying on us?"

"We prefer to call it watching."

Stacey started to object to any kind of surveillance, but saw that Zach showed no signs of being angry. She looked questioningly at her husband. "You suspected it was them, didn't you?"

"There are some really bad people in this new world we're living in," he told her. "We're still strangers to them. If I were in charge, I'd do the same. I'm glad it is them, and not someone we actually have to worry about."

"It's good to hear you say that," Peckham said. "Because of what is happening in the world, which is the reason we started this settlement, we put 'watchers' on all new people. You're the first ones Warren has been assigned to. Apparently, he didn't handle the job with great expertise." He looked toward the store. "Hey, Warren," he called, "why don't you come out and meet the people you're assigned to." He turned back to the Arthurs. "You know now, so he might as well watch you from up close."

A man in his early twenties opened the door and came over to the table. He was wearing a bright red shirt and carrying binoculars.

"This is Warren Sutton," Peckham told Zach and Stacey. He completed the introductions and then turned back to Warren. "You were spotted."

"I heard," the young man said sheepishly. "Sorry."

"I served as a Army Ranger in Afghanistan," Zach told Peckham. "If you'd like, I can give your people some training in surveillance and camouflage."

"That would be really helpful," Peckham replied.

"Warren, what do you think about. . . "

He didn't get any further with the sentence. The young man had the binoculars to his eyes, looking intently out to sea.

The young man handed the binoculars to Peckham, pointing to a spot past the harbor entrance. "Look there, by Bird Rock."

Peckham took the binoculars and trained them on the spot Warren had pointed to. After a minute, he whistled and handed the binoculars to Zach.

Zach took them and immediately saw what the other two were concerned about. A large boat, probably fifty feet long, was powering its way toward them. He counted nine men on deck. That didn't include the pilot, and there might be more below. Eight of those on deck were standing, grim-faced and holding assault weapons armed with ammo clips.

The ninth was on the bow, seated behind a machine gun that had loaded ammo belts hanging from its side.

Chapter 3

NO ONE made an effort to go out to meet the boat when it docked. The Arthurs and Peckham remained seated at the table. After a whispered word with Peckham, Warren went back inside the building.

One man with an assault weapon slung over his shoulder jumped from the boat and tied a bow line to a cleat on the dock. He then went back and tied another line from the stern to the dock. When the boat was secured, six more of the men with assault weapons jumped onto the dock. Another man came up from below and he, too, jumped on the dock. He didn't carry an assault weapon, but had a pistol in a holster at his side. One man with an assault rifle stayed on board to guard the boat, and the other man aboard stayed at his post behind the machine gun.

With the man wearing a gun and holster in the lead, the seven walked along the dock toward shore. The man who'd had his weapon over his shoulder brought it down, and all of the seven men with automatic weapons kept them at a ready position as they walked.

The man in charge saw Peckham and the Arthurs seated at the table, but didn't keep his eye on them. His gaze swept the area. The tractor was working the ground on the hill, and the men and women who had gone there with it were planting seeds. Quite a few people were working on their boats. He did not see any people on the hills on the other side of the harbor, but did see several buffalos and ten or twelve sheep grazing. He was smiling as he took the three steps leading from the dock up to the wooden platform where the table sat. Five of the seven armed men followed him up and took positions behind him. Each faced in a different direction, covering all but the shore area. The two men remaining on the dock covered the shoreline, one in either direction.

Peckham stood to greet the man, extending his hand. "I'm Harry Peckham, the acting mayor of Two Harbors."

Zach and Stacey stood, ready to introduce themselves.

The man shook Peckham's hand firmly, but cautiously. He immediately withdrew his hand and dropped it to his side, next to the holstered pistol, ignoring Zach and Stacey. "My name is Harlan McFee," he stated evenly. "I am the representative of the Governor of California."

"Governor?" said Peckham. "It was our understanding the governor died over a month ago when Sacramento was destroyed."

"The person who was governor then was killed, yes. I'm talking about the new governor."

"New governor?   I wasn't aware of any election."

"I'm sure you don't get much news way out here," said McFee, "but there was one."

"Where? Who voted?"

"In California. The people still alive there voted."

"This is part of California," Peckham noted. "We not only didn't vote, we didn't even know there was an election."

"Look, all the people around where we were voted.   Maybe next time you can vote, too, but right now you've got to abide by what we decided."

"Where you were? Which was?"

"Around Tracy."

"Tracy?" Peckham uttered.

"Yeah. It's a town about seventy miles south of Sacramento, and . . ."

"I know where Tracy is," Peckham cut in, "but what does it have to do with the election of a governor?"

"It's been set up as the new state capital. Sacramento is kaput."

"But, why Tracy?"

"That's where Mr. Silva is from," replied McFee.

"Mr. Silva?"

"Richard Silva. He's the new governor."

"What qualifies him as governor?" queried Peckham.

"He was an Assemblyman once, a few years back. He knows all about that kind of stuff."

Peckham shook his head. He turned to Zach and Stacey. "Do you have any questions?"

"I have one," said Stacey. She looked McFee, her eyes boring in on his. "Why are you here?"

"The first smart question you guys have asked," said McFee. "We're here to collect your first installment of taxes."

"Taxes? What taxes?" said Peckham.

"We've got a whole new state government to run. We need stuff."

Peckham studied the man. "Are you aware that what we used as money before no longer has value?"

"Sure, but what we need is food and equipment and other stuff like that. I saw lots of animals here when we came in, and I see you have crops growing. We need to take those, and we've heard you have things like canned goods, tools, rifles, ammunition. We need that kind of stuff."

"You need rifles and ammunition?" Zach asked.

"For the state militia." McFee put his palm out toward the men around him, indicating he was talking about them.

"They look very well armed," Zach pointed out.

"There are more of us," McFee told him. He looked meaningfully at Zach, and then at Peckham. "A lot more."

Neither man showed any signs of being cowed by what was an obvious threat. "Plus," Zach suggested, "it wouldn't serve your purposes to have others armed."

"As long as we got a militia to protect 'em, no one else needs to be armed."

"A lot of people would disagree with that statement," Zach said.

"Look, we're wasting time here," McKee protested. "Let's start . . ."

Peckham put up a hand. "Before we continue this, I need to talk to my man inside. I believe he's been on the phone with someone on the mainland, and he may have some information for us."

"Phone? There are no phones," McFee sputtered.

"It's not much more than a modern walkie-talkie, but it serves the purpose," Peckham told him. "Warren, come out here, please."

Warren walked out from the building, holding a walkie-talkie.

"Did you hear what was said out here?" Peckham asked.

"Every word," said the young man. "I relayed it on to Captain Kotchel."

"Who the devil is Captain Kotchel?" said McFee.

"He's the captain of what may be the only U.S. Coast Guard cutter left in the world," Peckham told him. "He and his men have been going up and down the coast trying to keep order."

"And," Warren said, "he says there's been no election for governor of California."

"If he's on a boat, he's out on the ocean," McFee pointed out. "He doesn't know what's going on away from the coast. I guarantee you there was an election and Richard Silva is now the governor."

"Captain Kotchel has contacts all along the

coast and inland," Peckham said. "He keeps pretty close tabs on what is happening on land as well as on the ocean."

"And he says there hasn't been any kind of consolidated effort statewide as yet," Warren interjected.

"Yeah, well, we consolidated around Tracy and elected a governor," McFee spit out. His eyes had narrowed and his face was getting red. The men around him were getting tense. Their weapons weren't pointing at the Two Harbors people, but they'd been raising up a little with each exchange of words.

"He says there are groups in several places in the state," Warren said. "Some are like us here on Catalina, people setting up a community. He says others are no more than gangs out stealing what others have put together. He hasn't heard of a legitimate group working to put together a community in the San Joaquin Valley area. That's where Tracy is, isn't it?"

"That's enough beating around the bush," McFee stated flatly. He straightened up in order to appear more dominant and took a half step forward. His men did the same. "Give us what we came for."

Peckham remained as he had been, standing casually beside the table. "I agree with your first statement," he said. "So, in order to not waste any more of your time or ours, I'll come right out and tell you that we are not going to give you a thing."

"In that case," McFee spat, "we'll just take it."

Pulling a revolver out of his holster, he pointed it at Peckham and raised a hand. When he did, they could hear a loud click from out on the boat. They could see that the man behind the machine gun had aimed it at the people on the hill. The click was undoubtedly something he'd done to get the weapon ready to fire. Three of the men with assault weapons pointed them at Zach, Stacey and Warren. The others were looking for targets on the boats and in the buildings.

"If one person lifts a finger to try to stop us," McFee seethed, "everyone on this island will be shot, beginning with the three of you."

To be continued...

My Thanks

Thanking people for their help when a book is published is a challenge when there have been so many who have helped, but I'll risk it.

I'll start with L. Michael Rusin, a master storyteller himself, who got me involved with writers groups, and with Kamel Press. This book would not exist if it wasn't for him, and them.

Curtis Cooper and Peggylou Beazley, two super writers with the Prose online writers group kept me from going too far off track by critiquing the entire book as it was being written. It's amazing how many errors a writer can make – and even more amazing how people such as those two can find them. They also came up with those key words and phrases I needed but was fumbling around trying to find. Writers Teresa Lampros, Stephanie Smith, Brett Pew and Mona Shroff also lent hands as the book progressed. What great suggestions they made.

After that, my good friend Gary Davis, who

has published a few books about life in Costa Rica himself, went through the whole book and came up with the "yellows," that spotlighted trouble spots that needed attention.

Editor Bob Brashears then came along and edited out some electronic monsters – errors that somehow raised their ugly heads while the book was traveling through cyber space. He was also able to discover the sneaky little typos and misspellings that somehow got by eight other pairs of eyes, and made sure the grammar was, well, grammatical.

Thanks to Deanie Deitterick, Chief Editor at Kamel Press, LLC, for that final touch – straightening out those last little things so that you now have a book that is very readable.

Calvin Cahail worked tirelessly to design a cover that is just right – often having to overcome ideas of mine that were a little too bizarre to work.

And, thank you, Kermit Jones, Jr., my publisher, for having faith.

Al Correia

About the Author

ALBERT A. CORREIA is a native Californian, having grown up in Tracy, located in that state's vast and agriculturally rich Central Valley. He had a rewarding career as a Chamber of Commerce executive in the U.S. before moving to Costa Rica.

While attending the California State University at Fresno, he interned at the Fresno, Oakland, and San Leandro Chambers of Commerce. Following graduation, he served as assistant manager of the San Bernardino and Berkeley Chambers of Commerce. He then went on to serve as CEO of the San Fernando, Pasadena, Pomona, and the Mid San Fernando Valley Chambers of Commerce, all in California. He was presented the Russell E. Pettit, "Executive of the Year Award," by the California Association of Chamber of Commerce Executives in 1986.

Since arriving in Costa Rica in 1995, Correia has devoted his time to the arts. In addition to his writing, he paints, and a number of his oils hang in prominent buildings in and around San Jose, Costa Rica's capital city. He is a devotee of Costa Rica's renowned symphony orchestra.

He lives in a quiet suburb of the capital with his wife, daughter, and two stepdaughters. Two of his sons live in California and the third lives in Alaska. When not in San Jose, he spends time in Jaco Beach where he lived a number of years before moving to San Jose.